LOOKING THROUGH DARKNESS

Center Point
Large Print

Also by Aimée and David Thurlo and available from Center Point Large Print:

A Time of Change
The Pawnbroker
Grave Consequences

LOOKING THROUGH DARKNESS

Aimée & David Thurlo

CENTER POINT LARGE PRINT
THORNDIKE, MAINE

This Center Point Large Print edition
is published in the year 2017 by arrangement with
Tom Doherty Associates, LLC.

Copyright © 2015 by David Thurlo.

The text of this Large Print edition is unabridged.
In other aspects, this book may vary
from the original edition.
Printed in the United States of America
on permanent paper.
Set in 16-point Times New Roman type.

ISBN: 978-1-68324-485-1

Library of Congress Cataloging-in-Publication Data

Names: Thurlo, Aimée, author. | Thurlo, David, author.
Title: Looking through darkness / Aimée and David Thurlo.
Description: Center Point Large Print edition. | Thorndike, Maine :
    Center Point Large Print, 2017.
Identifiers: LCCN 2017019186 | ISBN 9781683244851
    (hardcover : alk. paper)
Subjects: LCSH: Widows—Fiction. | Man-woman relationships—Fic-
tion. | Large type books. | BISAC: FICTION / Romance / Suspense. |
FICTION / Mystery & Detective / Women Sleuths. | GSAFD: Mystery
fiction. | Romantic suspense fiction.
Classification: LCC PS3570.H82 L66 2017 | DDC 813/.54—dc23
LC record available at https://lccn.loc.gov/2017019186

For Aimée
The love she had for storytelling is now a gift
to be shared forever with our readers.

Acknowledgments

To Peggy, Pete, Nicole, Jackie, Sydney, George, Herman, Isabel, Vivian, Herb, Melissa, Peter, and the others who were there for us not only during those final days, but for me in the weeks beyond.

Prologue

18 Months Ago

Kurt Vance had cheated on his wife, stolen thousands of dollars, and lied to almost everyone—and almost no one knew any of that. Everyone thought he was just a regular guy, and today he was doing a regular guy thing, going hunting with friends and coworkers.

He stopped beside a big piñon tree, standing very still, rifle ready, scanning the area for mule deer moving uphill from the orchards below. It was barely dawn and the steam from his breath rose in the cold air. He was in the center position, with a fellow hunter on both flanks, each about a hundred yards away. All three of them were wearing bright orange vests—no sense in having some nearsighted jerk mistake anyone for a deer and start blasting away.

Kurt yawned, wishing he'd taken that second cup of coffee. Though he and the guys had spent most of the night talking, he'd still managed to get out of his sleeping bag around 5:00 A.M.

If they got their deer on opening day, he'd be home by dark, maybe even in time to take Leigh Ann out for dinner.

He smiled to himself. He loved Leigh Ann. His

affairs meant nothing, and after all, he'd always come back to her. A few times he'd thought of coming clean and telling her about all the women he'd screwed and asking her to forgive him. Yet something told him that owning up to what he'd done would be a huge mistake. His conscience would feel better, but his wife sure wouldn't. He'd blow his marriage sky high for sure.

Shaking off those thoughts, he squinted into the tree line downslope, looking for movement. He checked his rifle for the third or fourth time: barrel up and safety on, his mantra to Leigh Ann each time she'd gone to the range with him. A small-town Texas girl, she was a natural with a rifle.

Many years had passed since Leigh Ann's days as head cheerleader and prom queen, but she was still drop-dead gorgeous. Him hooking up with other women . . . that wasn't about her. He wanted to prove to himself he still had what it took. He'd been the high school quarterback, the guy everyone had envied. Now . . . not so much.

He watched the far slopes as the sunrise slowly spread over the mesa. A few minutes ago, the light had been just a glow on the crest. Now the shadow line was halfway down.

It was so quiet he could hear his own breathing. Then he heard a snap from somewhere behind him and to the right. Close. Maybe a buck had come up undetected and was passing between him and Wayne.

He reached down slowly with a gloved hand and slid off the safety on his rifle. A slow turn was best, and less likely to spook the animal.

Suddenly there was a loud boom and his chest exploded in pain. Kurt felt his legs go weak as he fell backward. Lights flashing in his brain, he tried to understand what had just happened.

Seconds later, vaguely aware that he was on his back on the cold ground, he felt something warm flowing across his skin and realized he'd been shot. Karma. It had all finally caught up to him. He heard footsteps and a form loomed over him. He stared up, trying to see who it was . . .

One

The Present

Leigh Ann Vance stood beside the cash register and gave silent thanks that she still had a job. Business wasn't booming, but at least it was steady, and it beat the hell out of that waitressing job she'd had five or six years ago. Here at The Outpost, she'd never once had a beer spilled on her by a drunk or been groped by some horny cowboy.

The only plus back then was that the job got her out of the house and gave her spending money that didn't require her to justify the expenditure to Kurt. Life was definitely better now.

Waving at the last customer of the day as the woman stepped outside, she sighed. It was 6:00 P.M. and she'd been here since six in the morning. Although she was in her mid-thirties, at the moment, her energy level was down to zero and she felt ancient.

"You know that you don't have to put in such long hours, don't you?" Josephine Buck said with a weary smile as she double-locked the door and flipped around the closed sign. Jo owned The Outpost Trading Post, which was located just east of the border of the Navajo Nation in San Juan County, New Mexico.

"You can use a hand," Leigh Ann said. "Your workdays are even longer than mine."

"That's true, but I can't afford to pay you for the extra hours. The trading post is doing better now, but business is still not up to where it was before the recession."

"I don't mind helping out. Working here is better than going—" She stopped speaking abruptly. As friendly as Jo was, she was still the boss, and there were lines that shouldn't be crossed.

"It's your home, isn't it?" Jo said softly. "You don't want to live in that house anymore, do you?"

"No, I don't," Leigh Ann admitted in a quiet voice. "I can make ends meet since my sister Rachel is paying her share of the rent, utilities, and food bills, but I hate that place now. Every time I walk in the door, I think of Kurt, our screwed-up marriage, and his accident. He cheated with other women and left me nearly penniless, but I still feel guilty for not being able to mourn him. I'd sell the place tomorrow if I could, but with the housing market in this area what it is I wouldn't be able to get what it's worth."

"It's tough to make these decisions alone," Jo said with a nod, then glanced in the direction of

Ben Stuart's office. Leigh Ann was using it now as Jo's only salaried employee, but she knew it would always be Ben's office. Before that, it had belonged to Ben's father, Tom Stuart, the late owner of The Outpost. He'd left the trading post to Jo, but she and Ben now ran it together.

"You really miss him, don't you?" Leigh Ann said quietly. "How long has it been now, six months since his unit touched down in Afghanistan?"

Jo nodded. "Six months and eight days. We Skype a lot, but seeing his face sometimes makes the separation a lot tougher. He's right there on the screen, so close I can reach out and touch him, but still so far away." Jo shook her head. "At least he's alive and well, and that's all that matters."

"It's really nice that you two found each other again," Leigh Ann said, giving her a bright smile. "On that note, I better get going. I've got to climb into the attic, and I don't like going up there after dark."

"Problems?"

"Yeah, squirrels. Rachel began feeding them, putting raw peanuts along the back wall. I didn't mind—I figured it would keep them outside— but recently one's gotten into the attic."

"You sure it's a squirrel?"

"Pretty sure. I haven't seen any signs of mice yet, but squirrels are running everywhere in the yard. Rachel swore she was only feeding one, but I guess it brought its friends and relatives."

Leigh Ann drove home slowly in her old Jeep. She envied Jo. The young Navajo woman had ties to her culture that would sustain her no matter what the circumstances. She had rediscovered her relationship with Ben and had a wide circle of friends and a solid support system in place at the trading post. Ben had even helped her pay for the construction of a small hogan behind his house next to The Outpost, a place he insisted could be her medicine hogan someday.

Leigh Ann's own life was vastly different. She'd been alone long before her husband had died in a hunting accident more than a year ago. Their marriage had been nothing more than a sham. Even though she was now sharing her home with her sister, Rachel, they weren't close and mostly went their own ways.

She parked in the driveway and walked past the ADT sign in the front yard. She could no longer afford the security service, but she'd left the sign up, hoping it might deter anyone thinking of breaking in.

As she stepped into the small foyer, she saw Rachel coming down the stairs wearing pink sneakers, white exercise shorts, and a light blue, sleeveless, crop-top T-shirt. Rachel had dyed her beautiful ash-blond hair a garish shade of red that made Leigh Ann cringe. The color didn't do a thing for her, but Rachel loved it.

"You're home earlier than usual," Rachel said, leaning against the banister. "I picked up some takeout. Just pizza, but there's plenty left in the kitchen."

Leigh Ann forced a smile, looking down at her own jeans and turquoise knit Outpost polo shirt, complete with store logo. The jeans were feeling a little tight around the waist today.

She'd told Rachel she was trying to lose a few pounds but, as usual, Rachel couldn't remember anything that didn't directly affect her. "Thanks, I'll pass on that, but before you start your exercises, I'd like you to hold the ladder for me while I go up into the attic."

"Why? There's no telling what's up there—spiders the size of your fist, and maybe even mice. It's just not safe. Remember when I helped you store Mom's things? Except for that one spot, there's no flooring, just insulation and the Sheetrock ceiling. You can't put weight on that without falling through."

"Kurt placed some flat boards on top of the rafters to create walkways and more storage space. Otherwise his fishing gear and golf clubs would have fallen through ages ago."

Rachel gave her a wan smile. "Come on, Leigh Ann, it's really hot and creepy up there. Why do you care if the squirrel set up a nest? Let it."

"They chew through stuff and might eventually short out some electrical wiring. It's a fire hazard. There's way too much junk up there anyway, and I need to clear some of it out."

"Are you thinking about selling the house?" Rachel asked quickly, a touch of panic in her voice.

Leigh Ann knew that Rachel was saving a lot of money by living with her. By sharing expenses, they could afford this large, three-bedroom home instead of being stuck in one-bedroom apartments in Kirtland or Farmington, farther east.

"No, I'm not selling. This isn't a good time for that, but that's not the point. Besides the danger to the wiring, we don't want to provide homes for creatures who might bring in the plague or hantavirus."

"Okay, but you hate closed-in spaces and creepy crawlies as much as I do. Let's get someone else to do it."

"We can't afford an unnecessary expense like that, and I'm through putting this off. Something's been running back and forth there. If it's a squirrel, then I have to find out how it's getting in and out, and see what damage it's already caused. If it's mice or rats, then we need to set traps."

"Okay, okay. How can I help?" Rachel said with a sigh.

"Stay close by in case I need you."

"Once you're at the top of the ladder, I'll hand you a broom. If anything gross is dangling down from a spiderweb, you can swat it away."

Leigh Ann smiled. "You recall that cabin we squatted in the summer Daddy lost his job?"

"That place was beyond creepy. No windows in the bedroom, and you could hear things moving around at night in the walls and under the floor," Rachel said, and shuddered. "Remember that huge, hairy spider that crawled onto the pillow between us that night? Man, did we scream."

"To this day, I still can't stand spiders," Leigh Ann said. "That's why, as a general rule I've avoided the attic. Kurt and I made a deal. I cleaned the house and he was responsible for the garage and attic."

"It looks like it's our job now," Rachel said with a smile.

A few minutes later, at the top of the ladder, Leigh Ann aimed a flashlight around the hot, dusty attic. After a moment, she hoisted herself up the rest of the way, stepped onto a board, and pulled the long dangling chain connected to the single-bulb fixture. The confined space was suddenly flooded with light.

The place was so dusty it made her nose itch, but at least there was no damp, musty smell. The roof had never leaked. Of course they were in the middle of a drought and rain was as rare as unicorns.

She studied the layers of insulation and the simple board walkways, and looked closely at the electrical wiring and metal conduits that supplied the heat, air-conditioning, powered the ceiling lights and the various circuits. At least it seemed to be in good shape. Fitted together sheets of ply-wood placed across the rafters supported plastic containers filled with Christmas decorations, a metal book stand, fishing tackle boxes, and several fishing rods. Fine dust and spider webs covered everything.

Close by was a stack of long, flat boards. After a moment's thought, Leigh Ann realized that Kurt had probably used them to create temporary paths across the rafters. One false step onto the Sheetrock or insulation could be dangerous or fatal.

Farther across the attic where the pitched roof sloped down to the walls, she saw another makeshift plywood platform. Several cardboard boxes and one made of metal, maybe a toolbox, were nestled in a pile of fluffy insulation that must have been pulled loose. A couple of black plastic trash bags covered a long object, maybe another fishing rod. The loosened insulation seemed like a potential squirrel hiding place.

"Whatcha see?" Rachel called from below.

"Mom's stuff and a bunch of man toys. I'm going to check out a place I think the squirrel was interested in. I don't think it's there now, but I'll take a look and make sure nothing's damaged. Then I'm going to bring back some junk and hand it down to you. It'll be dusty, so be prepared to sneeze."

As she spoke, Leigh Ann laid one of the long, wide boards across the rafters in the direction of the possible nest.

"Want the broom, just in case?" Rachel asked.

Leigh Ann felt something brush against her leg and tried not to flinch. "Good idea. I can probe the insulation without putting my hand into . . . whatever."

Two minutes later, on hands and knees, Leigh Ann inched along the first board, broom and extra boards beside her across the rafters. As she moved, she'd pick up another board and position it in front of her as she created a path toward the boxes. Soon, she'd placed the last board in position and was less than five feet away.

She extended the broom toward the pile of loose pink insulation, then gingerly touched it to the top of the material. She cringed, hoping the squirrel wouldn't leap out and run right down the board.

Nothing. She wiggled the bristles of the broom around a little. All she saw was a little dust and some pink fibers drifting up into the light.

"So far, so good. Nothing's in the nest," she called out.

"Good!" Rachel said, her voice suddenly much louder.

Leigh Ann looked back toward the ladder. Rachel's head was sticking up into the attic. "Joining me?"

"Uh-uh. Sorry, Leigh Ann. This is as far as I go." Rachel seemed to study the situation. "Hey, maybe the squirrel is underneath those trash bags. Stir it up a bit."

"Not funny, what if it attacks?"

"Nah, it'll run toward the wall or a vent and maybe we'll see how it's been getting in," Rachel said.

"I don't want to get any closer until I'm sure it's not hiding somewhere." Leigh Ann inched forward, straining for a closer look. "I wonder what's in that gray metal box?"

She shifted the broom to the top of the box, pressed it against a small handle, and tried to pull it toward her. When she realized there was a string attached to the handle, she tried to break it away with the broom.

An enormous flash and boom shook the entire attic, yanking the broom right out of her hand. Stunned, Leigh Ann ducked, clapping her hands to her ears, and nearly rolled off the narrow board. Her ears ringing, she peered through the cloud of dust and debris, trying to make sense of what had just happened.

"Leigh Ann. Are you okay?" Rachel's voice seemed to floating in from the distance. "Leigh Ann? Leigh Ann!"

Leigh Ann shook her head, backed up a couple of feet, then turned around, looking at Rachel, who was halfway into the opening now. "Umm, I'm okay, but something just blew up."

"What did you do?"

"I don't know. I hit a string with the broom, then something exploded."

Rachel pointed. "Over there. Is that a fire? I see smoke."

As Leigh Ann turned, she saw shattered fishing gear and shreds of cardboard littering the top of the insulation batts. One of the truss beams that braced the connection between the roof and rafters had been peppered with holes and was shattered in half. Farther to the right, she glimpsed something she finally recognized. Sticking out of one of the black plastic bags was a big gun barrel. A thin wisp of smoke curled from the muzzle. "Nope, no fire. I smell gunpowder, though."

"Rachel, that's Kurt's pump shotgun," she added, still trying to make sense of things. "I wondered why I'd never been able to find it."

"Did you touch the trigger, or did it go off by itself?"

Suddenly things popped into place in her mind. "Neither. Kurt set a trap with that damn thing! He loaded the shotgun and aimed it at the front of the box. I saw a piece of string, which must have been attached to the trigger. If

I'd have moved that metal box myself instead of using the tip of the broom, my brains would be splattered all over the attic right now."

"Want me to call the sheriff?"

Leigh Ann was still shaking like a leaf. She couldn't move, and she was almost sure she'd wet her pants, but her thinking was crystal clear. "No. Hold off on that. This wasn't meant for you or me. Kurt knew we wouldn't come up here. This was meant for someone else. Before we get the police involved I want to look inside the box. It's no toolbox; it looks more like one of those petty cash containers. There's a lock on the side below the lid."

Kurt hadn't been violent, yet he'd been willing to kill to protect the contents of that box. She had to know what was inside.

Leigh Ann took a shaky breath and reached for the box, making sure that the string was no longer attached to anything. "No more secrets, you bastard."

"Leigh Ann?" Rachel called.

"I'm coming." She edged back on hands and knees, dragging the surprisingly heavy box with her, and made it down the small ladder a few minutes later, carrying the box by the handle on top, a piece of string still attached to it. "I can't stop shaking."

"It's little wonder." Rachel took the metal document box from her hands and tried to open the latch. "It's locked. Do you know where he kept the key?"

"No. I didn't even know this box existed until about five minutes ago. After I go get the shotgun I'm coming down. I'll get this thing open even if I have to blast it with buckshot."

It was getting late, and the darkness outside robbed Melvin Littlewater of the contrast between objects that provided him with orientation clues. His life had been shrouded in curtains of gray since the accident that had made him legally blind. Being told his vision was worse than 20/200 meant he could only discern objects in daylight that were within twenty feet or less. Faces, even point blank, were just a blur, and his reading material these days was in Braille.

He put away the clay sculpture of the antelope he'd been shaping with his hands, satisfied with the feel of the almost finished piece. After it was fired, he'd pack it up safely and deliver it to Director Nez at the tribal building.

Exhausted, he turned out the light and walked to the living room, knowing by heart how many steps he needed to take and where everything was placed. During the day he could find his way around his furniture and other large possible obstacles, but at night, outside, everything disappeared into a yawning black void.

He dreaded the night—the time when dreams came back to haunt him. Not yet ready to go to bed, he made himself comfortable in his leather easy chair and reached out to feel for the half-empty whiskey bottle he kept on the table beside it. The liquor was there to remind him that there were other demon-filled roads, some far worse than the one he traveled.

He switched on the TV and listened to a sitcom. Comfortable, yet weary, he soon drifted to sleep and back into the world of the sighted.

Unearthly, yet familiar dreamscapes unfolded before him.

He was on the road, behind the wheel of his truck, tired, and struggling to stay awake. Out of nowhere, he saw the bright headlight beams coming up fast behind him, blinding in the rearview mirror.

He pulled to the right, onto the shoulder of the road, taking his foot off the gas, giving the car behind him space to get around. There were two lanes in either direction and plenty of room.

With his horn blaring, the driver hurtled past him, then pulled back to the right too soon, cutting Melvin off and slamming into the front end of the truck.

At the impact, Melvin slammed on the brakes and fought for control. He saw the irrigation ditch beside the highway and steered left, trying to get away, but the car was shoving him inexorably to the right, tires shrieking.

Desperate to avoid crashing into the guardrail, he yanked the steering wheel hard to the right and broke free from the car. Somehow he avoided the steel guardrail and shot through a metal gate. The impact ripped into the driver's side door but didn't slow him down. Melvin struggled to steer, to regain control, but nothing made any difference. As his pickup struck the water, an air bag went off, nearly breaking his eardrums and slamming him back into the seat. He pushed the bag away and tried to sit up as the truck began to sink.

In the midst of the chaos, he saw the car roll, flip over the guardrail, then bounce into the water ahead of him, upside down.

With ice-cold water rushing into the cab of his truck, Melvin fought desperately to release his seat belt. He had to get out. Blood flowed down his face and his eyes burned so badly he could barely see. Everything seemed to be covered in a thin red veil.

The seat belt gave, but his leg was caught on something—the deflated air bag, he realized. He struggled, yanking at his pant leg with all his strength, and managed to free himself. Afraid of being pulled under as the truck continued to sink, he struggled out through the window and hauled himself onto the top of the cab. That's when he saw the girl, knee-deep in water, struggling to reach him, holding out her hands.

He was about to call out to her when his truck struck the bottom of the ditch. The impact knocked Melvin off the truck and into the current. He couldn't swim. As blackness encompassed him, he felt the presence of death, sweet, warm, and so enticing he almost surrendered.

It was the girl's insistent cries that broke through to him. He couldn't give up. He wasn't ready to die. Somehow, he kept his head above the surface, thrashing as the current tossed him around.

After an eternity, he felt hands pulling him out of the water. Pain followed, then blackness again.

Melvin woke with a start. As he tried to even his breathing, he wondered if he'd ever be able to put that night behind him. Like a man trapped in time, he seemed condemned to relive the moments that had changed his life forever. Yet what haunted him most was the girl.

Over the years, he'd spoken to nearly all the witnesses and responders, but no one else had seen her. At first, he'd thought she'd drowned that night trying to save him, but her body had never been found.

Everyone had tried to tell him that he'd imagined her, but as logical as their arguments had been, he knew better. She'd been much too real to be only a figment of his imagination.

Melvin found the sink and splashed cold water on his face. Fully awake, he now fought a different battle. Despair and frustration tugged at him, urging him downward into a hell he might never escape, an abyss where no hands could ever reach him.

Determined not to sink, he focused on Leigh Ann Vance. Everything about her, from the music of her voice, to the gentleness of her touch, called to him.

Everyone assumed they were friends, connected by her work at The Outpost, where he often sold some of his sculptures. To Melvin, however, their relationship defied labels. She didn't know how he felt about her, but that was as it should be. He'd never bring her into the nightmare his life had become.

Twenty minutes later, after a quick shower and a change of clothing, Leigh Ann joined Rachel in the room they'd converted into a home office. Rachel had brought in a pot of tea and was sitting by the desk. As Leigh Ann entered the room, Rachel poured two cups of tea, saying, "I decided to make herbal. I figured we both needed something to settle our nerves. I picked the Soothing Afternoon Tea that we bought last week."

Leigh Ann nodded absently and stared at the gray metal case.

"My boss has one like that for petty cash, but

without a key that's going to be tough to open," Rachel said, eyeing the box. "The hinges are concealed, too, so prying it open could take time."

"I've still got Kurt's pocket key chain. I tossed it in that drawer over there beside the one with the keys for the garage cabinets," Leigh Ann said, pointing. "Maybe one of those will work. We can try them all."

She found both key chains and inspected the keys, narrowing the possibilities down to two on the set he'd carried with him. As she tried the first one, her hands shook.

"Don't worry, Leigh Ann. He can't hurt you anymore," Rachel said softly.

She tried to remain focused on the box. When the first didn't work, Leigh Ann reached for the second and braced herself. She had a feeling that once she opened the box, her life would take a drastic turn for the worse.

"Maybe I should just destroy this, whatever it is, sight unseen," Leigh Ann said, but even as she spoke, she knew she couldn't back off now. Knowledge wasn't as dangerous as the lack of it—like the shotgun, which was now beneath her bed, unloaded.

The second key fit. As she opened the lid, her heart was beating overtime. The box's contents looked innocuous at first, and she lifted out the items and set them on the desk: a small notebook, a folder filled with receipts, and several folded printouts of bookkeeping spreadsheets. Beneath those papers she found a heavy .38 revolver.

"It's loaded," she said, opening the cylinder and checking. Holding a firearm came as naturally to her as barbecue and driving a pickup truck.

"Is that a passport?" Rachel asked, her eyes glued on the contents of the box.

"Sure looks like it, but what the hell was Kurt doing with one?" Leigh Ann picked it up and looked inside. The photo was of her husband, but the name listed on it was Frank Jones. Glancing quickly through the pages, she found no stamps or other markings. It had yet to be used.

"Frank Jones . . . I remember that name," Leigh Ann said. "After Kurt died, both Wayne and Pierre would drop by once in a while, or call to ask if I'd found a Frank Jones file in Kurt's papers. But it looks like Kurt *was* Frank Jones."

Rachel held the two spreadsheets against the window, one over the other. As light shined through them, she said, "These pages are nearly identical except for the column listing vendor payments. I think most people wouldn't even notice the differences, but it looks like one or more formulas have been altered, too, because the totals still come out the same down here." She pointed to another section. "I'm not a bookkeeper, but I work with spreadsheets and electronic ledgers every day. I think Kurt was doing some creative bookkeeping, and from what I can see, the last entries were made a few days prior to his death."

"There's a flash drive in here," Leigh Ann said. "Let's take a look at that."

Moments later, after loading the program into Leigh Ann's laptop, they went over several more spreadsheets. Finally Rachel spoke. "This is just more of the same, Leigh Ann. Again, there are two sets. One seems to be the real one, the other's doctored. The key differences are the payouts to Frank Jones Enterprises. They're steady and totaling around fifty grand. At a glance, I'd say your hubby found a way to cheat his partners."

"No way they knew," Leigh Ann said. "They considered him one of their buds. They'd even go hunting together. That's a guy bonding thing."

"Although the police and forest service ruled it an accidental death caused by a careless hunter, they never did find out who shot Kurt," Rachel said.

"I would have known if Wayne Hurley and Pierre Boone had found out Kurt was cheating them. Pierre, in particular, has a temper like Vesuvius. From the way they talked, I'm sure they thought Frank Jones was real."

"Neither of those men are fools," Rachel said.

"No, but then again it's easier to be taken in by a friend than it is an enemy. You never see it coming," she said, old hurts stealing over her.

"Do you think that's why Kurt rigged up the shotgun? He didn't want the guys breaking in when nobody was home, nosing around, and finding something that could get him arrested," Rachel said.

Leigh Ann nodded slowly. "He was obviously scared enough to do whatever it took to protect this."

"Why would he keep evidence that could have been used against him? Why not just destroy it?" Rachel said.

"I'm guessing it's because he was embezzling money up to the moment he died and needed to keep things straight so he wouldn't get caught. Kurt was no Einstein."

"What's in the little notebook?"

She looked through it. "I'm seeing a list of names: Sorrelhorse, Natani, Manuelito, Begay, Johnson, and Lee. Most sound Navajo, and I know there's a tribal official by the name of Sorrelhorse, but there are no first names here. Some have question marks next to them."

"Could they be potential clients, maybe?" Rachel asked.

"I have no idea." Leigh Ann continued leafing through the book. "There's also an address of a storage facility and a unit number." A folded piece of paper pressed between the pages slipped to the floor. "Whoops," she said, picking it up.

"This looks like a rental receipt. He was paid up for a whole year."

"I recognize the name of that place," Rachel said, looking over her shoulder at the receipt. "I stored some stuff in one of their smaller units before I moved in with you. They're cheap. You provide your own key and lock."

Leigh Ann checked the metal box again. Only one thing remained. "There's this little key with the number zero fifty-five on it. It doesn't match the number of the compartment he rented, but maybe that's it."

"I don't think so. Padlock keys usually have the name of the lock brand on them. It's more likely a desk drawer key, or one to a box like that one. The storage place he used recommends a sturdy lock, and the facility itself doesn't keep a duplicate of the key—to protect the client, they say."

Leigh Ann sifted through more of the papers. "Here's a receipt for a big padlock, but the key's not here."

"Do you suppose that Kurt hid the money he ripped off in that storage locker?" Rachel asked.

"Who knows? If he spent it, all I can tell you is that it wasn't on me."

"You need to go check out that place as soon as possible," Rachel said.

"I've got to find the padlock key first," Leigh Ann said, looking around the room slowly.

"He bought a Master lock," Rachel said, looking at the receipt. "That comes with a very distinctive key."

Leigh Ann looked through the top drawer. "Not here."

"So what happened to it?"

"I don't know, but since Kurt's dead, maybe I can get the storage company to open up his locker for me. I could show them the rental agreement and his death certificate."

"The rental agreement has expired," Rachel said, looking more closely at the receipt, "and I'm not sure how much grace time they give a renter. If they auctioned off the stuff inside, you can kiss that money good-bye. Someone's bound to have found it already."

"It wouldn't be mine to keep, anyway, but it won't hurt to follow up on this."

"If no one's come after the money, why not just keep it?" Rachel smiled and shrugged. "You could sure use a lump sum like that."

"Rachel, that money's *not* mine. Had it belonged to Kurt, I would cheerfully take it and spend every dime, but it belongs to the company. Anything I find has to go back to his partners."

"At least negotiate a finder's fee, Leigh Ann! If they haven't come to you for that money in all this time, they either don't know the money's gone or they wrote it off as a loss."

"You've just raised an interesting point. By

now, they have to know about the missing money, and fifty thousand dollars isn't exactly chump change. Yet they haven't said a word to me about that. Something doesn't add up right."

"You said they asked about Frank Jones. That means they knew something was going on."

She nodded. "They wanted to keep this from me. The question is why?"

"What are you going to do?"

"I'm going to hold on to that gun, for starters," she said, glancing at the .38. "I'm also going back up to the attic and see what else is up there."

"No, Leigh Ann, let it be. What if Kurt's got something else booby-trapped ?"

Leigh Ann shook her head. "Nothing else is covered up, but if I see any strings, wires, or fishing line, I'll use my remote control—the broom—or what's left of it."

"At least we know one thing," Rachel said. "That poor squirrel's gonna haul his nuts out of there."

"After everything's that happened, that's the best you've got?" Leigh Ann said, then laughed.

As Rachel went back out into the hall, Leigh Ann stared at the now empty metal box for a moment longer. Instinct told her that her problems were only just beginning.

Two

Leigh Ann arrived at the trading post early and used her keys to enter through the back door next to the loading dock. It was Saturday and Jo would be gone all day; she usually spent Saturdays with Rudy Brownhat, studying to become a medicine woman.

Leigh Ann flipped on the storeroom lights before crossing through the back offices and into the front room. The first thing that caught her eye was Melvin Littlewater's newest sculpture. She smiled at the sight of the mountain lion, depicted in midstride. That elusive, almost mesmeric lifelike quality had become his signature style and drew the gaze of anyone nearby. Jo had purchased the piece and kept it on view as a sample of Melvin's work, believing that it would lead to more commissions for him. The Outpost collected a fee every time they set up a deal for the sculptor, and even though the lion had only been on display for a short time, Jo had told Leigh Ann that buying it had been a good business decision. Leigh Ann knew, though, that Jo wouldn't have bought it if she hadn't loved it.

Her Saturday routine always began the same way, with checking the coolers to make sure everything was working, then walking down aisles verifying that shelves and merchandise in the main room were free of dust and attractively arranged. A year ago she'd run the cash register, now she was manager. The promotion hadn't come with much of a raise, but it had given her ego a much-needed boost.

Her life had unraveled after Kurt's death. Finding a video that had graphically revealed one of her husband's affairs had nearly destroyed her. Though a cheating husband was nothing new, she'd never seen it coming. After that, she'd questioned everything about herself, from her taste in men to her sex appeal.

Hurt, she'd avoided the opposite sex . . . until she met Melvin. Though blind, he could always tell when she was near. Every time he came to The Outpost, he made a point of coming over to talk to her. He made her feel special, a woman who had something more to offer than a nice rack, long legs, and a tight butt.

He was a complex man, and lately he'd become moody, reverting back to something she'd noted a year ago when they'd first met. Melvin was not only a talented artist, he was also very proud. He disliked anyone showing what he considered "excessive" sympathy.

Hearing footsteps behind her on the tile floor, she jumped and spun around. "You scared me half to death, Regina!" she said when she saw the woman at the other end of the short hallway.

At five-foot-seven, Regina Yazzie and Leigh Ann were almost the same height, but that's where the similarities ended. Regina's ebony hair was long and flowed freely down to her waist when it wasn't in a single braid.

Leigh Ann still retained her Texas high school cheerleader "big hair," teased, full, and mostly blond. Hair spray was her friend and she bought it at Costco in bulk. Today, instead of jeans and the turquoise polo, she had on a denim skirt just above the knees and a sleeveless white blouse. An Outpost name tag identified her as staff.

Regina had that natural look, with rich skin tones and a hint of copper lipstick. Today the young Navajo woman was wearing dark slacks and the polo with the trading post's name over the left pocket. They all had matching shirts that they could wear whenever they pleased. The simple silver cross Regina always wore around her neck shimmered against her turquoise top.

"Sorry, Leigh Ann, I didn't mean to startle you. I came in early hoping to catch you before the others got here."

"Is something wrong?" Leigh Ann had learned about Regina's marital problems a while back, accidentally overhearing her talking to her estranged husband on the phone. Regina had thrown him out when he threatened physical abuse.

Regina sat down on one of the stools, picked up a foam coffee cup from the stack beside the percolator, and added a packet of sugar. "It's Esther," she said, referring to Esther Allison, the trading post's senior employee. "Her husband's Alzheimer's is getting worse. Last night Truman walked out the back door and she had to call the police to help find him."

"Is he okay?" Leigh Ann asked quickly.

She nodded. "Reverend Moore and his wife went over to help. They're both fine now, but taking care of Truman is wearing Esther down. If she seems a little distracted at work, that's why."

Leigh Ann nodded slowly. "That explains why she hasn't changed the display lately." Part of Esther's job was to make sample garments using fabrics the trading post sold. Once people saw the finished products, they were more inclined to buy the patterns and the materials necessary to duplicate them.

"I'm guessing she hasn't had time to get anything ready for a while," Regina said.

"I'll mention it to Jo on Monday. Nobody here has given Esther a hard time about that, have they?"

"No, but I thought it best if you knew," Regina answered.

"Thanks," Leigh Ann said. ."From what I hear, you've got a heavy load yourself these days, working here during the day and teaching Navajo

40

at the community college at night. Three classes a week, is that right?"

She nodded. "I love it. Now that we're living with Mom and she's helping take care of Shawna, I don't have to worry. A two-year-old is a lot of work, but Mom adores her. The best part of all is that I finally get to use my teaching certificate. When Pete was around, he wanted me at home. Since I never liked leaving the baby with a sitter, I thought it was all for the best."

Leigh Ann looked up at the clock. "We've got a half hour before we open for business. Let's use that time to clear some more space up front. I need to set up a larger display area for Melvin Littlewater. He's bringing us another new sculpture this morning. His uncle John is giving him a ride."

Regina smiled. "He really likes you."

"Melvin's uncle?" Leigh Ann asked, teasing.

"No, Melvin!" Regina said, laughing. "I don't know exactly how he does it, but Melvin always seems to know where you are. He'll walk in, stand at the front for a moment, and turn right to you."

"He's not totally blind, you know. Under bright lights and during the daytime he can tell where someone is if they're not too far away. As for knowing it's me, it must be my perfume," Leigh Ann said, pride preventing her from admitting it was most likely the layer of hair spray.

41

Regina sniffed the air.

"It's a pretty subtle floral, but he has no problem picking it out, even in a crowded room."

Regina, who was a kind woman, smiled and nodded.

They cleared off a large display table, covered it with one of their colorful Navajo rugs and some locally crafted pottery, then placed Melvin's mountain lion in the center. "We'll remove some of the pottery to make room for the new piece."

Regina repositioned a hand-lettered sign with Melvin's name on it. "Have you spoken to him recently?"

Leigh Ann looked at her curiously. "No, I haven't, not since he told me he'd be bringing in something new today. That was a little over two weeks ago, and we didn't talk very long. He was kind of grumpy."

"Maybe it's because he hasn't visited the art classes at the elementary school in a while. I know the kids probably miss him."

Leigh Ann took a deep breath, suspecting his moodiness was the culprit. "He might be in the middle of some project. I know he loves the kids. To them, he's not a blind sculptor, he's just a guy who makes cool things out of clay."

"Yeah, that's what I've heard, too."

Leigh Ann was silent for a while, mulling things over. "You know, I used to think that

Melvin withdrew from everyone and focused on sculpting to get over bouts of depression, but if there's a plus side to that, I suspect that's when he's most creative. Or maybe it's the need to immerse himself in his work that makes him withdraw. It's his way of focusing solely on what he's trying to create."

Regina considered it. "I don't know Melvin that well, but my cousin knew him before his accident. She sometimes gives Melvin a ride when John's not around. She's also the one who told me about Melvin's past. He was a nature photographer who loved his work. He traveled all over the country, photographing wildlife for national magazines. Then he lost his sight—and his profession," she said. "Of course he's moved on and become a successful sculptor, but she's convinced that there's something else still eating at him."

Leigh Ann said nothing. She'd sensed that on occasion, too, but Melvin was very private, even with friends.

When they finally opened for business, there were people already waiting on the big, covered front porch, ready to shop. The business had been in a slump for months, but Saturday was usually always one of the busiest days at The Outpost.

The morning was even more hectic than usual, but Leigh Ann loved it when the place was like this. Time went by so fast, which made waiting easier, too. Although she was looking forward to seeing Melvin, she also knew there was no guarantee he'd actually show up. He came when his sculptures were ready, and that wasn't always predictable.

As hard as she tried not to dwell on it, every time the cowbell over the door rang, she'd glance up, hoping it would be him. It was close to eleven when Melvin finally arrived. He held the door open for his uncle, John Littlewater, a barrel-chested, slightly bowlegged man in his mid-fifties who was carrying a large wooden box.

"It's good to see you today, John, Melvin," she said, a special warmth stealing over her as she realized that Melvin had turned toward her even before she'd spoken. If it was just the hair spray, more power to it, she thought, smiling widely.

Melvin was a few inches taller than she was, with strong, broad shoulders and muscular arms. She'd never seen him without his shirt on, but she had a feeling he'd be easy on the eyes.

Taking Melvin's arm, she guided him to the display counter she and Regina had set up, John following close behind. "You know, Melvin, I have a feeling that you'd be able to walk around the trading post by yourself if you wanted to. You just like having me hold on to you," she teased.

"Busted," he said, smiling.

"So what did you bring us today?" she said, her voice rising slightly with excitement. "I can't wait to see it," she added, looking back at John.

"I think it's his best work yet," John said, carefully lowering the box to the floor. Leigh Ann quickly removed some of the pottery from the table, making space for the new piece while John opened the crate. He set the sculpture, shrouded in bubble wrap, on the table and carefully unwrapped it, revealing a bear. Standing on its hind legs, the work was finished in a satin black luster. Every detail had been crafted with care, from its paws and claws to the ghost of a growl Leigh Ann was sure she could hear coming from its muzzle.

"Wow," she said at last.

"Wait until you see the other one," John said.

"Two of them? That's great!" she said, tempted to clap but instead moving quickly to get the rest of the pottery out of the way.

The second sculpture was a stallion, also black but with less sheen, its head arched proudly, tail high. There was something in the cast of its eyes, an expression that was hard to define but immediately captured her attention. Sightless, they still appeared to see far into the distance.

"What an incredible piece," she said in a hushed tone.

"Do you like it more than the bear?" Melvin asked.

Leigh Ann considered it. "They're both amazing and very different, but this horse . . ."

"I knew it. Women and horses," he said with a grin. "There's a special connection there."

Leigh Ann sighed. "Maybe so."

"You'll sell both of them on consignment then, usual terms?" John asked.

"Yes, of course. We'll showcase and sell as many pieces as Melvin wants to bring us. His work is very popular with our customers."

Leigh Ann waved Regina over; the younger woman would position the signs for the works and relocate the pottery to other display areas.

"I wish you'd let me give you one of my sculptures as a gift, Leigh Ann," Melvin said. "The change in your voice when you see one of my pieces . . . It encourages me."

"I can't accept something like that, Melvin. It's your livelihood. It's right that you should get paid for your work."

John cleared his throat, getting their attention again. "So are we ready to go, nephew?" John asked Melvin. "We've got a lot of errands to run today."

"Leigh Ann, would you give me a ride home after John and I finish our errands? We should be done around five. John could drop me off here and meet his friends at the Totah Café

46

instead of having to drive me back," he said, then quickly added, "Unless you've got plans, of course."

"It's Saturday, so we won't close until six. You might have to wait for me," she said. "That okay with you?"

"You bet. I've put in long hours on these sculptures, so I've got a bad case of cabin fever."

A curious undertone in his voice caught her attention, but she didn't have time to pursue it as customers were approaching the register. "We'll talk later. Why don't you come over for dinner tonight? I'm a pretty good cook, if I say so myself."

"I'd like that."

Leigh Ann watched him leave. Though he often touched the shelves along the way to orient himself, his strides as he crossed the room were surprisingly sure, despite the fact that he usually chose not to carry a cane. Wishing they'd had more time to visit, she hurried over to the cash register, smiled at the first person on line, and focused on her work. There'd be time to catch up later.

After a while Regina came up. "Esther's still not here. Should I call?"

Leigh Ann shook her head. "Wait another fifteen minutes."

As she spoke, Esther hurried in through the front entrance. She was thin and wiry, but strong in every way. "I'm sorry I'm late, Leigh Ann. I had some trouble getting Truman settled before I left."

Leigh Ann could tell from the strain in her eyes that Esther hadn't been sleeping. "Do you need time off?"

The older woman shook her head, then looked away, a clear sign that she didn't want to talk about it. "I need to get busy. I have to change the display before I leave today."

"If you need a hand, holler."

As a customer stopped to take a closer look at Melvin's sculptures, Leigh Ann smiled. She had a feeling the horse and bear would sell within a few days. Even as the thought formed, the woman picked up the bear and brought it to the cash register.

"I've been looking for a birthday gift for my husband, and this is perfect. You take credit cards, right?"

Leigh Ann rang up the purchase, glad Melvin was coming for dinner. She'd fix him something special to celebrate. This sale was practically a land speed record.

As she wrapped the bear and placed it in a box, surrounded by tissue and bubble wrap, she wished she had the money to buy the horse sculpture. A piece of Melvin's heart went into each of his pieces, and that alone would have made it priceless to her.

She sighed. Some things were just meant to stay out of her reach.

Josephine Buck sat on a sheepskin rug on the earthen floor inside the ceremonial hogan. Rudy Brownhat was in a quiet mood today. In his role as teacher, Rudy sat at the rear of the hogan, behind the centrally placed fire pit, which was not in use on this warm day. Jo sat at the north end, facing him.

"She died a few days after the Sing. Went to the hospital with chest pains, I was told," Rudy said.

"She only came to us for a short pollen blessing. We did as she asked," Jo said, recalling the young woman who'd come to them a few weeks ago.

"There are those who feel that we somehow gave her false assurances."

"But that's not true," she said. "She had no symptoms and asked for no treatment other than the blessing."

He nodded and sipped tea from his sturdy white mug, which was stained from use. "Her family knows that and understands. I spoke with them after she passed."

"Then what's bothering you, uncle?" she asked, using the title out of respect, not kinship.

"The man she was going to marry, he's a *bilisaana*, red on the outside, white on the inside.

He doesn't respect our ways anymore. I realize he's been grieving for days now, but what happened concerns me," Rudy said in a heavy voice. "He came by angry yesterday and upset my wife."

"Did he threaten her or you?" she asked quickly.

He shook his head. "I returned from a Sing I'd done over in Waterflow and found the man waiting for me. He'd just learned of her visit here and demanded to know why I hadn't sent his fiancée to the hospital immediately," he said. "I explained that she hadn't been ill when she came to us. She'd been looking forward to her wedding and only asked for a pollen blessing."

"He believed you, didn't he?"

"I'm not sure. He was still very upset when he left. Grief . . . it changes people, and that much pain can twist a man's inner form. . . . I just wanted you to know in case he visits you." He took a long, slow sip of his tea. "It's time to begin your lesson. Have you memorized the Hogan Song that begins the night portion of the Blessingway?"

She took a deep breath. "I've tried, but it's long." A Blessingway Sing, which took several days, began with the Hogan Song and ended with the Dawn Songs.

"The Blessingway must be done perfectly. Through it, we bring our gods the gift of order."

Jo knew the risks. The slightest mistake in a prayer, however long, could bring about tragedy or disaster.

"Intent and the spoken word bring about completion, which gives us harmony. Think on that and begin."

Concentrating, hoping she'd be able to finish without mistakes, she beat on the overturned basket, using it as a drum. The monotone chant was invigorating and she felt its power coursing through her.

After several minutes, aware that her teacher hadn't commented and hoping it meant he was pleased, she looked over at him.

Rudy was blinking hard and clutching his chest.

Jo immediately stopped. "Uncle, what's wrong?"

Rudy pointed to his cup but his breathing was so rapid, he couldn't form words.

Jo dropped the basket and reached for her phone, dialing 911 as she walked to the Hogan door. "Victoria!" she yelled, calling for Rudy's wife.

She turned back toward the *hataalii* as the dispatcher came on the line.

A minute later, she ended the call. "Help is on its way," she told him. She'd asked for an ambulance and given their location, yet even as she spoke, she could see that he was getting worse.

Her teacher began brushing aside something only he could see. *"S-s-su!"* he yelled.

The word was roughly the equivalent of "scat" but she could see nothing near him, not even a fly or bee. Jo tried to calm him, but Rudy lashed out, pushing her away.

A second later Victoria Brownhat rushed into the hogan.

Seeing her husband thrashing on the floor, Victoria pressed a hand to her bosom. "What's happening to him?" She tried to go to her husband, but Jo held her back.

"No, give him room. He can't hurt himself where he is now, but he could hurt you without meaning to. He's having some kind of seizure."

"Why? What's causing this?"

"An allergic reaction, or maybe poison. The tea . . ." Jo looked down at the mug her teacher had dropped.

"Don't let him die!"

"Help will be here in just a few minutes," Jo assured her.

Fortunately, the Brownhats lived on the outskirts of Shiprock so the regional medical center was just minutes away. Hearing the sound of sirens, Jo went to the door of the hogan, watching for the EMTs. "Here they come."

Victoria nodded, her arms wrapped around herself in a hug. "First let the Anglo doctors help, and then do a Lifeway Sing."

Jo nodded. That was the way it was these days. The emergency room came first, then it was time for traditional medicine from a *hataalii*.

As the EMTs raced up the dirt road, Jo dialed the tribal police. Something told her they'd be needed, too.

The rest of Saturday went by quickly at The Outpost. Not long after Melvin's bear sculpture had sold, another customer expressed interest in the horse, promising to come back on Monday. Leigh Ann smiled, looking forward to giving Melvin the good news.

It was approaching six when she went to check on Del, the high school senior who worked for them during the afternoons and all day Saturday. The young man had kept to himself today, stocking the shelves and organizing the storeroom.

Leigh Ann walked into the storeroom and found him cleaning out the big double sink. "It looks great in here. Good job," she said. "About done?"

"Everything is shelved or on pallets, and I've just finished mopping the floor. I guess I better move fast and sweep the front. It's past closing time," Del said, glancing at the clock above the door.

Leigh Ann looked over and drew in a breath. It was five minutes past, actually, time to lock up if there were no more customers inside.

The afternoon had gone by in a blur. Melvin, who'd called earlier to say he'd be delayed—they'd had a flat—would be arriving soon and she still had to prove out the cash registers.

"It's later than I thought, too," she said.

Esther was still at the sewing machine, working.

"Esther, it's time to call it a day," she said.

"You've got one more customer," Esther replied, and gestured by pointing her lips, Navajo style.

Leigh Ann hurried to the cash register, where the Anglo businesswoman she'd spoken to earlier about the horse sculpture was waiting. The lady explained that she had decided not to wait to make the purchase, afraid someone else would get it first. Leigh Ann smiled. More good news to share with Melvin.

Once the sculpture had been carefully packed up, Leigh Ann escorted the customer out, holding the door open for her and wishing her a good evening. Then she closed and locked the door and hung up the closed sign. Turning back to the room, she saw Regina helping Esther add a new, obviously handmade western shirt to the clothing display. "That looks great!"

"It's still pinned in spots, but it will look fine to customers," Esther said. "I'll take some material home and finish another top tomorrow afternoon."

"You don't have to do that, tomorrow's Sunday," Leigh Ann reminded her.

"I need something to help me unwind," Esther said. "Days . . . are long at home—even the Lord's day."

As Esther walked into the back to punch her time card and collect her purse, Regina remained behind with Leigh Ann. "Del's already gone, and I've got to clock out, too. Mom's got a part-time job as a waitress at the Palomino Café in Kirtland so she has to get ready for her shift."

"Go. I'm waiting for Melvin, so I'll be here a little longer," Leigh Ann said, recalling her own six-month stint as a waitress at the Bullfrog Tavern, just off the Navajo Nation.

A café without a liquor license was probably a better gig than a bar, though she didn't know what was worse, an amorous drunk or a bawling child whose parents were oblivious.

Regina's mom could probably handle it. Leigh Ann had met the woman, and she didn't take crap from man or beast. The thought made her smile.

As soon as the others left, Leigh Ann turned down the lights, made sure the registers balanced, then put all the cash into the safe in Jo's office. She was just finishing when she heard a knock at the front entrance.

Leigh Ann stepped into the doorway of the

office and looked down the main aisle, spotting the familiar pickup parked in the lot. Grabbing her purse, she flipped off the light and walked out the door, keys in hand.

"Hi, guys!"

John gave her a nod. "You're all set, nephew," he told Melvin, who was standing on the gravel beside the passenger side door. "I'll be going now."

"See you later, John," Leigh Ann said.

"You ready to go?" Melvin asked, stepping forward, feeling his way over the concrete parking barrier.

"Yep. Let me lock up, then we'll be on our way," she said. "On the way home I'm going to make a quick stop, okay? I want to pick up some sparkling apple cider. It'll help us turn dinner into a celebration. I've got some good news for you!"

Three

Upon her arrival at the tribal hospital, Jo turned over the herbal tea container to the doctors treating Rudy. One of the lab people, a Navajo well versed in native herbs and regional plants, had been told of the symptoms and already had a theory. Based on her description of the symptoms and their onset, he suspected that Rudy's tea had been contaminated with chopped azucena de Mejico berries—belladonna. The berries tended to be sweet and masked easily by the traditional herbal tea the *hataalii* preferred.

"Tell me why you immediately suspected that he'd been poisoned," the Navajo tribal police officer standing at the nurses' station counter asked, questioning Jo as he filled out an incident report.

"I didn't know he'd been poisoned—*he* did," she said. "He pointed to the teacup and tried to tell me, but by then, he couldn't speak."

"You have no idea how the berries got into his tea?"

"If you're implying I had something to do with this—" Jo said angrily.

"Ma'am, I'm not implying anything. You've already stated that the *hataalii* was drinking from the cup when you arrived. I'm just trying to establish a timeline and sequence of events."

"I was in the middle of a Sing I'd been trying to learn for weeks, concentrating on that," she answered, mollified. "By the time I glanced over at him, he was already in distress and showing symptoms."

"Beside the patient and his wife, do you know who else might have had access to that tea?" the officer asked.

"Any of his guests or patients could have contaminated the container, I suppose. He keeps it in the medicine hogan on a shelf, but anyone could have gained access. The entrance is covered only by a wool blanket."

"That's according to the old ways," the officer said, nodding. "Do you know if your teacher has any enemies or if anyone has threatened him recently?"

She nodded. "As a matter of fact, I do. The fiancé of a former patient accused my teacher and me of not giving the young woman the proper treatment when she came to us. She died a few days after the pollen blessing."

"How, exactly, did she die?"

"The doctors here should know. From what I heard, it sounded like she had a heart attack," Jo replied.

"What's the man's name?"

She shook her head. "Names have power. My teacher didn't share that with me."

The officer nodded, then brought a small note-pad from his pocket and handed it to her with a pen. "Then write down the patient's name. I can get the boyfriend's name from her family."

The officer was respecting the Navajo custom of not speaking the name of the deceased aloud so soon after the fact, and Jo appreciated that. She wrote down the name: Rosemary Bernal.

Just then, a doctor came out of a double door and walked over to Victoria. "Excuse me a moment, please," Jo said, stepping over to join Rudy's wife.

"He's out of danger now," the doctor told them, "but some of the symptoms will persist for a while. With that in mind, we'd like to keep him overnight, just to be safe."

Victoria nodded. "May I sit with him?"

"Of course."

Jo remained next to Victoria as the doctor left. "Your husband's getting the best of care, but I'll be happy to keep you company."

Victoria smiled, and shook her head. "I appreciate the gesture, but it's not necessary. I know you have things to do, so don't worry. My husband and I will both be fine."

"All right then." Jo returned to where the police officer waited. "There may be more of that tea at the hogan. Would you like to follow me back there and collect it?"

"Good idea. Lead the way."

Jo walked out to her truck. All things

considered, Rudy had been lucky. If she hadn't been there . . .

She suppressed the shudder that ran up her spine. Though it had been a long day, she doubted she'd get much sleep tonight.

Leigh Ann happily served her sister and Melvin her specialty, what she called New Mexican lasagna. It was her own recipe, made with lasagna noodles, fresh green chile salsa and cheddar cheese. Since tonight was a celebration she refused to count the calories and put a good-sized portion onto her own plate.

Before long, Rachel helped herself to seconds. "I'm going to have to run for five miles to work this off," she said, "but it's just so darned good."

"It is," Melvin agreed and asked for another serving.

A phone rang somewhere in the room and Rachel said, "That's my cell, so it's probably Charlie. I think I'll skip dessert. Excuse me," she added as she stood and hurried over to the coffee table where she'd placed her purse.

"Charlie's her boss. They're dating now," Leigh Ann explained.

"That could get awkward," Melvin said.

"Guys, I'm taking off for a bit," Rachel said, walking back toward the table. "Charlie wants to talk to me about something, so we're meeting for drinks at the Bullfrog Tavern."

"You're going to have a conversation at the noisiest bar in the county?" Leigh Ann asked, surprised.

"I forgot you waitressed there for a while," Rachel said. "Now that I think of it, you might want to bring Melvin and come along. Back to your old stomping grounds, sis."

"I never stomped, I waited tables and ended up hating the place. Why would I ever want to go back?" Leigh Ann asked.

"Pierre Boone hangs out there," she said. "You need to talk to Kurt's former partners about what you found in that box and it'll be safer in a crowded, public place. They're not bound to get defensive there, even if you stick your foot in your mouth."

Leigh Ann said nothing for a moment or two. "No," she said at last.

"Suit yourself," Rachel said and shrugged. "See you later, Melvin. It was nice having you over for supper."

"Good talking to you, too," Melvin said, leaning back in his chair.

"You ready for some dessert?" Leigh Ann asked.

"Coffee would be great, but nothing else."

"You sure?"

"I'd rather just talk for a bit."

Leigh Ann got the coffeepot going and returned to the table.

61

"Rachel might be on to something," Melvin said. "If you've turned up information you think Kurt's former partners may not like, talking in a place like that may work to your advantage. Neither man is likely to give you trouble there, and even if the guys decide to follow up on it later, they'll have had time to cool off."

She sighed. "Not tonight. I need time to think it through. Kurt's entire life was a maze of lies and secrets."

"So what's this about a box? What's going on?"

"It's not about Kurt's women this time, at least." Months ago, in a moment of weakness and needing the comfort of his friendship, she'd confided in Melvin, telling him about Kurt's girlfriends. "This is something totally different, but I don't understand most of it yet," she said, then told him what they'd found in the attic.

"You know what bothers me most about all this? I spent years married to a man I never really knew. I saw only what I wanted to see. How could I have been so gullible?"

"Whatever Kurt did is out of your hands now. Maybe you should just let the past go."

"I can't. The past will keep finding me, just like that box in the attic, until I deal with it once and for all."

He nodded slowly. "You can't forget and let go until you have closure. I get it."

Once again she heard the edge of darkness that lay just beyond his sexy smile. She wondered about that side of him, the one he never showed the world. Yet as badly as she wanted to know more, she didn't push. That was a line neither of them ever crossed. Their friendship had boundaries.

"If you think Kurt hid stolen money in a storage locker," he said, "why don't we go over there right now and take a look?"

"I'm not sure the place is even open this time of night."

"Give them a call. I have a feeling they don't keep banker's hours. The people who use those places often have to go there after work and on weekends."

"Good point, but I still don't have a key."

He smiled, then reached into his pocket and pulled out a combination knife. "I used to be very good at picking locks."

She stared at him in surprise. "You were?"

"Practically gifted," he said, chuckling. "As a kid, I was always taking doorknobs and locks apart to see how they worked. It drove my parents crazy."

"Okay then." She found the number on a phone search and called. A minute later, she hung up. "I got a recording, but if it's up to date, they're open 'til midnight."

He stood. "Coffee can wait."

They were on their way moments later. Leigh Ann had grabbed a copy of Kurt's death certificate along with the rental receipt.

Are you sure you want to get involved in this?" she asked as she entered the city limits of Farmington, which was twenty miles to the east along the river valley. "I have no idea what I'll find except that it'll be something illegal. I may be getting you involved in a very dangerous situation."

"Leigh Ann, you worry too much. I'm a big boy. I can take care of myself."

"I'm just trying to look out for a friend," she answered.

"I know, and I appreciate it, but you're doing me a favor by letting me get involved."

"Really? How?"

"I'm between projects now," he said. "This is the time I'd usually go visit the art classes at the elementary school. Unfortunately, the semester is almost over and funding cuts have taken away most of the summer art programs for the kids. Volunteering at the schools, dealing with the kids . . . that's what helped me unwind. Without those visits I'm too alone with my thoughts, and that often takes me down some very dark trails. I need to be occupied, to keep my mind busy. Being around the kids helped me create new art—being around you . . . even more so."

"*I* inspire you?"

"You do in ways I find hard to put into words," he said.

"That's the nicest thing you've ever said to me," Leigh Ann said.

"It's the truth."

She parked at the curb outside the high wall of the storage facility, her hands now shaking so badly at the moment she almost dropped her keys. "We're here. The gated entrance is about fifty feet away," she said, but made no move to get out of the car.

"Relax, there's nothing to be nervous about. It'll be all right," he said quietly. "No matter what you find here tonight, we'll figure things out and go from there. Take it one step at a time."

"Good advice." She took a deep breath, sat perfectly still for a moment, then finally climbed out of the Jeep and walked around the front to the passenger's side. "There's a sidewalk, but you have to step up at the curb," she said through Melvin's half-open window.

He opened the door and stepped out carefully, feeling with the tip of his boot. "This is the time of day when I find it almost impossible to see anything at all. I can see shapes of people and objects when I get close enough, but at night even those disappear into the background unless there's really strong lighting."

"Do you want to stay in the Jeep?"

"Not if I'll need to pick a lock. It's true that I have a hard time getting around at night, but I may still be able to help you. I can detect scents that you wouldn't necessarily notice, for example, and hear the slightest whisper. My touch is heightened, too."

Leigh Ann's thoughts strayed as her anxiety was replaced with other emotions that led in another direction entirely. She'd always been more comfortable making love in the dark. It had been her way of hiding, of holding on to the piece of her soul she'd never surrendered. Now instinct told her that with Melvin there'd be no lines, no barriers left uncrossed. She bit back a sigh.

"The dark can reveal secrets we'd never share otherwise," he murmured.

A delicious shiver ran up her spine; there was a tiny hitch in her breath.

Melvin said nothing, but she saw the ghost of smile touch the corners of his mouth.

Forcing herself to focus, she wound her arm around his and walked to the storage facility's office, a small room just inside the tall, sliding panel, metal gates. As they entered, a young, attractive Hispanic woman smiled and rose from a tall stool behind the counter. "Melvin! I haven't seen you in ages."

Melvin paused for a beat, then said, "Jenny, is that you?"

"You remember!" she said, coming around the counter and giving him a hug. "I haven't seen you since you and Kathy broke up. I kept hoping you'd come by the house just to say hi," she said, snuggling into him.

Leigh Ann stared at the woman, hating the attention she was giving Melvin and the way he was eating it up.

"Truth is, I'd heard you moved out," Melvin said.

"Kath told you that, right?"

"Come to think of it, she did," Melvin said, and laughed.

Leigh Ann suddenly wondered if Melvin had volunteered to come because he'd hoped to run into Jenny. Not that she had any claim on Melvin, but until that very moment, she'd never even considered the possibility that there were other women in his life. At the trading post, she was the only guide he would accept.

Theirs was the best of friendships, one with no demands or expectations. There was much she didn't know about Melvin, and she'd wondered, since they'd met, if he was still burdened by the memories of the accident that had cost him his sight. Something was keeping him from speaking of his past, at least in any detail.

"This is my friend Leigh Ann, Jenny," Melvin said.

The young woman gave her a dismissive look. "Oh, yeah, hi, Lena."

"It's Leigh Ann," she hissed.

The young woman nodded, and moved closer to Melvin. "I'm so glad you came by tonight. It's been such a long time."

Leigh Ann wanted to shake her until she rattled, but managed a thin smile instead. "You two can catch up later," she said. "Right now, I need some help. My late husband rented storage space here, but I didn't find the paperwork until yesterday. According to this receipt, he was paid up for a year, but he's passed on and the rental payment is past due. I need to pay you for those extra months and retrieve whatever's inside."

"I'm sorry for your loss," Jenny said automatically, then glanced at Melvin again. "You're always ready to lend a hand, Melvin. That's so sweet."

Leigh Ann glared at the girl. It was hard to imagine the possibility that there could be anything between her and Melvin. Maybe Jenny was being her namesake—a female ass.

"Do you have the locker number, ma'am?" Jenny asked, glancing back at Leigh Ann. "We usually don't close out unclaimed lockers right away unless we run out of space, so maybe you'll get lucky and everything will still be there."

Leigh Ann read it off the receipt.

Jenny stepped over to the computer keyboard and typed for a few seconds. "Compartment eighty-four C? You sure?"

"Yes, that's what it says here," Leigh Ann said, holding up the receipt.

"Sorry. That storage unit was closed out on October eleventh, almost eighteen months ago. The customer was given a prorated refund. We rented the unit again a few weeks later and that client is still using the compartment."

"Check again," Leigh Ann said crossly. "That can't be right. My husband died on October ninth, two days before that date. Dead people rarely come by to pick up their stuff."

"Ma'am," she said again, making Leigh Ann painfully aware of the difference in their ages, "this is all I have to go by." She turned the computer screen around so Leigh Ann could see it.

"Looks like someone passed themselves off as my husband," Leigh Ann said, reaching the only logical conclusion.

"Ma'am, that's not possible. No one can get into the storage units without using their personal key. We don't keep duplicates for security reasons. It's on our rental contract." She pointed toward a large sign on the wall that detailed the basic agreement. "If we'd had a break-in at around the time, that would explain it, but we haven't had any problems here, like, in forever."

Which begged the question how long was "forever" to someone her age, but Leigh Ann held her tongue. This wasn't the time to lose it.

"Also every time a unit is unlocked, especially on the night shift, an employee of the facility has to be present. It's an extra security measure. We don't allow people to just wander around back there. If the attendant accompanying your husband had noticed anything suspicious, like he was trying to pick the lock or use bolt cutters, he or she would have called the cops."

"If your dates are accurate, it couldn't have been my husband," Leigh Ann said flatly. "I notice your contract mentions security cameras. Can I see the video for that date and time?"

"Oh, of course!" she said, but after a beat, added, "Oh, wait, it's long gone. The DVDs are recorded over every few months. That helps keep down the costs to our customers."

"What about your personnel records then? Any idea which staff member was on duty at that time?" Melvin asked. "Kath was working here back then, wasn't she?"

Leigh Ann glanced at Melvin, and realized that she was getting so upset she hadn't even thought to ask that.

Jenny looked at the display again. "Yeah, but the person on duty that night was a guy named Joey Smart. See his name on the receipt? Your husband—" she started, then seeing the look on

Leigh Ann's face, amended it, "the person who said he was your husband must have fit the description, because we take a photo copy of the renter's driver's license and compare it with the customer's face before we let them access any units."

Leigh Ann stared at her in surprise, then after a beat added, "And no one here has a duplicate key to the renter's padlock?"

"No. Every renter has to have their own key *and* know the number of the unit. We don't give that information out."

"Joey Smart . . . The name sounds familiar," Melvin said, interrupting. "Wait a sec. Is that the same guy I heard about on the news? He identified his neighbor, an elderly lady with short hair, as the serial killer he'd seen on a reality TV crime show the night before?"

"Yeah, that's him," Jenny said, laughing. "He apologized to avoid a lawsuit, but picked up the nickname 'Not Smart' along the way. Then he got into a fight here with a customer and was fired."

"So we're not dealing with a genius," Leigh Ann said softly.

"At least Kurt and the person impersonating him were probably both males," Melvin said.

"That doesn't narrow the field much. Do you have any idea where we can find Joey now?" Leigh Ann asked. "Maybe you have a forwarding address?"

"No we don't, sorry. After he got fired I heard he moved to Mississippi. I don't know where."

Leigh Ann led Melvin back to the Jeep and opened the passenger's side door for him. "There's no way Kurt would have told anyone about the storage unit or willingly surrendered the key. He was paranoid and determined not to get caught—case in point, the shotgun in the attic," she said.

"Maybe he left the key someplace, like his desk, and someone stole it."

"I doubt it. Kurt was really careful and kept everything on two rings—the house keys, car, post office box, business, on one, which he always carried, and the garage cabinet keys on the other, which were usually in a kitchen drawer. I'm certain Kurt kept the padlock key with those in his pocket."

"But it wasn't there when you got his personal effects from the police?"

"Not that I recall," she said, pulling out into the street.

"Are you're thinking he was murdered by his partners?" Melvin asked.

"Who else had a motive? Maybe one or the other found out he'd been creating phony accounts and embezzling money. They squared off and things got out of hand."

"You're thinking manslaughter as opposed to premeditated murder?"

"I suppose it could be either," she said slowly, having time to think now that they were at a stoplight. "But Kurt wouldn't have willingly told either of them about the storage space . . . unless he was bargaining for his life. That points to premeditation."

"Sure does. Do either of the partners resemble Kurt enough to pass for him at the storage place?"

She shrugged as they continued down the road. Traffic was light, with only a few cars out at the moment. "Wayne Hurley is about the same size and build as Kurt. He'd be a good match except for eye and hair color. Wayne has short, light brown hair, and Kurt's was longer and dark."

"Sunglasses, a wig, or a cap might have fooled 'Not Smart,' especially because he was working the late shift and may have been tired and inattentive."

"You may be on to something there. It's been my experience that nobody's security is as good as their company slogan," Leigh Ann said.

"Now we have a theory, but no way to prove it," he replied. "You're going to have to think hard about your next move, Leigh Ann. If you start asking questions, you're bound to make enemies. Kurt was killed, and you could be next."

"I hear you," she said, checking the rearview mirror.

"But you're not going to let it go, are you," Melvin said.

She smiled, noting that it hadn't been a question. "How do you do that? Nobody's ever been able to read me as easily as you do."

"I listen to you—not just to your words, but to what's in your heart when you speak."

A delicious sense of awareness rippled over her, making her feel bare and exposed. Realizing the danger, she pushed the feeling back. She had to remain more guarded around Melvin. Neither of them was ready to advance their relationship beyond friendship—not yet.

"Where to now?" he asked.

"You're going home. It's getting late."

"The road to my place is hard to travel at night. There are no lights around. Remember to go slow and look for potholes."

"My Jeep doesn't have a problem with off-road, and there's a full moon tonight," she said. "Don't worry. I won't get lost or wander off course."

"It's a rough ride no matter how you slice it," he warned. "You might consider spending the night and leaving tomorrow at first light."

Her heart jumped to her throat and for a moment she couldn't answer.

"I can't do that," she said at last. "It'll get . . . complicated."

"You can have the guest bedroom—or sleep

with me." Guided by her warmth, he touched her arm and traced a lazy pattern over her skin. "I could make it a night you'd never forget."

She shivered, and aware of it, he smiled. "You're denying something we've both thought about and want."

"Maybe so, but intimacy requires more than either of us is ready to surrender, Melvin. There's a line you and I have never crossed—things we've each chosen to keep private. We both need and want those barriers there."

He nodded slowly. "Respecting that balance is what allows us to be such good friends."

"And that's something worth protecting."

After a brief silence, Leigh Ann changed the conversation, wanting to lead her own thoughts back onto safer ground. "Have you decided what you'll be sculpting next?"

He shook his head. "It'll come to me in its own time. I can't force it."

As Leigh Ann glanced back in the rearview mirror, she saw the same car she'd seen behind them earlier at the first stoplight past the storage place.

It was probably just someone else driving to the Rez. There was only one major highway heading west out of the city. After another quarter mile, the car turned onto a residential street and she gave it no further thought.

Four

It was noon on Sunday and although the trading post was closed for business, Jo and Samantha Allison, Sam for short, were there, configuring and tweaking the computer software.

"Are you sure working on Sundays isn't going to create a big problem between you and Esther?" Jo asked, finishing the sandwich she'd taken from the deli bar.

"Grandmother hates it when I work on what she calls the Lord's day," the half-Navajo girl answered, sipping an oversized cola, "but I'm not a practicing Christian. I'm more into math, science, and technology," she said, focusing on the monitor for Jo's desktop computer. The blue upload progress bar was moving, but slowly.

At twenty-one, Samantha was the quintessential computer geek, hoping to gain real-world business experience by working at The Outpost. Jo had hired her to adapt and configure some new software. The Outpost had unique, individualized contracts with local artists—sculptors, potters, jewelry makers, and more. Sam's tweaks had made it possible for Jo to keep a continual tally on all merchandise under consignment as well as the specifics of each agreement. A database stored all the information Jo needed to reorder or commission new stock. What made it almost perfect was that Sam had set things up so that the pertinent data was automatically transferred to the store's tax accounting software.

"Your car's not outside," Jo said, casually glancing out. "Is it still at the shop?"

"Yeah, I'll get it back tomorrow. It needed transmission work. Jack Colburn dropped me off earlier. Which reminds me, Jack wanted me to ask you if he could deliver the bales of bedding straw later this afternoon instead of on Monday. If you're okay with that, he said he would stack it himself. I should be through by then though, so I can help him."

"That's fine," Jo said. She wasn't planning to stay long at The Outpost; in fact if she hadn't felt it necessary to get this computer work finished, she wouldn't have come in at all. As soon as she could get away, she wanted to check on Rudy. He'd spent the night at the hospital, and if the doctor released him today as planned she wanted to be on hand to offer him and Victoria a ride home.

"Oh—and can he put up a notice on our bulletin board?"

Jo glanced back at Sam, realizing that she had tuned out the young woman's last few sentences. "I'm sorry, what were you saying?"

"The bulletin board. Jack wants to expand the number of free riding and grooming classes he offers to children of military veterans. His Saturday classes are jammed, so he's going to start teaching Sunday afternoons, too. He wanted to place a notice on our bulletin board to help get the word out."

"No problem at all. He's really doing a great job. I've heard some of the moms and dads bragging about how much their kids have learned from Jack."

"Jack's a natural, being the son of a big rodeo cowboy. Since he's also half Navajo and remembers all the traditional stories his mom taught him, the kids think he's really cool. Of course they're a little surprised at first by his prosthetic arm, but after a while, they don't even notice it."

Hearing the way Sam's tone of voice changed when she spoke of Jack, Jo smiled. "You got a thing for him?"

Sam smiled. "Yeah. Not that he'd ever notice."

"So you two aren't dating?"

"Nah, I help him with the horses and the kids when I can, but that's about it." She shrugged. "That's okay. I don't plan to stick around the Rez much longer. There's really not that much work available around here for a computer tech—at least right now."

"That'll change—sooner rather than later."

"Maybe, but I have to be ready to go wherever the work is, and although it'll be hard to leave, it'll be exciting, too. A new adventure might be out there waiting for me."

"You sound just like Ben did when he graduated high school," Jo said, remembering.

"He joined the army and has seen the world. Europe, the Persian Gulf, the Middle East. Afghanistan . . . Now there's an adventure," Sam said wistfully. "Testing your limits . . . finding out about yourself . . ."

"More than you want, sometimes," Jo said quietly.

"Yeah, it can be like that, too. When you test yourself, you don't always get the answers you want, but look at Jack. He served in the army, fought the enemy, and like Ben, became stronger for it."

"Is that what you want—to join the military?"

"No, I'm not a fighter—not the gun-carrying kind anyway. Jack needed the structure and discipline of the military to find himself, but I'm after something different. I don't have a big college degree, just a lot of good course work. I'm good with computers, though, and I love math. What I need now is some experience and the contacts to eventually build a business of my own. I want to be the go-to IT source in the Four Corners."

Jo smiled. Although they were only seven years apart, Samantha seemed more like a teenager than a woman to her. Sam had been sheltered and protected all her life. Jo, on the other hand, had cared for herself and her shattered family for as far back as she could remember.

"Have you heard from Ben lately?" Sam asked. "Grandma says he usually calls via Skype on Thursdays and that you were disappointed last week when you didn't hear from him."

That was one of the reasons she'd come in early today. Sometimes when Ben couldn't contact her during the week, he would call on Sundays instead, but so far she hadn't heard from him. No email, no call.

As Sam's focus shifted back to the computer, they suddenly heard a loud *thump,* followed by breaking glass, coming from the back.

Sam jumped up and ran to the rear window. "Nobody's out there. I thought maybe Jack had come back early and run into something."

Jo stepped into the hall and looked across the interior of the store toward the front parking lot. A dark-colored truck was speeding up the drive in a cloud of dust. "The driver must have circled the building. I wonder what he did? It's easy to see that we aren't open for business today . . ."

"Let me grab the baseball bat and go out with you," Sam said.

Jo continued to look outside, but didn't see anyone. "No, Sam, stay put. I'll step out onto the loading dock and check my truck and the trading post's vehicles. If you hear me yell, call 911."

"Don't go out there alone, Jo. Let me go with you. I can fight. I grew up with three brothers."

Jo chuckled. "Okay, but bring your cell phone."

Once they stepped onto the loading dock, it was easy to see what had happened. A glass jar filled with blood red paint had been thrown against the overhead door. The jar had shattered, creating a big splatter that was trickling down in rivulets and scattering shards and chunks of glass everywhere.

Jo glanced around and breathed a sigh of relief as she saw that her car and the store's van were untouched.

"Petty vandalism," Sam said and smirked. "With graduation coming up, the high school seniors are just itching for some action. Things can get awfully dull around here."

Jo sighed. Dull. She'd welcome that. Some days she was so busy she barely had time for meals.

Sam looked over. "Should I call it in?"

Jo shook her head. "No, don't bother. The sheriff won't be able to do much. We didn't get a license number or see a face."

She stepped closer to the paint, making sure not to step on the splatter, and sniffed the air. "It's water-based, which means I should be able to wash it off before it dries if I move quickly enough. I'll bring the pressure washer we normally use for cleaning the dock and add a little detergent to the spray."

"I'll hook up the hose," Sam said, running off.

Jo stared at the paint. The color . . . the timing . . . After what happened to Rudy, she couldn't know for sure, but it was possible that this was more than just petty vandalism. Someone might be sending her a message.

Sam brought the hose out of the storeroom. "Do you need my help here, or should I go back to setting up the software?"

"Hook up the hose, then focus on the computer. That's your skill set. I can take care of this."

Jo put on a pair of rubber gloves, then collected all the pieces of glass she could find and put them in a bucket out of the way. Using the pressure washer's high-impact spray, she rinsed the paint from the loading dock's door. It didn't take long. She was just cleaning off the washer with some paper towels when Sam beckoned to her from the employee door.

Hoping it was a call from Ben, Jo ran inside. "It's Victoria Brownhat," Sam said softly, gesturing to the phone.

Jo answered quickly. "I'm here. Is everything all right?"

"Yes. I'm calling because I need to talk to you. Can you come by the house today?"

"You're already home?"

"Yes, my cousin came by the hospital to visit and offered us a ride."

Jo glanced up at the clock. "I'll be there as soon as I can." As she hung up, she glanced over at Sam. "Can you lock up without me when you finish? I have to go."

"Of course," Sam said, "and before I leave I'll also make sure the bedding Jack's delivering today is properly stored. Is everything okay?"

"I don't know." Thinking of the vandalism and suddenly worried about Sam, too, she added, "When's Jack supposed to be here?"

"He said around four, but no prob. I'll be fine," she said, as if reading Jo's mind.

Jo shook her head as she checked the time. It was two thirty. "No. I'll wait."

"You want me to call Jack and ask him how his schedule is running? He's usually early."

Jo nodded. "Normally I wouldn't ask but . . . these are special circumstances."

Sam nodded and had just picked up her phone when they both heard the roar of a powerful truck engine. She went to the window and smiled. "Jack's here. As I said, he's always early."

"Good. Grab dinner before you leave, on the house, but don't forget to lock up everything and set the alarm."

"I'll ask Jack to take one last look around, too, just to be on the safe side."

Jo smiled. "Thanks, Sam."

"No problem," she said, sipping from a jumbo cup of highly caffeinated soda.

No wonder Sam stayed so skinny, Jo thought. The girl loved those fast-food energy drinks and was always on hyperdrive.

Jo grabbed her purse. The bright silver tote sparkled in the sunlight and she just loved it. She'd always had a thing for purses, the wilder the better. They cheered her up, and at the moment, she needed all the boost she could get.

Leigh Ann was dressed casually today, wearing jeans, a sleeveless blouse, and comfortable sneakers, appropriate attire for the Sunrise Café, a popular roadside diner in the community of Kirtland. She was waiting for her cousin, Dale Carson. He'd served with the state police for a decade before transferring to the county sheriff's department, wanting a smaller area to patrol. Although he hadn't been involved in the investigation surrounding Kurt's death, she knew he was familiar with everything that had happened.

The tall, blond sergeant, out of uniform and wearing a dark blue polo shirt and jeans, stepped into the diner and Leigh Ann waved. In a moment he'd joined her at her table.

"Day off?" Leigh Ann asked.

"Yeah and not just because it's Sunday. I've been working the graveyard shift. Next week I go back to days again." He ordered coffee, leaned back, then placed his arm across the booth's low back. "What's up, cuz?"

"I've got a mess on my hands, Dale." She told him what she'd found in her attic.

"You turned that stuff in, right?" Seeing her shake her head, he added, "You've got to do that, Leigh Ann, and be aware that once you do, things are going to get a lot tougher for you. You were Kurt's wife, which means you'll become an instant suspect in his embezzlement scheme. Did anyone ever ask you about Kurt and that missing money, or about the fake vendor, Frank Jones?"

"Wayne and Pierre have both asked me about business files pertaining to Frank Jones. They thought Kurt might have brought them home or transferred them to his home computer. I looked around, but I didn't find anything at the time."

"It sounds like they *did* suspect Kurt. Once officers go talk to both men, the partners may claim that you've been holding out on them."

"That's not true. I didn't know anything about all this until I found that box."

"Maybe so, but look at it from a different perspective. It could be argued that you knew Kurt had been cheating on you. When you found out about the money, you decided to kill him, make it look like a hunting accident, and take the cash."

"Oh, crap. I'm a pretty good shot, too," she admitted in a muted voice, fear winding through her. "I used to go with him to the gun club and shoot the rifle he bought me for our anniversary. What a gift, right? Conveniently, it was the same rifle he'd wanted for himself for years."

"Consider getting a lawyer," Dale said, looking serious.

"Are you kidding me? I barely have enough to cover my bills." She stared at her hands, lost in thought, trying to come up with a plan. After a moment, she looked up at him. "I realize that at first glance it may look bad for me, but if people stop to think it through they'll see I'm not guilty. If I were, I wouldn't have turned the box over to them."

"It's not that simple. You could have decided to shift the focus back to Kurt's illegal activities, hoping that would protect you from his partners. Since they knew about Frank Jones and the embezzled money, it was only a matter of time before they came after you. At the very least, they might have sued Kurt's estate for restitution."

"But I almost got shot getting that box," Leigh Ann said, trying not to lose it now.

"That shotgun booby trap could also work against you. Even if it could be proven that you didn't fake it, it suggests Kurt was keeping the theft from you and was willing to risk you getting killed. That begs the question, why didn't he trust you? Couple that with the fact that you didn't have an alibi for the day he was killed and it doesn't look good."

"I was at home that entire weekend," she said, swallowing hard, her voice whisper thin, "but I shouldn't have to prove my innocence. They have to prove my guilt."

"That's true, but while they look into things your life is going to get mighty complicated," he said. "Here's another question. When did you first learn that Kurt was cheating on you?"

"Not until after he died."

"Can you prove that?" Seeing her shake her head, he continued. "Infidelity is a common motive for killing a spouse. Add to that the money Kurt stole, and you've got the makings of a pretty good circumstantial case. The detective in charge of the investigation will undoubtedly consider the possibility that you've got the money hidden somewhere right now, or have been spending it a little at a time."

"This was a mistake. I shouldn't have called you," she said, almost in tears.

"Leigh Ann, we're family," he said, patting her hand. "I had to let you know what you're acing. I'll do my best to protect you. In the meantime, you need to watch your back. Give straight answers, but don't volunteer any information."

She felt sick but managed to nod. "Okay, let's go to my place. All things considered, I'd rather hand the box over to you." *Everything except for the .38.* It was loaded with six rounds, and she'd already put that somewhere safe. She had a feeling she might need it.

Leigh Ann sat just outside the French doors on the patio, looking into the garden. Dale had told her he'd pass the box along to the detective who'd investigated Kurt's death. The white collar crimes division would also be informed. Someone in one or both of those divisions would call on her soon.

On edge, she stood and paced, praying that Dale's worst-case scenario would end up being nothing more than a scary story. She'd assumed the police would be on her side, but it seemed she might be in more danger than ever. If Kurt had been murdered, she'd just awakened a sleeping tiger, a dangerous adversary who, up 'til now, had gotten away with his crime.

Last night, after dropping Melvin off, she could have sworn she'd seen a dark-colored sedan following her and had briefly wondered if it was the same one she'd seen when they'd left the storage facility. The car had veered off before she'd reached the turnoff to her home, so she'd stopped worrying about it. Now she wondered if she should have paid closer attention and tried to make note of its license plate.

Rachel came out the French doors with two

mugs of tea, handed one to Leigh Ann, then sat down in the other patio chair.

Leigh Ann looked at her across the small bistro table in surprise. "What's all this?"

"I have something to tell you and I wanted you to have some of your favorite vanilla caramel tea while we talked."

"What's up?"

"Since you're so intent on finding out what Kurt was up to, I decided to give you a hand. I made copies of everything that was in that box. I figured you might need to check that information and duplicates might come in handy somewhere along the way."

"That wasn't a bad idea at all," she said, considering the circumstances. "Thanks."

"I also ran into Pierre Boone last night at the Bullfrog. I told you he hangs out there, remember?" At Leigh Ann's nod, she continued. "He and Wayne were having a drink, and while the band was taking a break, I went over to talk to them."

"You did *what?*" Leigh Ann sat up. "Rachel, what exactly did you say to them?"

"I was casual about it, but I told them that some of Kurt's personal papers had raised some questions for you and that you'd probably be calling them to see if they could help you find answers."

"Rachel, I really wish you hadn't done that," Leigh Ann said.

"Those two have always liked me, so I wanted to open the door for you."

Leigh Ann thought back again to the sedan she'd seen last night. Didn't Wayne drive a similar make and model? Then again, so did half the county. She took a deep breath. "You shouldn't get involved in this, Rache."

"Once they find out you've turned everything over to the cops, they're not going to hold you responsible for anything Kurt did. They'll leave you alone."

"It's not that simple." Leigh Ann gave her a short version of what Dale had told her.

"Damn," Rachel said softly. "I didn't think of that. There's only one thing you can do then. Stop looking into this right now, Leigh Ann. Maybe the whole thing will blow over if you just let it be."

Leigh Ann shook her head. "It's too late for me to back off, but even if I could, I wouldn't. I spent a lot of years closing my eyes to whatever I didn't want to see. I can't be that person anymore, no matter what the risk."

"You've changed a lot this past year, Leigh Ann. You're harder . . . tougher, you know? You don't back away anymore, but that can get you into a lot of trouble."

"Maybe, but I'm through hiding my head in the sand." Leigh Ann stood, grabbed her cup, and went inside.

There was one important thing she'd have to

do as soon as possible. She needed to let Jo know what was going on. She didn't think that whatever she'd stirred up could affect the trading post, but Jo deserved a heads-up.

The trading post people had become like a second family to her. They'd all faced danger together before, after Tom Stuart was murdered, and she knew they'd have her back.

She picked up the phone next to the kitchen cabinet and called Jo. Maybe they'd be able to talk tonight. If not, it would have to be tomorrow at work—hopefully, before a detective showed up to question her.

Jo sat across from Victoria in the Brownhats' small living room. Property belonged to the women, according to tribal customs, and that was evident inside the house. Just as the hogan was Rudy's domain, everything here held a feminine touch. The walls were adorned with beautifully crafted Navajo rugs of various styles. Victoria's mother and Victoria herself were skilled weavers. There were wildflowers in pots all around the room, too. Some Jo recognized, having become familiar with the Plant People, as Rez plants were called by Traditionalists.

Victoria sat in her favorite chair next to a small end table. At her feet were the beginnings of a woven basket. "My husband's resting now, but he asked me to give you a message."

Jo waited. Long pauses were common, and interrupting them was considered extremely rude.

"The fiancé of the woman who passed away days after her pollen blessing is a very angry young man," Victoria said. "The first time he came by, my husband was making tea from the herbs he keeps in the hogan. The man may have come back later during the night and added the poison to the container. The hogan is always open."

She handed Jo a piece of paper with the name Edmund Garnenez. "That's his name. I've been told by several people that he claims you and my husband witched her."

"That's a very serious accusation and a complete lie," Jo said, fighting to control her temper.

"Yes, but stories like those can take on a life of their own," Victoria warned. "They grow from the telling."

"People will see that it's his grief talking." Knowing that Victoria had enough to handle, Jo added, "I'll try to track the man down and talk to him."

Victoria shook her head quickly. "No, that's precisely what you shouldn't do. He's not thinking straight right now. I ran into him at the pharmacy and he said some bad things right to my face."

Although Jo knew that an apprentice *hataalii*

couldn't afford to succumb to anger, she felt a slow rage building inside her. There was no way she'd allow anyone to try to intimidate her teacher's family.

"Your first instinct may be to confront him, but remember that a *hataalii,* even an apprentice one, has to remain above things like this," Victoria said.

Jo swallowed hard and nodded. Her teacher's wife was right.

"My husband said to warn you that the young man may try to poison you next. You need t be careful what you eat and drink."

"I'll stay on my guard. Don't worry," Jo said, and stood. "If you need me, day or night, just call."

"Walk in beauty," Victoria said, accompanying her to the door.

As she headed for the trading post, Jo's thoughts shifted back to Ben. He was never far from her mind, but he'd been out of contact for several days, and she was worried about him. Since she didn't have access to Skype at home, she intended to hang around the office today as long as possible.

Hope . . . It was often a cheat, but sometimes it was all a person had.

Five

Leigh Ann liked to come in early on Mondays, but no matter when she arrived it seemed like Jo was already there. Today, she was determined to beat her boss to work and have coffee ready by the time Jo got there. She'd bring some of her special homemade biscuits, too. She used her mother's secret recipe and the baked goods practically melted in your mouth. Add just a touch of butter, and you had heaven.

Leigh Ann reached The Outpost at five minutes before six in the morning. To her surprise, Jo's truck was already there.

Leigh Ann shook her head in amazement as she got out of her Jeep. How dedicated was Jo to be in an hour early? Carrying a basket with a dozen biscuits she let herself in through the back, as usual. Jo was probably in her office, so Leigh Ann walked toward the employee area.

Light streamed into the hall through Jo's open office door. Leigh Ann looked in and saw Jo bent over in her chair, her head resting on her folded arms atop the desk.

The soft sound of Jo's rhythmic breathing told the story. Jo had undoubtedly spent the night waiting to hear from Ben. Leigh Ann knew that Jo had a laptop at home, but only dial-up, which meant Skype was out of the question.

Leigh Ann considered letting her rest, but, knowing Jo, realized her boss would rather be awakened before the store opened. Leigh Ann stepped into the room, placed a hand on Jo's shoulder, and called her name softly.

Jo sat up and groaned. "Aw jeez, I fell asleep . . . My back . . . ow." She straightened slowly.

"Did you hear from Ben yet?" Leigh Ann asked gently.

"No, not a word, but maybe . . ." Jo reached out and moved the mouse, bringing the screen out of sleep mode. Leigh Ann didn't look closely but could tell that Jo was checking her email inbox. The younger woman shook her head. "Damn."

"He may just be stuck somewhere that has no Wi-Fi service."

"I know." She stretched slowly from side to side and glanced up at Leigh Ann. "You're here way early, even for a Monday. Is everything okay?"

"I was hoping to talk to you before the others showed up," Leigh Ann said, not answering directly. "I brought biscuits to go with your coffee. Hungry?"

"Yeah, and those smell absolutely amazing. Unfortunately I need to go home, shower, and change," Jo said, indicating her paint-splattered jeans and shirt. "There's no way I'm greeting customers looking like this."

"I'll tell you what: Let me give you a ride home and back. You can eat on the way and we can talk."

"Sounds good to me," Jo said. "I'm too stiff and sore to drive right now anyway."

Within minutes they were on the way. Jo carefully cradled a lidded, foam cup of hot instant coffee in one hand and one of Leigh Ann's biscuits in the other.

"Better now?" Leigh Ann asked after the first biscuit disappeared.

"Much. My back's not screaming in protest, either." Jo glanced over and shifted in her seat so she could face Leigh Ann more squarely. "Okay, what did you want to talk to me about?"

Leigh Ann told her what she'd learned about Kurt and how she'd handed the box over to the sheriff's department. "I don't see any reason for this to spill over onto the trading post, but I felt you had to know. Dale warned me that I might get a visit from a detective today."

"I appreciate you telling me, Leigh Ann, but don't worry. We're not responsible for the actions of others," she said. "I know you're not a thief, much less a killer."

Leigh Ann breathed a sigh of relief.

"Let me know if I can help you in any way," Jo added.

Leigh Ann smiled. "Jo, you have no idea how much it means to me that you even offered." She glanced down at Jo's shirt. "What were you painting with such a bright red? A warning sign?"

Jo told her what had been happening, starting with Rudy's poisoning.

"Do I know the guy who might have done this?"

"I'm thinking it might be a guy named Edmund Garnenez. I knew him back in high school, but I haven't seen him since. He's not a Traditionalist, more like a Modernist, and I think he lives outside the Rez."

"I'll keep a lookout around The Outpost for anyone who's not acting right." Leigh Ann glanced in the rearview mirror and saw a dark sedan keeping pace with her Jeep. Uneasy, she tried to remember if she'd seen that car earlier today. Lately, she'd become paranoid, and for a good reason.

"There's a reworked turnoff to my place. It's just ahead on the left, about a quarter mile off the highway. The road used to be nothing more than potholes and dirt, which is why I always took the long way. Now it's all been graded and graveled. Take the turn kind of slow, though, because there's still a drop-off from the asphalt."

Leigh Ann didn't slow down, instead taking another quick look at the car behind them.

"Jo, I'm going to go past the turn, just to make sure."

"Sure about what?"

"There's a dark sedan that might be following us. I think I've seen it behind me before. . . ."

"You *think?*"

"It's probably nothing, but if the guy is tailing us, I don't want to lead trouble right to your doorstep." Her mouth was feeling really dry at the moment, and it wasn't from thirst. Suddenly she wished she had that revolver in the glove compartment.

Jo turned to look back. "Looks like he's decided to pass us."

"I'll slow down and give him plenty of room to get by," Leigh Ann said, easing up on the gas.

The driver closed the gap between the vehicles. As the big old car drew even with Leigh Ann's Jeep, she glanced over for a look at the driver, but couldn't make out his features. A ball cap pulled low kept his face in the shadows.

"Go ahead," Leigh Ann said, waving at him. Suddenly the black sedan swerved and, with a sickening crunch, slammed into the driver's side of the Jeep. The jarring collision almost made Leigh Ann lose her grip on the steering wheel, and her heart was pounding.

The Jeep bounced to the right, tires screaming as they barely avoided running off the highway.

"What the hell?" Jo gasped, grabbing the seat with both hands.

"Hang on, Jo!" Leigh Ann yelled, trying not to lose it. She pumped the brakes just as the sedan cut right again, crashing into her left front fender.

An ear-shattering screech of metal rattled her teeth, as the two cars locked together for a second. Leigh Ann felt the back of the Jeep lift off the roadway. Another few seconds and they'd roll for sure. Somehow, she had to get away. She took a quick look ahead.

"Screw this," Leigh Ann muttered, slamming on the brakes and whipping the Jeep to the right. They broke free, slid in neck-snapping jerks for an endless three seconds, then ran off the shoulder of the road onto the tall, dry grass of the drainage slope.

Somehow the Jeep stayed on all fours, finally rattling and bouncing to a stop. Dust enveloped them in a cloud, and in the chaos, the black car disappeared.

Leigh Ann stared at the white knuckles on each of her fingers, which were locked around the steering wheel in a death grip. Then she turned and looked over at Jo, who was leaning back, head up, muttering something in Navajo that sounded like a prayer.

"Are you okay?" Leigh Ann asked her, shaking.

"Yeah, but what the hell just happened?" Jo

sat up and reached for her cell phone. "I'm calling the tribal police."

"You think it was Edmund what's-his-name?" Leigh Ann said.

"I don't know, but whoever it was, he tried to run us off the road, maybe even kill us. There was nothing accidental about what he was doing. How'd you learn to drive like that?"

She laughed nervously. "Bumper cars at the county fair, I guess. Besides, there was no other choice but to leave the road and hang on."

Leigh Ann waited until Jo had finished her call to the tribal police. "I realize we're on the reservation, but this highway isn't exactly private, and I'm almost sure I've seen that dark-colored sedan before."

"You could ID the car?"

Leigh Ann shook her head, and filled her in on the details.

"Do you think it could have been one of Kurt's partners?"

"Wearing a baseball cap?" Leigh Ann shook her head. "Maybe, in disguise, but I really doubt it. Both those men go for cowboy hats. It could be that they hired someone to keep an eye on me and run me off the road if the opportunity came up."

"Are you suggesting that either one of us could have been the target, particularly if Kurt's partners have something to hide?"

100

"Yeah. Lucky us."

A woman tribal officer responded within thirty minutes, a fast response time for the tribal police. The force was stretched thin these days.

After getting the details of the incident from Jo and taking photos of Leigh Ann's car and the skid marks on the pavement, the dark-haired officer continued questioning them. She took notes as they spoke. Leigh Ann told the tribal cop about her suspicions regarding Kurt's death and Jo explained what had happened to Rudy, adding her theory regarding his poisoning.

"You gave me three names of men you think might have done this, yet neither one of you is able to describe or identify the driver. I need some actual evidence, ladies, not just speculation," the officer concluded.

"You could have someone at least pay them a visit. If one of their cars is damaged on the right front end . . . ," Jo said, leaving the sentence hanging.

"I'll check Mr. Garnenez's vehicle and have the sheriff's office run a make and model on any cars Mr. Boone and Mr. Hurley own or operate. I'll have a notice sent to local auto body shops as well. That's all I can do unless some physical evidence is uncovered or a witness comes forward. At this point, I have to consider this just a random act, possibly caused by a drunk driver."

"I understand. However, if you find out something, will you let us know?" Jo asked.

She nodded, handing Leigh Ann a business card. "You'll be notified if we find anything. I'll recover a sample of the chipped paint left behind as a result of the collision. In the meantime, you might want to call a towing service."

Leigh Ann gave her a wan smile. "I know it looks like it's gasping its last breath, but this Jeep can take almost anything I throw at it. The tires are intact and the damage is all cosmetic. It'll start and keep going."

The officer gave her a skeptical look. "Better get that driver's side front signal light fixed before another officer pulls you over."

Leigh Ann checked the support bracket, which had been bent almost ninety degrees. The cover glass had been smashed, and she'd have to get the wiring checked, but the bulb still looked intact. "Of course, Officer."

As she'd predicted, the Jeep started without any problem. Leigh Ann asked the officer to watch while she turned on the signal—which lit immediately.

"Okay, it still works," the officer said, shrugging. "It's as good as a lot of vehicles I see out here. But you should get a cover over the bulb before it gets wet."

"I'll take care of it," Leigh Ann said as Jo

climbed into the passenger seat. The tribal police officer got into her vehicle and pulled away, quickly disappearing down the highway.

"One way or another, we've got to find out who the target was—me or you," Leigh Ann said, checking her seat belt and shoulder strap.

"We will," Jo answered as they got underway. "Just don't let your guard down in the meantime."

Leigh Ann kept her eyes on the highway. Despite the paint incident at the trading post, she was sure that this violent, open attack had more to do with her than Jo. "If this turns out to be my fault, I can find another job, at least until I get matters settled."

Jo looked at her in surprise, then shook her head. "Trouble's part of life, Leigh Ann. No one's immune. The Outpost can handle whatever comes. I can't think of a better set of people to depend on when times get tough."

"You're right. We're family—the best kind, too—one that's bound by choice."

Jo was alone in her office when she finally heard the soft Skype ring tone and saw the box on her monitor with Ben's name. She clicked on the video button, put on the headset to keep it private, and within a few seconds Ben's face appeared on the computer monitor.

As usual, he was seated in a metal folding chair

in front of his laptop, which rested upon a makeshift table of what looked like plywood. Behind him was a white painted wall of undetermined composition, and against it two bare wood shelves piled with duffel bags and wire metal containers full of army gear and personal items. Fatigue uniforms were hung from a metal rod and there was a cot barely visible to one side. A photo of her was tacked on the wall above the bunk.

"Hi, darling," he said and flashed his usual grin. She'd gotten used to the slight delay and frequent jumps in imagery long ago. It was a small price to pay to actually be able to see Ben and talk in real time.

"Hi," she said, touching the screen. "I miss you." Her heart went out to him. She'd never seen him look more exhausted, yet he still managed to smile.

"Sixty-two days left in this deployment, and I won't re-up this time," he said. "I'm ready to come home for good."

"You look tired," she said in a gentle voice.

"Been training for the last eighteen hours," he said and shrugged. "It goes with the job." He looked at her for a moment. "I may be off-line for a while after today, just a heads-up."

"What's going on?" she asked, instantly alert. "What can you tell me?"

"Just that I'll be fine," he answered without

hesitation. "I'm on alert twenty-four/seven, so if you don't hear from me for a few days, don't worry, okay?"

"Yes, sir," she said and smiled.

"No, don't call me 'sir.' I'm a workingman, not an officer."

She smiled.

"You look pretty tired yourself. Are you getting enough sleep?" he asked.

"Yeah, it's just stress. Leigh Ann and I were in a fender bender with a drunk on the road, but nobody was hurt."

"What else?"

She smiled. He could read her better than anyone else ever had. "I'm worried about my teacher, the *hataallii*. Rudy drank some contaminated tea and it made him ill."

"Your medicine man mixed the wrong herbs?" he asked, surprised.

"No, he was poisoned, and it wasn't an accident either. He ended up in the hospital. He's okay now," she said, giving him the highlights.

"You probably saved his life. Just remember that you're his assistant now, so you'll have to be careful, too."

"I am," she said, refusing to tell him how close the threat had come to home.

Hearing a commotion behind him, and seeing him turn his head suddenly, she sat up instantly. "You okay?"

"Yeah, but I've got to go. Time for me to earn my pay. Love you!"

With that, he was gone. She had no idea when she'd hear from him again, and the thought tugged at her, but she fought back the tears. Ben was serving his country. The least she could do was hold it together and take care of things until he came back home.

She took a deep breath and took off the headset. It was time for her to get busy. She touched the screen with her fingertips. "Come home soon, Ben," she whispered, brushing away an errant tear.

For a few days they'd been taking intermittent mortar fire from the hills, and that last round had hit close to the fuel dump of their FOB, forward operating base. A push to sweep the hills to the north for the Taliban mortar team was already in the works, so maybe this was meant to be a spoiling attack. The fact that it was still light outside showed how desperate the Taliban had become.

Since his quarters were protected by concrete and sandbag barriers, it would take a direct hit by a 120mm bomb or bigger to do more than raise a little dust. Thinking fast, Ben selected Ambrose John's name from his Skype address book, clicked the right boxes and waited, listening to the ring tone. Three minutes later, his longtime high school buddy's face popped up on the monitor. Back then, Ben had stood up for Ambrose when gay bashers had confronted him. Now Ambrose, a very successful silversmith, returned the favor and watched out for Jo while he was deployed. "Hey, Ben, how's the weather?"

Ben chuckled. A.J. knew that it was either hot and dry or cold and dry at this FOB, and had to rub it in. Ben hated the sandbox, one of the printable names for Afghanistan. "Just working on my tan, A.J."

"What's up, pal?"

Ben watched the image flicker a little bit because of the signal delay. Live conversations had a tiny time lag due to the satellite relays and that halfway-around-the-world thing.

"Remember when you promised to keep an eye on Jo and the rest of The Outpost crew for me? I hear Jo's been catching some grief lately."

Ambrose nodded. "She's never said word one to me, but I've heard that somebody's trying to give her and Rudy Brownhat, the medicine man, a hard time. One of their patients died and rumor has it that the dead woman's boyfriend is raising hell."

"I'm going to need you to stick close to her and The Outpost. I'm probably going to be out of touch for a while." A big operation was hours away, first clearing the hills, then moving up the valley. Intelligence sources had indicated that there were several hundred Taliban in the area. His mission was clear. Go in, treat, extract, and transport the wounded until the operation was completed.

"Give me an idea. Are we talking days, weeks, or more?" A.J. asked.

Ben shrugged. "Can't say. You may hear about it on the news in a week or two, once it's over."

"Okay, stay safe, and don't worry about Jo or the crew at the trading post. Watch your back, and I'll take care of things around here."

"Appreciate it, A.J.," Ben said.

"Anything else?"

"Nah, that's about it. Take care of yourself. Things can get damned hot at home, too."

"Gotcha, Ben. Now get some sleep, you look like crap."

"Tell me about it."

Ben felt a mortar bomb hit close by, then the screen flickered, and went blank. He wasn't worried. A.J. knew what to do now and would take care of things for him back home.

Two more blasts followed nearby. Mentally shutting out the noise, he went back to his bunk to try to get some sleep. All things considered, he wished he were back in his easy chair watching a Rockies home game instead of sweating away the hours in this hellhole.

• • •

Later that morning, John Littlewater stopped by the trading post. Seeing him, Leigh Ann stopped dusting the candy display beside one of the registers and went to greet Melvin's uncle.

"Hi, John. Are you here for Melvin's check? It won't be ready until this afternoon."

"Thanks, that's great, but the reason I came by was to ask you a question: Do you think the trading post would be interested in displaying some of Melvin's maquettes? They're small, preliminary models he usually makes of his sculptures. He was going to break them up and throw them out, but I think they could be put to better use. If you can display them as samples of what he can do, it might drum up some extra business for him and for the trading post."

"Does Melvin need the extra work right now?" she asked, wondering if she was reading John right.

John shrugged. "It's not a big emergency or anything, but he has some repairs that need to done at his house. Just don't bring it up, okay?"

She nodded, having gone through the same situation recently. Last year she'd managed to get the roof patched instead of redoing the entire thing, but that was a temporary measure at best. Before long it would have to be completely replaced. When you owned a house, there was always a maintenance or repair issue.

"I'll ask Jo about the display and let you know as soon as possible," she said, changing the subject.

John nodded, opened his mouth as if to speak, then turned away.

"There's something else, isn't there? Is Melvin really hurting for money?" she asked.

"No, that's not it. I have another question for you though, just between the two of us?" he asked softly, looking around to make sure nobody was listening.

"Of course. What's wrong?"

"I don't know if you've noticed, but something's been bothering Melvin lately. He hasn't been getting much sleep. I've asked and all I get in return is that he's been having some nightmares, I shouldn't worry, and that he'll deal with it. Has he said anything to you?" John asked. "I know Melvin respects your opinion."

"No he hasn't. If he can't sleep, I think maybe it has to do with his accident. I can't imagine anything more traumatic than that. You almost die, then wake up blind or nearly so, with no hope of ever having your sight restored."

John nodded. "That makes sense. I just don't know what to say about it, or even if I should bring it up at all. Any time I mention the accident he locks up on me or changes the subject. There must be more to it than he's willing to tell."

"Well, he's the only one still alive that experienced the entire incident. I guess we have to let him make the first move. If there's anything I can do to help, let me know, okay?"

"Thanks, Leigh Ann, for hearing me out. Just don't mention I brought this up, though. I have to respect his word when he says he has his own way of dealing with this," John responded.

Or not, Leigh Ann thought as Melvin's uncle walked away. Some things needed to be talked about, or they'd eat you up inside. But how could she persuade Melvin to open up? That was the problem.

Barely ten minutes after John left, Leigh Ann saw what looked like a SJCSO department vehicle pull into a parking slot just outside. Dale had warned her to expect a visit from someone in the San Juan County Sheriff's Office. Something told her this was it.

Six

Leigh Ann took a quick look around the front room. There were only two customers and Jo was at the front register. Leigh Ann signaled her, pointing out the window.

"Go ahead, Leigh Ann," Jo said as the door opened and a tall, slender man in gray slacks and a light blue jacket entered the store. The man had closely cropped brown hair, steel-blue, intelligent eyes, and wore a gold badge on his belt. Barely visible beneath his jacket was a handgun in a black holster.

After the officer introduced himself, Leigh Ann led the man down the hall and into her office. "Have a seat, Sergeant Knight," she said. "If I recall, I spoke to a Detective Alvarez when my husband was killed. Is this your case now?"

"Detective Alvarez was on the violent crimes unit, Mrs. Vance, but he's retired now. I work white collar. Crimes involving corporate theft, such as embezzlement, end up on my desk. The metal box and contents you turned in went to Detective McGraw, who replaced Alvarez, then came to me."

"So Detective McGraw doesn't think this is connected to Kurt's death?" she asked, wondering if she should be disappointed or relieved.

"Your husband's death was determined to be a hunting accident, and the individual responsible has never been identified. Unless substantial evidence suggesting otherwise comes to the department's attention, we'll be investigating what you found as a potential case of fraud. Would you please tell me, in detail, how you came to discover this box?"

Leigh Ann knew that Sergeant Knight had probably heard all about it, but she took her time and told him everything. The only thing she left out was finding the .38. Later, if a weapon like that became part of the investigation, she'd turn it in. Until then, she'd hang on to it.

Knight listened carefully, asking questions and taking notes during her statement. Leigh Ann explained her theories about the list of names in the notebook and told him about the storage compartment Kurt had rented. The detective commented that he planned to speak to the employees at the facility.

At last he seemed satisfied and put away his notebook, then said, "Do you have any questions for me?"

"Yes. From what you've seen of the evidence, do you think my late husband really stole that money?"

"At this point, that's not at all clear. I spoke to his former business partners at Total Supply and both denied that any money had been taken.

The largest discrepancy they'd found in the books was one that resulted from a five-dollar entry mistakenly entered as fifty dollars."

"But the spreadsheets in that box show how the numbers were concealed. How do Kurt's partners explain what I found?" she asked.

"According to Mr. Boone, you and your husband were having some marital problems around the time of his death. He speculated that you were still angry and are now trying to destroy your husband's reputation retroactively. Mr. Hurley, interestingly enough, didn't agree. He thought it was more likely that what you found was one of Kurt's many gags, one he'd never had the chance to put into play. According to him, Kurt was a practical joker who loved watching people squirm."

There was some truth in what Wayne Hurley had said, but even for Kurt, this seemed to be a lot of work for a joke. "What did they say about Frank Jones, the vendor that my husband clearly made up? Total Supply company checks were sent to my husband, payable in Jones's name."

"Hurley and Boone both said they had no record of a client or supplier by that name and that no checks had been made out to Jones. They also denied asking you about any files, other than those needed for the partnership settlement after your husband's death. Were there any witnesses to either man asking you about Frank Jones?"

She shook her head. "No, but they're lying. They repeatedly asked me about Frank Jones."

It was becoming clear to her that Wayne and Pierre were covering something up. Had they all been underreporting to avoid taxes, or was something else going on?

"Unless I come across evidence that an actual crime has taken place, there's not much more I can do. If something changes, I'll get a forensic bookkeeper to go over Total Supply's business accounts and records. Until then, I've got no case."

"What if I find more evidence? Can I turn it over to you?"

"Of course, but here's a piece of advice, Mrs. Vance. Be careful not to do or say anything that might be considered slander in regards to Total Supply or your late husband's associates. They weren't happy to hear about your discovery, and they might decide to get in touch with their lawyer if you keep pursuing this issue."

"I appreciate your advice, and I'll keep your card, Sergeant."

"Thanks for your cooperation, Mrs. Vance," Sergeant Knight said, standing to shake her hand. "I'll be in touch if the situation changes." He headed for the door. "I'll find my own way out. Take care now."

• • •

The day went by quickly after that for Leigh Ann. She and Jo, whose mood had improved immensely after talking to Ben, kept a lookout for strange cars, but there were no further signs of trouble.

"Maybe the driver who hit us has already done his worst. He wanted to scare us or get even, and now he's ready to move on," Leigh Ann said. "That vandalism with the paint could be nothing more than kids acting up right before graduation."

Jo didn't reply right away.

"You don't think so, do you?"

Jo shook her head. "I have nothing more than a gut feeling, but I trust it. Keep watching your back."

Knowing it was almost quitting time, Leigh Ann brought up the possibility of displaying Melvin's maquettes. "What do you think?"

"That's a great idea," Jo said. "It'll give everyone who comes in something new and interesting to look at and consider."

Leigh Ann said good-bye and, promising to visit Melvin that evening to give him the news, headed out.

Alone on the highway, Leigh Ann's thoughts drifted back to Jo and Ben. It had to be a special kind of hell to have a loved one fighting a war eight thousand miles away. She had a feeling that Jo never really stopped worrying. Yet, despite that, she still envied her.

Jo loved Ben and he loved her. Their relationship was one based on mutual respect and seemed virtually unassailable.

Leigh Ann sighed. Maybe someday she'd find that same kind of deep, steadfast love herself. Unfortunately, she was a rotten judge of men. From day one, she'd seen only what she'd wanted to in Kurt. Then by the time she'd realized her mistake, it had been too late. Reality had torn her apart like a Texas tornado, leaving her broken, and afraid to try again.

Now, when she looked at Melvin, she wondered if she was really seeing him for who he was, or whether her fantasies were getting in the way. After all, she knew about Melvin's dark side, but not the reasons for it. Her conversation with John had suggested where it might have originated, but that was something Melvin had kept private. If she brought it up now, that might just compromise John's relationship with his nephew without gaining anything helpful for any of them.

Pushing back those thoughts, she focused on the present. Leigh Ann tried calling Melvin on her way over to his home, but he wasn't picking up. Although he often didn't answer the phone, he'd given her a key and an open invitation to drop by whenever she wanted.

She smiled. That was one of the things she liked most about being friends with Melvin. He was always glad to see her, making her feel special and valued just for being who she was. Although their friendship had boundaries, or maybe because of that, it had also set her free.

Jo went home early, and although she'd spoken to Ben, she was more worried about him than ever. Everything he did as part of a medevac team was dangerous, and no matter how hard Ben tried to reassure her, the reality was he was fighting a war. There were few certainties in his life except that he faced danger and death nearly every hour of every day.

Although she wasn't always successful, Jo tried not to show her fears or ask too many questions whenever he Skyped. Navajo ways taught that to talk about bad things was to attract them. Yet the constant uncertainty had a way of wearing her down.

As Jo drove up to her home and parked, she saw a coyote lurking around less than fifty yards away. Coyote was the Trickster in Navajo creation stories. Maybe his appearance today was a reminder that uncertainty was part of the pattern, too.

Leigh Ann arrived at Melvin's while there was still daylight. As she pulled up, she saw Melvin, shirtless and wearing low-slung jeans, standing on his back porch. He looked beautiful in an earthy way, as much a part of the New Mexican desert as the sun-drenched mesas on the southern horizon. His copper skin glowed in the half-light and his muscular chest looked hard and toned to near perfection. Everything about him spoke of strength and the courage to endure.

Shrouded in equal parts of light and the long afternoon shadows, there was an air of mystery and danger about him. He lived at the edge of a perpetual mist so vast she couldn't even begin to fathom it.

She sighed.

Then he turned toward her and waved.

Of course he'd heard the car—the Jeep's engine had a definite roar and there were no other sounds out here except those that came from nature. She laughed as she got out of the Jeep.

"Be right with you," he said, turning to go back through the house.

Fingers crossed, she hoped he wouldn't stop to put on a shirt. He'd looked so sexy—a man alone at home, listening to the quiet.

"I'm glad you came," he said, meeting her by the door. He'd put on a shirt, but it hung open, teasing her imagination.

"I tried calling first—"

"I disconnected the phone," he said.

She heard the odd, hollow sound in his voice.

For a second he looked . . . haunted. Maybe it was just the lack of sleep. "Are you okay?"

He nodded and led her inside his house. "While searching for an idea for my next sculpture, I tested out a few concepts, but I wasn't satisfied with any of them. This time around, I'd like to create something different. I want a figure that speaks to the loneliness in all of us."

"Any idea what kind of figure you'd like it to be?"

"I've never sculpted people before, but that's what I want to do next. I won't be duplicating a person or using a model. What I want to depict is something more elusive . . . a human figure that captures a longing for something destined to remain out of reach. . . ." He took a breath, then said, "What I feel when you're near."

For a moment, she found it hard to breathe. To have him sculpt a figure based on his feelings for her . . . the possibility was thrilling—and a little scary.

"No one would know the part you played in its creation but us," he said, his voice seductively husky. "Will you help me?"

"How?" she managed after a beat.

"At this point you won't have to pose, or model. What I'd like you to do is talk to me. Let me listen to your voice. Or you could sing."

"Sing? Oh, good heavens, Melvin. I'd drive

you straight out of the house!" she said and laughed. "I don't sing, I wail."

"Not true, I've heard you singing to yourself at the trading post a few times. You can carry a tune, and you have a beautiful voice that resonates with happiness, or sadness, depending on your mood. That's part of what I want to keep in the foreground of my mind as I sculpt. Will you do this for me?"

She swallowed hard. "Yeah, I'd like that, but remember, I work full time."

"Then come over in the evening. It doesn't make that much difference to me. One more thing—you won't be able to look at my work until it's finished. Agreed?"

"Oooh, that's going to be really hard," she said, her voice trembling with excitement.

"Once it's done, you'll be the first to see it, and I'll want your honest opinion. If you think it's no good then it'll never leave my work-shop."

"Melvin, I'm not exactly unbiased. I like all your work, but I have a feeling this one's going to be amazing." Instinct also assured her that this would be an experience she'd never forget. She might even learn something about herself in the process. Yet there was no denying the danger . . . for her . . . for him.

He stepped closer and ran his hands over her face with a tenderness that made her weak at

121

the knees. "You're excited and looking forward to this."

"I am," she said, not bothering to deny it. The low, masculine sound of his voice, his touch and nearness filled her with a delicious longing.

"First, I'll see the image in my mind, then I'll feel it become a part of me. Once that happens, we'll begin."

"You'll let me know when you're ready?"

"Yes."

To see herself as he did . . . What an amazing thing that would be. More than anything, she wished she could have commissioned it right there and then, but there was no way she could afford anything she didn't absolutely need.

As her thoughts returned to finances, she remembered the reason she'd come. Leigh Ann told Melvin about the special display they could set up using his maquettes if he allowed it. "It would be an easy way to drive business to you on a more regular basis, but of course, it's up to you."

"The models aren't very detailed. They are more like an architect's blueprints or an artist's preliminary sketches."

"If you were just going to get rid of them, like John said, why not allow us to use them? Most people have never seen something like that and it'll generate interest in you, your work, and the creative process."

He considered it silently.

"If my opinion counts, they're beautiful," she said, looking at the ones that had been placed up on the shelf.

"They're fragile and tend to crumble. They're not finished sculptures and will never be fired."

"They're still beautiful," she said.

He came closer. "You're easy to please," he said, standing before her, just inches away.

She knew he was attracted to her. His voice always gave himself away, even when he wasn't flirting. And now he was tempting her. Melvin's shirt hung open and the urge to touch him, to run her hands over his beautiful hard chest, was nearly overpowering.

"You're holding your breath. Just relax, I won't run away," he murmured.

The temptation to touch him was too great, and now they were alone. She placed her palm on his chest and ran her hand lightly over his skin, feeling his muscles tense in the wake of her touch.

Raw masculinity . . . that's what he was. She'd dreamed of a moment like this. He was all hardness and strength. Using only her fingertip, she traced the top of his waistband, seeing his body strain against the fabric of his jeans and imagining what lay just beyond her reach.

Leigh Ann heard him suck in his breath and that's when she suddenly realized that she'd crossed a line and was playing with fire. She stepped back quickly.

"It's okay. Nothing will happen. You have my word. Touch is just another wonderful way for us to . . . communicate. You can see my face and know my thoughts, but all I have to go by is your voice and your touch—and in brighter light, your presence. Communicate more, if you wish."

"All right." She ran her hands slowly over his shoulders and upper arms and caressed his chest again, loving the way his muscles rippled and tightened.

His breathing quickened, but she knew he was a man of his word. He would allow her to caress him and enjoy that magic for as long as she wanted without making any demands.

After a moment, her heart racing, she moved back. "That's what *I* feel when I'm with you."

He smiled. "As with me, your heart's in your touch. You've just told me everything I wanted to know."

Although he seemed to have an iron grip on his emotions, the same couldn't be said for her. She took another step back, trying to stop trembling.

With effort, she forced her voice to remain even. "So tell me, may I take some of those models to the trading post?"

"Sure, but hand each one to me first and let me check them in case they're damaged."

She did as he asked, and watched his hands glide over the hardened clay pieces, feeling for nicks, bumps, or edges. After making sure they were okay, he gave them back to her.

Carefully wrapping each piece using some of Melvin's packing supplies—tissue paper and foam packing peanuts—Leigh Ann placed the maquettes into cardboard boxes.

"I have some photos of the finished pieces, too, after they were done. John insisted on that, but they don't do me much good. Would you like them?"

"Absolutely. They'll show how you transform a simple concept into a beautiful, finished sculpture."

He went to the shelf and brought out a big scrapbook, almost dropping the cumbersome volume before catching himself. "You'll have to look through this."

She took it from him, placed the scrapbook on the table, and began to leaf through the pages. She'd seen this before on the shelf, but had never asked to see it, observing the boundaries of their friendship. The early pages held photos of Melvin in high school. "So you were a football player?"

He laughed. "Don't sound so surprised. I was a pretty decent receiver once upon a time."

"It's hard to think of you as a jock. Your hands create such beautiful things."

"Catching the pigskin is a thing of beauty, too."

She laughed.

"The photos John took are in the back, I think."

She flipped to the end and found the photos of Melvin's sculptures. "These are great! I'll design a special display and when you get the chance you can come inspect it. I'll describe how it's laid out and you can give me your feedback."

"Great."

The change of light in the room told Leigh Ann that the sun was now setting. Though she'd previously traveled the roads to and from his home in the dark, she decided that today, she didn't really want to be out on this stretch of empty desert alone after the sun went down. "I'm going to have to get going."

"The sun's set?"

"Almost, yeah, but how could you tell?"

"The shapes of objects begin to fade and I lose any sense of depth of field in what vision I do have. In many ways, this time of day is the toughest for me. The shapes of close objects just slip away and all I can do is accept it."

Her heart went out to him, but instinct told her that the last thing he wanted from her was pity. "Melvin, have you ever considered one of those laser-type canes for getting around in really low light? I saw one on TV."

"That's pure fiction. They don't exist for the public, not yet. But to be perfectly honest, I'd rather have your hand or arm," he added with a grin.

"And you're welcome to them," she said, "but for when I'm not around? Maybe there's something besides the white cane . . ."

"Someday there might be, but right now, the white cane's all that's available. I have one, but since I can discern the presence of most larger objects during the day and navigate around a room, I don't need a cane. I might use one at night, yes, but normally I'm not out and about at that time," he said, then added, "The bottom line is that I don't want to become reliant on an aid."

"There's nothing wrong with doing whatever you can to retain your independence."

"Some say that seeing-eye dogs and canes increase independence, and maybe they do that for other people, those with even less vision, but I see it as relying on something else that could be taken from you."

She considered this. That stubborn pride defined everything about Melvin. Although life had tried to force him down to his knees, he continued standing, fighting the odds.

"If you were me, would you find it easy to depend on an aid?" he asked.

After everything she'd gone through with Kurt, both during their marriage and after his death, she found it hard to completely trust

127

anyone or anything outside herself. "No, I guess not. In that way, you and I are alike."

"That's what I thought."

"I better get going," she said, picking up the box, ready to load the maquettes into her Jeep.

He walked her to the door.

"Would you like me to pick you up sometime tomorrow and drive you to the trading post so you can check out the display?"

"No, that's not necessary, Leigh Ann, I trust you. But I enjoy it when you drop by, so come over anytime."

Leigh Ann drove away slowly to avoid jostling the box. Her visits to Melvin's were always filled with the unexpected and today had been no exception. She still wasn't sure if she'd made a mistake by agreeing to let him sculpt her, but saying yes to him had come as naturally as the next beat of her heart.

Seven

Leigh Ann drove down a narrow, wavy asphalt lane between two thick rows of poplars that must have been thirty or more years old. They were sickly looking and in need of pruning.

The trees lined the road near an abandoned housing development that had been built for employees of a natural gas company long gone from the area. The entire place gave her the creeps. Decades ago, this complex could have been overrun with children, but now there was only emptiness and an eerie silence.

A pickup pulled onto the road from one of the turnoffs to the development. It turned half toward her, blocking her way, then stopped.

"Crap, now what?" she muttered, tensing up.

The driver stepped down out of the pickup and Leigh Ann saw, despite the fading sunset, that he was wearing a ski mask and carrying a baseball bat, or club.

She slammed on the brakes and put the Jeep in reverse. Looking in the side mirror, she discovered that she was cut off behind, too, by a van that was parked across the asphalt. It must have come from a street behind her while she was watching the pickup.

The second driver was also wearing a ski mask

and carrying a club of some kind, maybe an axe handle.

This was no carjacking; this was an ambush. She reached for her purse, then remembered that her .38 was still at home. Without a concealed carry permit, she hadn't wanted it around when the sheriff's department stopped by to question her. *Stupid!* She should have kept it in the Jeep.

Trapped, she tried to figure out what to do next. She could try to run one of them over, but even if she did, she'd never get around their vehicle and through the trees fast enough to get away. Her only chance was to jump out and run before they got any closer.

Leigh Ann threw open her door and raced across the road, slipping between two trees heavy with low branches, then into the thick undergrowth beyond. Thank goodness she was wearing loafers instead of western boots, slacks, and her Outpost knit shirt.

Though the brush scratched her arms, she forced her way through until she broke into a clearing to the west. Ahead were four houses in a row, flanked by empty concrete pads where other buildings might have sat years ago.

Maybe she could find someplace to hide in one of the empty homes. Then, once it was completely dark, she'd make a run for the highway.

Leigh Ann dialed 911 as she raced toward the closest building. It was clearly unoccupied, judging by the broken windows.

She glanced back and realized no one had come after her, but she still wasn't about to slow down. Maybe they'd gone back to their vehicles and planned to chase her down that way. Or maybe they were trading their weapons for something with more range, like a rifle.

Hearing a voice, she brought the phone to her ear.

"911, what is the nature of your emergency?" a woman said calmly.

"My name is Leigh Ann Vance, and two men wearing ski masks and carrying clubs came after me. I had to leave my Jeep and make a run for it. I'm in the old housing area west of the gas road turnoff in Kirtland."

Leigh Ann stopped to catch her breath. She looked back, but still couldn't locate either man. Yet, peering through the trees, she could see all three vehicles still on the road.

"Where are your assailants now, Leigh Ann?"

"I don't know. They might be hiding where I left my Jeep, waiting for me to come back."

"Keep moving away from the vehicles, Leigh Ann. Can you see anyone else?"

"No. Maybe they wanted to steal my Jeep. Hell, they can have it."

"Help's on the way, Leigh Ann. Keep moving

and stay on the line. Can you see the main highway?"

"Yes, it's about a quarter mile away, to the south."

"Head there. There's going to be traffic and that'll work in your favor."

"Okay."

"You're doing fine. Stay calm and keep moving. A patrolman's heading your way now."

"Tell him to hurry," she managed, breathing hard as she ran.

Five minutes later, Leigh Ann was standing beside a sheriff's department cruiser, breathing normally again, almost relaxed now as she tried to recall all that had happened the past quarter hour. The deputy, a slightly overweight man in his late forties with a bald patch, was on the radio, directing other patrol units that were searching for the two men who had threatened her.

Her description of the attackers wasn't very detailed. "I'm sorry, but the two things I noticed most were their masks and their clubs. All I could think about after that was running away as fast as I could."

"Under the circumstances, that was the right thing to do," the officer said. "We've put out a BOLO for their vehicles, but without license plates or a better description . . ."

"You're right. What does 'BOLO' stand for, anyway? I hear it on TV a lot."

"It's law enforcement jargon: 'be on the lookout for,' ma'am."

"Makes sense."

"Come on. I'll take you back to your Jeep. I want you to check and see if anything's missing."

A few minutes later they pulled up in front of her Jeep, and in the glow of the vehicle's dome light, she could see that both doors were open. "This makes no sense, Officer. As far as I know, they never even chased me. So why the trap? Look at my old Jeep. Did they want to steal it, then change their minds once they got a closer look?"

"From your statement, I'd say you were the target, but after you got away, they decided to see if you had anything of value in the Jeep."

"Like my purse," she said. She hadn't taken it with her. She'd bolted instantly, knowing her cell phone was in her shirt pocket.

She stood by the driver's side of the Jeep and looked inside, her anxiety returning as she accessed her losses. The box with Melvin's clay figures had been opened but she could see that the figures were still hidden in tissue paper, which hopefully meant that they were intact. The glove box was open, too, and her owner's manual and insurance card were on the floorboard, along with the tire gauge and a credit card receipt for gas.

Her purse had been dumped out on the passenger seat, but her wallet, two credit cards, and the photos of Melvin's sculptures were all still there. The little bit of cash she'd carried, however, was gone. "All this for ten bucks?"

The deputy shook his head. "That's doubtful. Based on what I see, I think their intent was to scare you off, then take the opportunity to search your vehicle for something specific." His laser sharp gaze remained on her.

"Like what? Drugs? All I've got is a few aspirins."

"You tell me, ma'am. According to what I read on my MDT, the computer terminal in my cruiser, you were involved in another incident on the Navajo Nation just yesterday. Someone in a big black sedan ran your Jeep off the road. So this is no coincidence, is it? What are these people after, Mrs. Vance?"

"All I'm sure about is that it wasn't my Jeep either time. This old thing is held together by duct tape, wishes, and a prayer. Not exactly the ride of a rich woman."

Even as she answered, she realized that there was something else she hadn't taken with her before rushing off. She looked at the ignition where one set of keys had hung, then looked at the scattered contents of her purse for the other set. "Crap! They took my keys!"

"What were they to?"

"The Jeep, my house, a friend's home, my sister's car key—and the trading post," she said, her eyes widening. "See the logo on my shirt? I work at The Outpost."

"Targeting a business makes a little more sense," the officer said. "You need to tell the owner to change the locks. You should do the same thing at your home, and warn your friend and sister, too."

"None of the keys were labeled, but I'll tell everyone. Am I free to go?"

"Do you have an extra set of keys to the Jeep or should I call a tow?"

"I'm fine," she said. There was a magnetic key holder inside the wheel well.

Minutes later, she was on her way. Her hands were shaking even as she gripped the steering wheel. What the heck was happening to her life? Two attacks in two days . . . Kurt—this had to be connected to him. He'd never been anything but trouble, and now he was having the last laugh from his grave.

"You mangy old toad," Leigh Ann muttered under her breath. "I'll straighten out your mess, and after that I'm going back to my maiden name. I don't want anything more to do with you. I'm going to bury the memories, just like I buried you."

Jo arrived at the trading post early as usual the next day, still thinking about yesterday's brief conversation with Ben. Months ago Ben had told her that she'd get a visit from an area army officer if anything ever happened to him. At times like these her gaze continually searched the parking lot for a government motor pool car.

Jo walked up the steps leading to the back door, fumbling in her purse for her keys. Leigh Ann had called last night to let her know what had happened and warn her to rekey the locks as soon as possible. Since none of Leigh Ann's keys had been labeled, Jo figured it wasn't an emergency. She'd get to it later today, or early tomorrow. After all, unless the person coming in quickly turned off the alarm, the security service and police would respond almost immediately.

As Jo stepped up, key in hand, she suddenly froze. Hanging from the doorknob was a medicine bag made from the skin of a horned toad—clearly a gift from a skinwalker.

She placed her hand over the deerskin *jish* Rudy had made for her. The little bag was fastened to her belt and contained Talking Rock medicine, scrapings from a rock found in a cave with a pronounced echo. That, along with other items in the bundle, protected Jo against Navajo witchery.

Jo circled the trading post, entering though the front entrance and quickly turning off the alarm. After cleaning her hands using a lotion made from a Game Way plant, she pulled on a pair of work gloves and opened the back door from the inside.

She removed the toad-skin pouch, then built a small fire in the gravel of the parking area and burned the artifact, being careful not to inhale the fumes. Holding an arrow point in her left hand, she carefully recited a prayer and concluded by throwing tiny bits of turquoise into the air.

Neither the Modernist police nor most of the trading post employees would really understand this kind of danger—but she did. It would be up to her to keep them safe, and that's precisely what she intended to do.

Leigh Ann made it to work just in time, apologized to Jo once again for losing her store keys, and made the changes in the display showcasing Melvin's work. By nine, she was finished. After studying the result for several seconds, she turned to her boss, subtly straightening her long, lavender broomstick skirt, which nearly reached the tops of her western boots. Today, with a Western-style blouse and a tooled leather belt, she was dressing the part of a trading post employee. She even wore a ponytail.

"What do you think, Jo?" she asked, anxious to show off her work.

"It's perfect," Jo said. "Take a photo of it with your cell phone and send it to Sam. She asked me to collect images of all the displays and events at the store for our Web site."

Leigh Ann did as she asked, then took up her station at the cash register. It was a slow morning and time dragged, with the only interruption being the coming and going of the locksmith, who was smooth and efficient during his half-hour visit.

Regina, across the big room, was lucky. She'd elected to straighten out the dairy cases and could, at least, keep moving.

She was surprised when the door opened to admit John, with Melvin right behind, holding his arm. Leigh Ann's heart quickened. As usual, Melvin turned slowly and smiled directly at her.

"Hi there," she said, stepping up to him and taking his hand just as he was about to bump into a wire rack filled with cookie packets. "Let me lead you to your display. Everything's been carefully staged on a Burntwater Navajo rug woven in sand, gold, and white. It's very eye-catching. Your maquettes are on the center of the table on top of small wooden boxes of various heights."

She guided his hand over them. "Photos of the

138

finished pieces are placed next to each," she added.

His touch was so light that nothing was displaced. As she watched him, her thoughts wandered, imagining his fingers touching her that gently, and her skin prickled. She stiffened. This was neither the time nor place to revisit any fantasy.

Leigh Ann mentally pulled herself together, adjusting her blouse, adding silent emphasis to her resolve. She saw a knowing smile on Jo's face and realized she'd given herself away.

"This was well thought out. Thanks for the care you took," Melvin said, his voice softening just a little, but not too much.

Remembering what John had said about Melvin's cash-flow problem, she said, "This is going to give business a boost, for you and for us."

"No rush. I have a special project in hand now and since it's very different from what I usually do, I'd like a little bit of time to settle into it."

"Did I hear right?" Jo asked. "You're doing a new kind of sculpture?"

Melvin nodded. "I needed the challenge."

"So what's your new project?" Jo asked.

He shook his head. "I don't want to talk about it yet. I need time to get a better feel for what it is I'm trying to create and what I want the sculpture to say."

"Fair enough, but you'll bring it here first?"

He nodded. "You're the only retailer I deal with these days."

"I know it's halfway to lunch now, Melvin, but have you had breakfast yet?" Leigh Ann asked.

"If you call a Coke and Hershey bar breakfast. We nearly ran out of gas and had to find a station in a hurry," he said, and laughed.

"It wasn't a dire emergency, but I figured I better play it safe and not push it," John said quickly.

"I don't know how you define 'emergency' but I heard you curse the orange gas pump symbol, and that's a sign the truck's almost out of gas," Melvin said, a tiny smile tugging at the corners of his mouth.

"Memory like an elephant," John grumbled. "Yeah, that's true enough. But I can usually make it another fifteen or twenty miles. I . . . tested it once."

Melvin burst out laughing. "That means you've run out of gas before. Where did that happen?"

"On that highway west of Morgan Lake. I had to hike six miles to the Chapter House to catch a ride," he admitted grudgingly, then glanced up at the clock. "I'd better hurry. I'm meeting a man about a horse and I'm late. I'm sorry that I have to drop you off so early at the doctor's,

140

Melvin, but they've got a comfortable waiting room so you'll be fine."

"Melvin, if you'd like you could have a late breakfast here and we'll find someone to give you a ride later," Jo said. "After all, you're one of our most talented artists. You're also welcome to pick up a breakfast burrito on the way out, John. They're fresh. My treat."

"I'll take breakfast and the ride," Melvin said.

"I'll be on my way then," John said. "Thanks for the breakfast offer, Jo, but I'm good." He nodded to Leigh Ann and hurried out.

Melvin chuckled as he heard the bell over the door. "I think I've pissed him off."

"How so?" Jo asked.

"Uncle John hates being wrong, and he especially didn't like a blind man suggesting that he almost ran out of gas," he said. "The thing about John is that he takes care of the big things, like picking me up, but tends not to bother with the details," he said.

Regina, who'd finished her work at the dairy case, came over.

"Hello, Regina," Melvin said easily.

"How did you know it was me?" Regina asked.

"It's the way you walk. You move with very little sound, like on tiptoes. You're very light on your feet."

Leigh Ann's stomach tightened. She suspected that Regina had acquired that ability as a way of not attracting attention after years of being married to an abusive man.

"Hey, who called the staff meeting?" Esther said, coming over with a smile on her face.

Leigh Ann looked over at Jo. "Since most of us are here, do you think this would be a good time to tell everyone what's been happening lately and why the store locks had to be rekeyed this morning?"

"I haven't heard all the details of last night's incident from you either, Leigh Ann. So why don't you start?" Jo asked.

"Last night?" Melvin asked quickly. "Does this have something to do with the deputy who dropped by my house about nine P.M.? Once he figured out I couldn't have seen anyone, he asked if I'd heard any vehicles passing by. He mentioned something about an attempted car-jacking?"

"I ran into some trouble after I left your place, Melvin," Leigh Ann said, then told them about the van and the men wearing masks and carrying clubs. When she finished, all eyes were on her.

"And all they took were a few dollars and your keys?" Regina asked, surprised.

"Yeah, but they searched the Jeep from top to bottom, even dumping out the contents of my glove box. The deputy thought they were looking for something specific—just what, I'm not sure," she said, then added, "My sister is having our house locks rekeyed this morning. You should do the same, Melvin."

"I'll get it done, don't worry," he answered.

Jo filled everyone in about the poison in Rudy's tea, the vandalism at The Outpost, the time when Leigh Ann and she had been run off the road and, lastly, the medicine pouch she'd found on the back door this morning.

"Are we all in danger again, like when Tom was killed?" Regina asked, looking at the faces around her.

"From what I can see, Jo and I are the only targets," Leigh Ann said. "As for why Jo's being targeted . . . That could be the result of being with the wrong person, me. Keep in mind that I was alone when those men came after me."

"Is this all connected to the deputy who came by to talk to you?" Regina asked. "I couldn't help but notice."

Leigh Ann wasn't quite ready to share all the details, but she wouldn't lie to them either. "I found some papers in my attic that indicated my late husband may have been involved in some shady business practices," she said, then added, "That may have been what the Jeep-jackers were looking for—more papers—but I'd already handed everything over to the detectives."

"Uncle John works at a farm supply business

that competes with Total Supply," Melvin said. "He told me that every time they bid for a tribal contract, Total Supply manages to under-cut their price by a small margin. John thinks that there's some under-the-table dealings going on with tribal officials, but he can't prove it."

"That's interesting," Leigh Ann said, "but the papers I found only involved my late husband, and had nothing to do with tribal contracts. At least I don't think so."

"Leigh Ann and I will stay on guard, but it wouldn't hurt for the rest of you to do the same," Jo said. "If you notice anything out of the ordinary, or you think you're being watched or followed, call the sheriff immediately."

Leigh Ann looked at her watch. "Melvin, you'll have to eat now if you're going to have breakfast before your doctor's visit."

Esther took his arm. "Let me show you where we keep the good stuff."

Regina walked to the front cash register, where a customer with a shopping cart was headed, as Leigh Ann took a quick look around. No other customers were in the store so she decided to join Melvin and Esther in the break room.

Before she could, Jo touched her arm and held her back. "We need to talk."

"If this is about Melvin's new sculpture, I don't know much more than what he's already told you."

"That's not it. I want to go to my teacher's house. I called him earlier today to make sure nothing bad had been left at his place, but found out they're staying with Victoria's cousin for a few days. Since my teacher's still unable to drive and is relying on relatives to take him and Victoria whenever they need to go, he asked that I go check."

"Let's both go and I'll help you look around. We'll drop Melvin off first, then keep going. Right now we should travel in pairs as often as possible."

"I agree. Do you mind if we use your Jeep? My truck's at Benny's Garage right now, getting a tune-up," Jo said. "I won't have it back for another couple of hours."

"That's fine, but I'm curious. You never drive the truck that belongs to the trading post. How come?"

"I use it for business on occasion, but it really belongs to Ben now."

"And everything in it reminds you of where he is, and the danger he's facing," she said, not bothering to turn it into a question.

"Yeah, it's like that," Jo admitted.

"Let me see if Melvin's ready, then we'll go."

"Wait." Jo reached into her medicine pouch and gave Leigh Ann an arrowhead.

"What's this?" Leigh Ann asked her.

"Flint. I know you're not Navajo, but I hope

145

you'll keep it in your shirt pocket. If we find something bad at my teacher's place, it'll protect both of us."

Less than ten minutes later they set out. Jo insisted on sitting in the back, so Melvin took the front passenger's seat. Noticing that he was being unusually quiet, Leigh Ann asked, "Are you worried about your doctor's visit?"

"No, it's only a check-up," he said. "I was thinking about my new sculpture. I need to work out some details."

A gust of wind blew in through her open window and Leigh Ann shook her head, trying to get the strands that had worked loose from her ponytail away from her face. Using one hand, she tried to tuck her hair back beneath the rubber band, but the elastic snapped.

"Melvin, will you reach into the glove compartment that's directly in front of you and feel around for a hair scrunchie? There should be one in there."

He did as she asked. "There's a pencil, some paper, and a . . . piece of metal with a hole. A bent-up washer, maybe?"

Leigh Ann felt her breath catch at the back of her throat. "Beg your pardon?"

He brought it out so she could see.

Leigh Ann stared at it in shock, then quickly focused back on the road, hoping Jo hadn't noticed her reaction. That had been Kurt's lucky piece. He'd taped a quarter to the bull's-eye of a target one day, and shot a hole right through it. Since then he'd always carried the coin with him. Yet it hadn't been among the items the police had brought back to her. She'd wondered where it had gone, but really hadn't given it much thought. At the time, she'd had a lot more important things to occupy her mind.

Now, here it was. She knew it hadn't been in that compartment before because she washed the Jeep and cleaned out the glove box once a week. A chill settled over her as she realized that she'd searched to see what might have been taken from the Jeep, but had never thought that anything might have been added.

"Leigh Ann, are you okay?" Melvin asked.

"Yeah, I just hadn't seen that coin in a long time." There was only one possible answer. The lucky piece had been taken by Kurt's killer, and he wanted her to know he had his eye on her.

"Here's the hair band," Melvin said at last.

She took it from him, but decided to leave her hair loose for now. Her hands were shaking, and trying to fix her hair while steering probably wouldn't be a great idea.

"If you don't mind me interrupting, Melvin, tell me about your new project," Jo said from the back, unaware of what had just happened.

"It's something I've wanted to do for a while, but wasn't sure how to go about it," Melvin answered. "It's going to take some time though. This kind of piece needs to develop in my mind first." He looked over at Leigh Ann and smiled.

"So, in the meantime, what should we tell customers wanting one of your animal sculptures?" Jo asked.

"We'll work things out. My new project isn't something I can work on continuously, at least at this point. In the interim, my animal sculptures will help me stay focused and relaxed."

This time, when he looked over at Leigh Ann, he winked. It was clear he was going to keep this a secret between them, at least for now.

Minutes later they arrived at the medical center. Leigh Ann found a handicapped parking space and pulled in. "Okay we're here, Melvin."

Leigh Ann got out of the car, circled around, and took his arm as he climbed out. "Jo, I'll walk in with Melvin and be right back. You might want to move the Jeep, though. I don't have a handicapped sticker."

"Sounds good," she said.

As they walked into the building, Leigh Ann tried to stay calm. She'd disliked hospitals as far back as she could remember—the antiseptic smell, the white uniforms, the carts, the odd sounds . . .

"You hate hospitals?" he noted in a quiet voice.

"Yeah, how did you know?"

"Your muscles tightened up the second we stepped inside, and you've got a tight grip on my arm," he answered, placing his hand over hers.

She eased up instantly.

"It's okay. You don't have to walk me in. A lot of people hate hospitals, particularly traditionalist Navajos, though their reasons are undoubtedly different from yours."

"How so?"

"Since death occurs here, hospitals aren't considered safe places to be," he said. "John isn't a traditionalist, but he still won't go past the entrance unless he has no other choice. He drops me off and I rely on the staff to take me to any new destination."

"With me it's nothing more than a dumb phobia. I'm fine," she said, and pressed the elevator button that would take them to the second floor.

"When are you going to tell me about that metal piece—the coin with the bullet hole in its middle?" he asked as the elevator began its ascent.

"We're here," she said as they came to a stop. "That story will have to wait." After getting his doctor's name, she led him down the hall. "Here's the office," she said.

"One thing before you leave. I'm going to have my own locks rekeyed, but hang on to the old key until I can give you the new one. I want to remind you that you still have an open invitation to my home."

"Thanks for doing this," she said. It was more than just the key, he was letting her know he still had faith in her. A lump formed at the back of her throat. "It means a lot," she added in a thick voice.

As soon as they walked into the office, the receptionist came over and took Melvin's arm. "It's good to see you again," she said in greeting.

Knowing he was in good hands, Leigh Ann stepped back. "If you can give me an approximate time when you'll be through here, I'll make arrangements to pick you up," she said.

"Thanks, but there's no need. John will come get me, we'll have a late lunch, and afterward he'll drive me home."

"All right, Melvin. See you later."

As Leigh Ann hurried out, she decided not to tell Jo about Kurt's lucky coin. She knew traditional Navajos stayed away from the possessions of the dead. They were said to be contaminated with the *chindi*, the evil side of a man that was condemned to remain earthbound after death.

As for herself, she wished the danged thing would have stayed lost. Everything connected to Kurt brought back toxic memories and trouble.

Eight

"If you tell me what I should be looking for, I'll be better able to help you," Leigh Ann said as she drove toward the Brownhats' home, following Jo's directions.

"It's hard to say precisely. Look for anything that appears to have been left there for others to find, or something odd that doesn't seem to belong. We'll start by checking the front and back doors. The way I figure it is this—if the person who left that witch bag at the trading post went to my teacher's place, too, he'll want whatever he leaves behind to be seen. His goal is to instill fear in his victim."

"That doesn't seem like the work of the same person who threw paint on the side of the building," Leigh Ann said.

"I know. I think we're dealing with at least two different people," Jo answered.

Rudy lived just west of Shiprock, north of Highway 64, and less than ten minutes from the clinic where they'd dropped off Melvin.

"Go down that dirt track." Jo pointed toward the turnoff. "It leads directly to the medicine hogan. His home is about a hundred feet beyond there."

As Leigh Ann approached, Jo sat up. "Slow down and stop about fifty feet from the hogan."

"Sure," Leigh Ann. "Is there a reason?"

"I want to check for tracks. The ground is fine sediment here, soft enough to leave impressions."

"Oh, you want to do some amateur police work?"

"Yeah, and keep an eye out for any animal tracks leading up to the house, okay?"

"Like coyotes? I know they're supposed to be bad luck," Leigh Ann said.

"Coyote is known as the Trickster. He can bring whatever he wishes, but it's generally not a good sign if you see one hanging around."

Leigh Ann parked well away from the front of the hogan. Jo circled the hogan alone, searching the ground. Not finding any fresh signs, they made their way together to the house.

They checked the front entrance first, but saw nothing but two sets of shoe prints. "These look like they belong to my teacher and his wife," Jo said.

They circled to the back next, and Leigh Ann helped Jo look around, but neither of them found any tracks other than those Jo had already identified as Rudy's. Leigh Ann was ready to call it a win until she saw Jo crouching near the back door.

"What did you find?" she asked.

"A trace of fur, maybe from a coyote or wolf."

"Like stuff a skinwalker uses?"

Jo shot Leigh Ann a hard look. "Don't use that word, especially here."

"Sorry," she said.

Jo reached into her medicine pouch and sprinkled a substance that looked like cornmeal on the ground.

As Jo chanted, Leigh Ann listened closely. She had long felt that there was something entrancing about Navajo Songs. Though many were basically monotonic, they often had a haunting quality that spoke of power and tradition so closely interlaced that neither could exist without the other.

After several minutes, Jo stood up. "Wait for me here," she said. She walked around the corner of the house and out of sight. Soon another chant filled the air, softer, yet no less compelling than the first.

When Jo finally returned, she seemed more relaxed, as if a great weight had been taken off her shoulders.

"Now we can go back to work," Jo said.

"What did you do?" Leigh Ann asked.

"I conducted a blessing to take care of the danger to my teacher."

"But the person, or people, are still out there," Leigh Ann said, thinking of whoever was after her, too.

"That's true, so we'll have to be careful, but

keep things in perspective. These people will eventually be caught. No matter how bad things get now, it won't last forever."

Leigh Ann nodded thoughtfully. Jo was right. Nothing ever stayed the same—even when you wished it could be so.

"Thanks for taking care of the locksmith today, Rachel, and for making copies of all those papers I turned over to the sheriff's department. That ended up being a good call," Leigh Ann said, filling her sister's glass from a soft drink can.

"After what happened to you last night on the way home from Melvin's, I think they might be even more important than we thought," Rachel said.

"Nothing about this mess is simple or clea cut. Pierre and Wayne obviously lied about the money, so there's something else going on."

"What now?" Rachel asked.

"We need to get some damning evidence, anything the police will accept that'll also clear me of any wrongdoing."

"That's going to be tough," Rachel said. "Leigh Ann, do you think you and I will ever be able to settle down with nice guys and live happily ever after? The guys we choose . . . Well, the word 'pricks' comes to mind."

Leigh Ann laughed. "There are some gems out there."

"Like Melvin?" She saw Leigh Ann nod, and continued, "You used to go for those ultra-macho guys—like Billy Ray Jackson who went on to play pro football, or Jake Faulkner, who's now racing cars down south. Melvin . . . seems like a stretch."

"He's more of a man than either of those guys, Rache. Believe it."

"Too bad he doesn't have a cool-sounding name."

"What difference could that possibly make?" she said, laughing. "Besides, ever heard of Mel Gibson?"

"True," she smiled. "But Melvin's not at all high impact, you know?"

"Make up your mind—not high impact or pricks?"

Rachel laughed. "Good point." She leaned back in her chair. "How are things going between you two? Is it getting serious?"

"No, that's something it can never become. It's just too complicated," she said. "But when I'm with him, I feel like a whole woman again, Rache. It's the most amazing feeling in the world." Leigh Ann stared at the soda can in her hand, lost in thought. "There are lines neither of us will ever cross, though. We both carry a lot of baggage."

"You guys don't have much of a future unless you can be open with one another."

"Some demons are hard to expose to the light, sis, and I have this Kurt thing hanging over my head. Friendship is as far as it can go between us."

"But you'd like it to be more."

"Someday, maybe, but I'll keep what I have for now."

"If things are right, don't let him slip away, Leigh Ann. You've finally found a man who isn't attracted to you just because you've got big boobs."

Leigh Ann laughed, allowing herself to feel relaxed for a moment. Then she sighed and told her sister about finding Kurt's lucky coin.

"I thought that was missing from the stuff the police gave you when his body was released," Rachel replied.

"It was. I got back Kurt's wallet, key chain, and credit cards. I also checked the list of items the police kept as evidence, but that was mostly the clothes he was wearing at the time of his death."

"So you're thinking his killer took the lucky quarter?"

"I'm positive Kurt had it with him when he left on that hunting trip, but I haven't seen it since," she said. "Now, out of the blue, it turns up in my glove box? What other explanation could there be?"

Rachel considered it. "He didn't have the Jeep with him that day, did he?"

"No. I did. The three of them went in Pierre's SUV."

"Then I have no idea how to explain this," Rachel said at last. "So what do you want to do about it?"

"I honestly don't know," Leigh Ann said, and sighed. The phone rang; Leigh Ann looked at the caller ID, saw it was Jo, and answered immediately.

"Is everything okay, Jo?" she asked quickly, knowing Jo never called after hours except in an emergency.

"Two detectives from the sheriff's department came by and asked me some questions about you. It was just routine, they said, but they wanted to know about you, your marriage, and Kurt. I told them you came to work for me *after* your husband died, and that I'd never met you or him before that moment, so I couldn't help them," Jo said, sounding a bit anxious.

"That's true," Leigh Ann confirmed.

"Once I told them that, they wanted to know about your spending habits, whether or not you had a boyfriend now, and if so, how long you'd been involved with him."

"What did you say?" Leigh Ann asked quickly, hoping Jo hadn't ended up sending the cops to Melvin's doorstep.

"That I know virtually nothing about your private life, other than the fact you share your home with your sister."

Leigh Ann breathed a silent sigh of relief. "Who came to question you?"

"Detective McGraw, from the county's violent crimes unit, and Sergeant Knight, the same officer who spoke to you the other day at The Outpost. It sounds like a lot more than just those papers you mentioned finding. What's going on, Leigh Ann?"

Jo sounded worried now, so she gave her a quick update. "Sooner or later, they'll discover the truth about Kurt and what's going on over at Total Supply. I'll make sure of it."

"Let me know if you need any help," Jo said.

Leigh Ann hung up and filled Rachel in.

Rachel said, "I wish we'd thrown out that box of Kurt's instead of turning it over to the cops."

"It's what I get for trying to be honest and playing by the rules," Leigh Ann said.

"Someone wants to make sure you get the blame for whatever Kurt did or didn't do. You're going to have to start digging even deeper into his past."

"I don't even know where to begin."

"Maybe with this?" Rachel said, holding up the small key that had been in the box with Kurt's papers. Leigh Ann was startled.

"Rachel! What did you do?"

"I kept it."

"Aw, jeez, Rache," Leigh Ann whispered.

"Hey, you kept the revolver."

158

"True enough. But why the key?"

"I'm sure it has something to do with Pierre and Wayne. Think about it, sis. They found out Kurt was stealing from them and Kurt ended up dead, but they still haven't found the cash. That's why one of them cleaned out that storage compartment, and why they kept asking you about Frank Jones."

"Let's assume they did find out what Kurt was doing. They couldn't turn him over to the cops maybe because they had their own secrets to hide. Now I've become a liability because I've started nosing around. I'm drawing unwanted attention to them and Total Supply."

"So they've got to make it look like you're the bad guy."

"I have half a day off tomorrow, I think I'll pay them a visit," Leigh Ann said.

"You're going to drop by and just say hi? Oh sure, Leigh Ann, that's a great idea," Rachel said sarcastically. "That won't seem suspicious at all, walking into the enemy camp."

Leigh Ann shook her head. "I was planning to play the dumb blonde card and go in to buy a humane squirrel trap. They're a ranch and farm supply place, so they'll be able to get one for me."

"Be sure to talk to Wayne. I think he's sweet on you."

"Yeah, maybe," Leigh Ann said. "I'll chitchat,

then naturally let him know that I went up to the attic to chase out a squirrel and found a stash Kurt had hidden up there. I'll say that it was a bit of cash and several business folders. Then I'll watch his reaction. If he doesn't say anything, I'll ask if he and Pierre are still interested in Frank Jones, just in case I happen to come across something with that name."

"Detectives have already questioned them about that. Wayne's sure to know you're trying to play him," Rachel warned. "What you're doing could be really dangerous."

"The police are checking up on me and seriously exploring the possibility that I shot Kurt. I've got to do whatever I can to help myself."

The doorbell sounded. Leigh Ann went to the door and saw two men standing outside, pistols on their belts. One was Sergeant Knight. Her stomach sank.

Leigh Ann reluctantly opened the door and gave the sergeant a nod, then glanced at the other man, a slender, dark-haired man in his early thirties wearing a gray jacket, light blue shirt, and tan slacks. "May I help you?"

"Mrs. Vance, this is Detective McGraw," Knight said. "He's with our violent crimes division. We'd like a moment of your time. May we come in?"

She stepped back and waved them into the

large, open space that combined the living room, dining area, and kitchen. "What's this all about, detectives?" she asked, trying to sound confident, or at least not intimidated. McGraw had penetrating pale blue eyes and sharp, narrow features that reminded her of a hawk, for some reason.

Seeing Rachel at the dining table, McGraw said, "Is there someplace we can speak in private?"

"Sure. How about my office?" Leigh Ann suggested.

"That sounds fine, ma'am," McGraw said, eyeing Rachel a moment longer than necessary.

Leigh Ann led the police officers down the hall, to the first room on the left. She closed the door once they were inside, knowing full well Rachel would cross over to the sofa and listen in anyway.

"What can I do for you?" she asked, now a little more in control, hopefully.

McGraw spoke first, his voice softer than she'd expected. "Sergeant Knight recently learned that your husband had a bank account at the Rocky Mountain Bank in Cortez, just over the state line. Two days before he died, your husband withdrew a sum close to fifty thousand dollars. Do you know what became of that money?"

"No, sir. If I did, I'd have a nicer car, new

furniture, and this season's heels," she said seriously.

The two detectives exchanged a look.

McGraw continued to speak softly, though his expression had hardened a bit. "We've also followed up on that storage locker he rented in Farmington. It was closed two days *after* his death by someone who posed as him. How do you explain that?"

"I discussed that with Sergeant Knight. As I told him before, that wasn't me. Frankly, I'd have a hard time passing as my late husband. He was taller," Leigh Ann responded, straightening her back, which projected her breasts even more prominently. If Rachel could distract him, maybe she could, too.

"Do you find this amusing, Mrs. Vance?" McGraw replied, his voice no longer soft, and his expression cold, almost glaring. Knight, however, was unable to hold back a smile.

"No. It's your methods I find . . . humorous, as does your companion, obviously. You knew my answers to these questions already. I have no idea who it was, but clearly it wasn't me. I'm not going to confess to any crimes I didn't commit. Should I get an attorney?"

"Do you think you might say something that will incriminate you?" McGraw snapped.

"Listen carefully, detectives," Leigh Ann said, more annoyed than worried now. "I did *not* harm my husband, and I'm *not* a thief. Look closely at my lifestyle—my bank records, my two credit cards. Do a credit check. My meager income goes to bills—the regular kind, like food, water, gas, and so on."

"The bank account was in your name, too," McGraw said.

"Kurt never said a word about it to me, and you won't find my legitimate signature on any checks or application forms. I assure you I never saw a dime of that money, and, no, I have no idea where it is right now."

"So you've said," McGraw answered, and shrugged.

"I am *not* Kurt's killer. If I were, wouldn't I have just kept my mouth shut and let things lie?" she said, no longer concerned about showing her anger.

"Interesting that you're now proposing that your husband's death wasn't an accident. Sergeant Dale Carson mentioned that all three partners frequented a local shooting range and recommended we check out Wayne Hurley and Pierre Boone's association with that facility. He suggested that perhaps the weapon that killed your husband was rented or purchased there, maybe a private sale that was never recorded," McGraw said.

"I suppose that makes sense," Leigh Ann answered, suspecting from McGraw's tone that her cousin had inadvertently made things worse for her. "But where are you going with this?"

"We paid the range a visit and the gunsmith at their shop provided us with some interesting information. It turns out your husband was considering the purchase of a used rifle, so he brought it in to be checked out first. The gunsmith recalled that the weapon was going to be a gift for you," McGraw said, scowling.

"Yeah, Kurt bought me a rifle and we went shooting a few times. The last time I fired it was the summer before he died," Leigh Ann said.

Sergeant Knight spoke, his tone almost apologetic. "Can we examine the rifle, Mrs. Vance? According to the gunsmith's records and our forensics lab, it's the same caliber as the one that killed your husband."

"Shouldn't you have a warrant for that?"

"Yes ma'am, here it is, and it also includes your husband's laptop computer," McGraw said, a smug smile on his face as he brought out a handful of folded paper from his pocket.

Leigh Ann's stomach sank. She realized now that she'd been set up, maybe in more ways than one. If the killer had stolen the rifle, killed Kurt, then put it back, she was about to be royally screwed. Her hands shaking, she looked at the pages of the warrant. It all looked legal. She saw the judge's signature and the description of the rifle, undoubtedly provided by the gunsmith at the club.

"Well?" Detective McGraw said. "You wanna show us, or do we have to search room by room? It'll make a mess."

Leigh Ann shook her head. "No problem, except I sold Kurt's laptop months ago at a garage sale after erasing the hard drive. I needed to pay some bills. My rifle is here, upstairs. Follow me."

She walked out of the office, glanced at Rachel, who was now sitting on the sofa pretending to read a magazine, and then led the two officers upstairs. Once inside her room, she pointed toward the bed. "It's under there beside Kurt's shotgun, inside the gun case, which isn't locked. It's probably covered with dust, so be ready to sneeze."

McGraw nodded to Knight, who got down on his knees, peered underneath, then brought out the pump shotgun and a long, black plastic container. "Yeah, it's dusty," Knight observed. "No smudges anywhere. This has been sitting here, undisturbed, for weeks, maybe months."

"Bet your wife doesn't vacuum under the bed that much either," Leigh Ann muttered.

Knight shrugged. "My ex-wife didn't vacuum at all."

"Enough small talk. Open it up, Sergeant," McGraw grumbled.

Knight opened the three suitcase-style latches and lifted the top.

"Crap," McGraw growled.

"Dammit to hell," Leigh Ann blurted out at almost the same time. "Somebody stole my rifle."

"Don't think this is going to get you off the hook, Mrs. Vance," McGraw said.

Leigh Ann didn't answer. A few minutes later, after double-checking the rest of the bedroom, they went back downstairs. She stayed perfectly still on the living room sofa as he continued hurling questions at her. Rachel, meanwhile, had gone into the office and Sergeant Knight was searching the rest of the house and the garage.

"Wherever that rifle is, I didn't take it, hide it, or use it in any crime," she replied. "I've allowed you to search my home and garage freely. Now I'm through cooperating. Until that rifle turns up, you need to leave me alone," she said.

Sergeant Knight walked back into the room, and looking at McGraw, shook his head. "Nothing," he said, handing Leigh Ann the keys to the garage cabinets, which she'd freely offered.

"We're done here," Leigh Ann said, standing. "Investigate all you want. I'm innocent. More than that, my life's in danger and I'll do whatever it takes to protect myself."

"We'd advise you to stay out of this, ma'am," Sergeant Knight said. "Let us do what we're trained for. If the rifle was really stolen from this house, it'll turn up eventually. We have the serial number, and once the weapon's found, ballistics will be able to determine if that was the rifle used to kill your husband."

"And if it was, count on another visit from me," McGraw added. "We're not done, Mrs. Vance. If you're really innocent, keep your eyes and ears open. If you learn something, give us a call." He handed her his card.

"Count on it, detectives. Once I figure things out, I'll let you know—through my attorney."

A few minutes later, as they were driving away, Rachel came out of the office and stood beside her. "Way to go, sis. So who's your attorney?"

"Are you kidding? I can't even afford to pay the light bill until I get my next paycheck."

"So you were bluffing?"

"Yeah, but not about clearing my name. It's all I've got left, and by damn, Kurt's not taking that from me."

"Change it. Go back to your maiden name—Carson."

"No. I'm not going to try and hide from this. I'm tackling the mess head-on. Tomorrow, I'll be walking straight into the lion's den."

Nine

Leigh Ann drove over to Total Supply right after eight the next morning, this time with the revolver in her purse, just in case. As she parked in the graveled lot in front of the large sheet-metal building, she realized that her hands were shaking. It wasn't fear—it was excitement.

She wanted answers, and for the first time in her life she was taking the proverbial bull by the horns instead of waiting for someone else to lead the way.

That was what Kurt's death had done for her—taught her to stand on her own two feet. The pretty little girl from a small town in Texas had finally grown up.

Back in high school, popularity had come as easily as breathing to her. She'd been head cheerleader and homecoming queen.

Right after graduation, filled with big dreams, she'd married the hunky high school quarterback.

Instead of the fairy-tale romance she'd hoped for, reality had pushed her dreams into the sand, sucking the life out of them. They'd struggled and put off having kids, waiting for a "right time" that had never come.

In her mid-thirties now, she still had her looks, though her innocence was long gone and trust didn't come easily to her anymore. She tried her hardest to be friendly and cheerful, but cynicism had, for the most part, replaced hope. These days, she had a tendency to assume the worst and be pleasantly surprised if circumstances proved her wrong.

As she walked into what was essentially a large warehouse with compartmented offices, she saw Wayne Hurley helping one of at least five customers visible at the moment.

Wayne and his client were standing in one of the long rows between tall metal shelves piled high with samples of their product line, everything from horseshoe nails, lubricants, irrigation valves and sprinklers, and even scale models of hay balers and irrigation pumps. She waited until Wayne completed the transaction, then caught his eye, waved, and walked over to join him.

"You're a sight for sore eyes, Leigh Ann," Wayne said, adjusting his bolo tie and sucking in his middle-aged gut. "What brings you here this fine morning?"

"Remember when you and Pierre told me I'd get a wholesale discount whenever I needed something?"

"Of course, and that offer still stands. Whatcha need, some fencing or maybe a backyard shed?"

She gave him her best smile. All things considered, she preferred dealing with Wayne.

Pierre was polite and nice enough, but they'd never hit it off. He and Kurt had been friends though, so maybe that was part of it. On the other hand, Kurt had never much cared for Wayne, often griping that Wayne wasn't hungry enough to be a good salesman. It seemed to gall Kurt that Wayne tended to give their big-ticket clients and the small, walk-in buyers equal time and service.

"I'm looking for a live trap—something large enough to catch a pesky squirrel, but not harm it."

"You got one setting up a den under the house?" Wayne asked, stepping behind a U-shaped counter that held computer terminals and cash registers.

"No, this one is wandering into the attic, and those little sharp-toothed rascals can create all kinds of trouble, making nests in the insulation and such. Since I don't want it trapped and dying up there, I've got to catch it before I seal off any openings. Once it's in the cage, I'll release it down in the bosque."

"I know exactly what you need," he said, conducting a quick search on a computer. "How's this?" he said, turning the monitor so she could see the low wire cage with slanting doors at each end.

"Is it easy to use?"

"Yes indeed, and once the squirrel touches the

bait, the doors slam shut and it's trapped. I've sold dozens of these over the years and I'll go over it with you when you pick it up. I can have one here early next week if we order now. Will that do?"

"Sounds fine, Wayne. How much will it run me?"

"You've never come to us for anything, so this first order is at cost: fourteen ninety-five plus tax, which includes shipping. You okay with that?"

"You bet. I really appreciate it, too," she said with a smile. "You know, the months after Kurt passed away, things were really hard for me. I don't know if I ever properly thanked you for buying back Kurt's share of the business at such a fair price. If you guys hadn't done that, I wouldn't have been able to pay the bills and hang on to the house."

"I'm sorry that you had such a rough time of it," Wayne said. "It's hard to go from being a couple to being alone."

Remembering that Wayne's marriage had ended up in a divorce several months ago, she nodded. "I'm sorry you and Cathy didn't make it. I thought you two would be together forever."

"So did I," Wayne said. "We had our problems, sure, but I always thought we'd work them out."

"I know you tried a marriage counselor."

"That was a waste of time," he spat out. "Cathy played me."

"I know how that feels."

He avoided her gaze and that spoke volumes to her. Had everyone in the entire county known that Kurt was cheating on her? How could she have been so blind?

"I've been sorting through a bunch of old household junk and it turns out Kurt left me a few more surprises," she ventured, her voice casual. "Are you still looking for files on what's-his-name . . . Frank something?"

"Frank Jones?" Wayne said quickly. "I'd forgotten all about him, it's been so long. What'd you find?"

"Nothing but his name, so far, but you know my cousin, Dale Carson, a former state police officer. He's with the sheriff's department now. Maybe I can ask him to look into this Jones guy for you? Would that help?"

"Don't bother, it's no big deal. If you happen to find any papers on the guy, though, let me know and I'll come get them," he said. "But I'm curious. I was under the impression that you'd cleared out Kurt's things months ago."

"That's what I thought. It turns out Kurt had little stashes all over the danged place."

"Little stashes?"

"Yeah. Not long ago, we found two hundred dollars hidden in the attic. Then, when Rachel and I got ready to paint the office at home, we moved that big desk, and found another hundred taped to the underside, along with a passport. Can you believe it? He never used it, but jeez, a *passport?* Who runs off to Mexico when you've only got three hundred dollars in your pocket?"

As she talked, Leigh Ann saw that Wayne kept shooting glances at Pierre, who'd come in from the back and was now standing beside a desk not fifteen feet away.

"Hey, Wayne," Pierre called out, "don't you think you better go check on that field fencing before the customer comes to pick it up?"

"What fencing?"

Pierre scowled. "You took the call, remember, just after we opened?"

"Oh, yeah. The field fencing. I'll handle it. Can you help Leigh Ann? She wants to order a humane squirrel trap—the one on the display. I told her she could have it at cost."

"Sure, glad to help," Pierre said, coming over. "Hi, Leigh Ann, sorry to interrupt. I'm glad to see you again. You know that if you ever need anything for your place, you can come to us, right?"

"That's very kind," she said.

"Kurt left you with bills and a huge mortgage. The way I see it, you're going to need to keep that house fixed up because it's your biggest asset. If you ever need painters, plumbers, whatever, call me. I'll put you in touch with the right people, businesses that won't try to rip off a woman."

"I really appreciate that," she said. It wasn't like Pierre to be this nice—or patronizing. She wondered when the other shoe would drop.

"I heard you mention to Wayne that you've been finding little stashes Kurt left all around the house. Kurt was like that in his office here, too. We each had our own personal file cabinets, but he stowed away paperwork like a squirrel gathers nuts."

She could tell he was curious about what she'd supposedly found, but was being careful not to mention Frank Jones. She wondered if that was because they'd denied any knowledge of Jones to the detective. Maybe Pierre had sent Wayne to the back because he'd heard his partner slip once already.

Instinct told her to play it cool right now. "Kurt was a pack rat, rest his soul," she replied.

"One more thing, Leigh Ann. I know you're a proud woman, and you don't like asking anyone for help, but if you ever need a loan, or if there's any way we can help, just say so. We're here for you."

"I really appreciate that, Pierre. Thank you."

He looked at the monitor. "You still have the same address and phone number, correct?"

"Yes, but I'll be picking it up here, right?"

"Yeah," he said with a nod. "If you need the trap sooner, I can try and put a rush on it."

"No, it'll be fine by early next week. Give me a call?"

"No problem."

Walking out, Leigh Ann could feel Pierre's eyes on her. Despite all his kind words, she could sense the man didn't trust her one bit. Maybe, like the cops, he also thought she'd been in on Kurt's embezzling scheme.

She took a deep breath as she got into the car. She'd stirred up a hornet's nest, all right, but she wouldn't back away from this fight. She'd see it through to the end.

She'd switched on the ignition and put the Jeep in gear when she heard the smartphone tone that signaled an incoming email. Shifting to neutral, she checked the phone's display and smiled. It was from Melvin. He had a Braille keyboard hooked up to his computer and often sent her short messages.

When she finished reading, she called him. "Hey, I just got your email," she said. "You're really ready to begin the new sculpture?"

"Yeah, but I need you here to help me get started. This time what I'd like you to do is sit on a sheepskin rug, so you'll be comfortable, and just talk to me."

"I can do that," she said. "Should I come over

right now? I don't have to be at work 'til noon today."

"Great! I'll be waiting."

"Why the floor, though?"

"You know that I see dark figures and outlines but few details. I've learned to let my imagination fill in what I need. Having you sit on the floor will give me an idea of proportion without having to guess when you're in a chair or on the sofa. Will that be a problem?"

"Not at all," she said. "I'm comfortable wherever."

Placing the phone on the console beside her, she pulled out of the parking lot and headed west. She was really looking forward to these sessions. It would be nice to spend time with Melvin.

Today, while he worked, at first she'd keep the conversation light and not distract him, but then she'd try to find out what was bothering him, starting obliquely by talking about what needed fixing at his house. She knew he was short on cash and she was a pretty good handyman, handywoman, handyperson? She didn't know the politically correct term, but if it leaked, chipped, or bowed out, she knew how to fix it. At the same time, maybe he'd open up a little to her.

Ten

Leigh Ann was almost at Melvin's when her phone rang. She normally didn't get that many phone calls during the day. Seeing it was Regina and suspecting it was trading post business, she answered.

"Hey, Regina, what's going on?" Leigh Ann asked.

"I need a favor. I want to switch around my hours so I can take off an extra day next week and Jo suggested I work something out with you or Esther. I'm scheduled for half a day, but since you already have this morning off, I wondered if you could use the entire day? I could stick around, and trade with you next month to even things out."

Leigh Ann considered it.

"Leigh Ann, I know things have been a bit crazy for you lately, so if you can't don't worry about it. I can ask Esther."

"Actually this works for me, too. Let's do this, but please let Jo know, okay?" She'd wanted a chance to talk to Melvin about everything that had happened to her, as well as what was bothering him. Maybe if she opened up first, he'd do the same, and together they'd find new insights.

As she pulled up at Melvin's, she saw him step out the front door. Of course he'd heard her Jeep. Only the stone deaf could miss it.

"When are you going to fix that rattle? Do you even know what it is?" he asked, his forehead furrowed.

"It's nothing. The Jeep still runs fine and that particular noise isn't coming from the engine."

He nodded, though she could tell she hadn't convinced him. "So tell me more about your new sculpture," she said, changing the subject.

"I don't want to talk about it 'til it's done. Be patient," he said, then gestured inside. "Come on, it's already warming up here. Do you want something cold to drink?"

"My mouth's dry, but it doesn't have anything to do with the weather."

"You're nervous? Why? All you have to do is talk to me."

"You may have lost your sight, but you see the real me more clearly than anyone I've ever known."

"I hope so. That's the ability I'll need to rely on most now. I'm trying to give form to your inner self, your wind breath, as my people would say. It isn't meant to be a duplicate of what you see when you look in the mirror."

"That's scary," she said, then chuckled nervously.

"Your voice is filled with uncertainty—but

hope as well. That's all part of what I want my sculpture to reflect. If I do my job right, our combined spirits will define the figure and breathe life into the clay."

"I know your work. There's nothing you can't do. I'm curious. Why haven't you attempted a human figure before?"

"For the same reason I don't do just any animal. Something has to whisper to me and compel me to create it." He led her to the sheepskin rug he'd laid out in the middle of his den. "Last call. Do you want something to drink?"

"Water would be fine," she said.

"You sure? I have the Mexican Cokes that you like—with real sugar, not corn syrup. They're phasing them out, so this might be the last one you'll ever have."

"One of those would be great. And don't bother with a glass. In the bottle's fine."

He brought it to her, then moved across the room to a table with a folded up wing that blocked her view.

"You picked that particular table so I couldn't see?"

"It does keep the work from being seen, that's true enough, but the back is up so nothing falls. I've already begun a wire armature to give the piece internal support, but until I get the pose just right, the internal frame won't stand securely on its own. If you hadn't noticed, I sometimes misjudge distances and bump into things."

She made herself comfortable on the floor. "I love sheepskin rugs. They're so soft."

"Describe the way you're sitting," he said. "Cross-legged?"

"No, I have my right leg straight out and my left leg tucked underneath my right thigh. I'm leaning back a bit, with my left arm behind my back, supporting me. My right upper arm is to my side."

"Hmm. I get the picture. Makes my knee hurt just thinking about it."

She laughed. "It's real comfortable for me."

"If you say so," he said, and chuckled.

"What are you doing now?" she asked after several quiet minutes had passed.

"Kneading the clay," he said, "but I don't want you focused on me. Tell me about you, your day, and what's been happening in your life."

She told him about her visit to Total Supply. "It went smoothly enough, I guess, but I don't know any more than I did before, except that they lied to the detectives about Frank Jones."

"Yeah, but you already knew who Frank Jones really was, so what exactly did you hope to find out?"

"Just how far they were willing to go to continue the lie," she said. "They not only told the detectives that they'd never heard of Frank Jones, they also said that no money had been stolen from the company. What's interesting is that when I brought up the name, Wayne tried to get me to give up whatever I had on Jones. Then Pierre heard what was going on and sent Wayne away before he could make things worse."

"Pierre sounds like the brains of the two, which makes him the most dangerous. So be careful. Letting them know you're onto them is like playing with fire," Melvin said.

"I know, which is why I'm carrying the .38 revolver in my purse right now."

"You have a concealed carry for that?"

"No, but I have more important things to worry about, and as long as it helps me fight back and stay alive, I'm willing to take the risk. I'm more worried about them than I am about getting caught with a weapon."

"Hope you never have to use it, Leigh Ann," he said. "Now let's think a little farther ahead. Say that a year from now, you have all the answers you've searched for and you're ready to move on. What would you like to see in your life then?"

Him, but she couldn't say that. "A house that's finally all fixed up," she said with a thin smile.

"No, tell me about *you*—where do you see yourself in a year?"

181

"Are you asking where I'd like to be, or where I'd see myself realistically."

"Answer both," he said.

Although she couldn't see his hands working the clay, exertion tightened the cords on his neck, and angled toward his shoulders. What she wouldn't have given to see him working shirtless. She bit back a sigh.

"And tell me what made you sigh under your breath like that."

She laughed. "Hey, you don't miss much."

He grinned. "Does that bother you?"

"Bother, no, wrong word."

"Then what is?"

She took a deep breath. "You make me feel as naked as a jaybird sometimes."

"And you want us to be on more equal footing," he said with a nod. "Navajos believe in balance. So, shall I strip and work naked?"

She'd just taken a sip of Coke and instantly choked. "Good gravy, Melvin! That's not what I meant." She'd thought about it, sure, but she'd go to her grave before she admitted it.

Hearing him laugh, she realized he was deliberately teasing her.

"We should still strive for balance, so how about I strip off my shirt," he said.

"You don't have to do that," she said, but as hard as she'd tried, her voice lacked conviction even to her own ears.

He grinned. "No problem. I'll volunteer. It's warm in the house anyway. In fact, let me turn on the swamp cooler. Adding moisture to the room will help the clay."

"If you're going to be lowering the temperature, you'll want to keep your shirt close by," she said, trying unsuccessfully to hide her disappointment.

"It won't cool off that much. There's something wrong with the unit."

Leigh Ann watched him tug off his shirt and toss it aside. Though he hadn't seemed to be aiming, he obviously knew precisely where the closest chair was. The garment fell neatly over the arm.

"Nice."

"Me, or the throw?"

"Both."

As he continued working, she could now see the muscles on his upper arms and chest ripple. The light dusting of hair that arrowed downward from the center of his chest and disappeared into the nether regions below teased her imagination. With effort, she forced her breathing to stay even—well, almost.

"That's what I want to hear—temptation, a touch of longing, the struggle."

"I haven't said anything!" she protested.

He laughed. "It's your breathing . . . It changes, though you're fighting it. And when you paid me a compliment, there was a tiny hitch in your voice."

"I think you should definitely consider a second job as a CIA analyst—or a psychic," she said.

The house stayed warm, just as he'd predicted. Uncomfortable, she shifted in place, feeling sweaty. "When you're ready to take a break, how about letting me buy you lunch?" she asked, thinking that he needed to save money for a new evaporative cooler. Going without wasn't an option. Summers on the Rez could be brutal. Fans just moved the hot air around. Without a cooler, a home out here in a basically shadeless environment would rival the hottest corner of hell.

"You're modeling for free, so lunch is my treat," he insisted.

Pride. She could hear it echo clearly in his voice. "How about if we split the bill? You need funds for a new cooler, and my Jeep's going to need tires and a tune-up, so I have to watch my spending, too."

"No deal. Lunch's still on me," he said, checking his back pocket for cash.

"How can you tell one bill from another? That's got to be tough."

"I put a little fold on my fives, two on the tens, and so on," he responded.

"Smart guy."

"Nah. Just someone who knows about survival."

"I hear you," Leigh Ann answered. Maybe his mention of survival was a sign he might be open to discuss whatever was keeping him awake at night. She tried to figure what to say next to move in that direction.

"Come on. I'm starving," he said, covering the figure with a sheet of black plastic, setting it on a shelf, and then reaching for his shirt.

"We'll come back here afterwards, and you'll work some more?"

"Maybe. Let's see how it goes."

Spending the morning watching Melvin sculpt shirtless . . . It didn't get better than that. Since she'd given her hours to Regina, she had the afternoon to look forward to also.

They were just getting into her Jeep when her cell phone rang. She recognized Rachel's tone. "What's up, sis?" she asked, answering the call.

"They came to my work, Leigh Ann. I'll be surprised if I still have a job tomorrow."

"*Who* came to your work? Calm down and make sense," she said, her heart beating in quick time.

"The detectives. They asked me all kinds of questions. They wanted to know about my job, and how much bookkeeping it entailed. I was in the break room, but I know Charlie was listening."

"They're just fishing, Rachel, following up on

my interview, maybe hoping to get something new. Don't worry, they can't touch either one of us because we've done nothing wrong."

"No one wants someone suspected of embezzlement working for their company. Ever since they left, Charlie's been asking me all kinds of questions about Kurt's business and why the detectives came to talk to me."

"Just tell him you don't know what's going on."

"I did, but I don't think he believed me any more than the cops did."

"Calm down, Rache. The more nervous you appear, the guiltier you look."

"Yeah, well, I ran into the restroom and threw up after the cops left. Then I clocked out and I'm on the way home. Only there's someone following me."

"Who?"

"I think it's the cops in an unmarked car—one of those generic sedans. They asked where you were right now, and I said I didn't know. They must have thought I was lying about that, too. What do we do now?" Rachel added.

"We'll have to play it by ear. That's all we can do." Hanging up, Leigh Ann put the Jeep in gear and got underway. "I've got to find answers fast, Melvin, before this mess destroys my life. Getting past all the secrets and finding the truth is like peeling an onion. The closer I get to the center, the more it stinks."

"Surprises and secrets—that combination usually spells disaster," Melvin observed.

She heard it again—that haunted quality in his voice. Melvin's past was a closed book, and maybe that was the way it should remain. If she pressed Melvin with personal questions, she might lose what connection she already had with him.

"Let's go to lunch and forget all this for now. I'm tired of fighting, of trying to stay strong. I've had it," Leigh Ann said.

"You have a hard fight ahead, Leigh Ann, but don't forget that you've got plenty of backup. The trading post folk are a tough bunch. You can count on them—and me."

"Thanks, Melvin," she said softly. "I'm glad we're friends."

As she spoke, she saw his expression tighten. He wanted more, and so did she, but fear had built a wall between them. That was the problem with people who'd been to hell and back. Life had taught them how rare it was to find a friend who really cared, one you trust to the end, and some things were just too precious to risk.

Eleven

Jo sat alone in her kitchen. It was late and she was tired, but she still couldn't sleep. Her stomach had been upset all day. As soon as the teakettle whistled, she brewed another cup of the herbal tea her teacher had recommended.

Lost in thought, she stared at the teacup. Gray sunflower, the Navajo name for the herb, not only helped with stomach upsets, it was used as a good-luck plant. It was said that Horned Lizard had become frightened during a very bad thunderstorm, and had run under Gray Sunflower for protection. Although lightning had struck all around them, neither plant nor lizard had been harmed.

Considering what Ben was going through, she wondered if she'd be allowed to send him a medicine pouch with that herb. The plant wasn't illegal.

Glancing at the clock, she was surprised to discover it was one in the morning. If she didn't get some sleep now, she'd be dragging later for sure. With a sigh, she got up and walked to her room, turning off the lights as she went.

The silence in the house enfolded her and assured her that all was well. In contrast, Ben lived in the middle of chaos. She vividly recalled what she suspected were explosions as they'd spoken via Skype. How did he cope and stay sane?

Lying down, Jo took a deep breath and shut out those thoughts. Unless she focused solely on her breathing, she'd never get any sleep.

She wasn't sure when she finally drifted off, but it seemed to her that she'd only just fallen asleep when she woke abruptly. A glance at the clock told her it was four in the morning. She lay still, wondering what had awakened her and trying to calm her pounding heart and get back to sleep.

Just as she started to drift off, a squeak jolted her awake. Someone was walking across her wooden front porch. She listened closely and heard the footsteps again, along with another, more muted sound she couldn't quite identify.

Bringing out the rifle she kept beneath the bed, she levered a shell into the chamber, then picked up the phone and called the police. She made her report quietly, moved silently to the living room, then held her rifle up and ready.

Jo flipped on the outside lights and called out loudly. "I'm armed and you're trespassing." She'd found out a long time ago that the more confident she sounded, the more of an advantage that gave her.

There was no response.

Jo went to the window, approaching from the

outside edge of the curtain, and peered out. If the intruder was also armed, she wanted to make sure she didn't turn herself into an easy target.

Hearing a rush of footsteps, she pushed the curtain aside slightly and saw a figure wearing a hoodie running away down the road. He raced around the curve, and the piñon and juniper trees along the road quickly blocked him from view.

Jo waited and listened. Soon she heard a car engine rev up and a few seconds after saw dust rising from the road in the moonlight. Rifle still in hand, she looked through the peephole and tried to identify the odor right outside her door. Something sure stunk out there. The scent was familiar, too. . . .

She unlocked the door and stepped out onto the porch. In the next instant she realized she was smelling kerosene. A red gas can, lying on its side, was glugging its contents onto the porch.

Reacting quickly, she immediately set it upright. Knowing kerosene could ignite from just a spark, Jo raced to the garden hose coiled up beneath the outside faucet. Leaning the rifle, barrel up, against the wall, she began washing down the porch, using a coarse spray from the adjustable nozzle, just like she'd done with the paint and the loading dock. This was getting old.

She worked methodically, taking care not to

splash kerosene onto the wall of the house. Once the scent dissipated, she turned off the hose, grabbed her rifle, and went back inside to wait for the police. Out here, response times were often half an hour or more. There were too few tribal officers and their patrol areas were enormous. Since Tom Stuart's murder last year, she'd taken to keeping a loaded rifle handy.

Forty minutes after she'd placed the call, a Navajo tribal police force white-and-green SUV pulled up outside. Jo stepped out to greet the officer, who was clad in the department's khaki uniform.

Jo felt calmer, but as she set her rifle against the wall again, she realized her hands were still shaking. She jammed them into her jacket pockets and walked over to talk to the officer, who'd parked about twenty-five feet from the porch. He was tall, in his mid-thirties, and fit.

"Miss Buck? You called 911 about a prowler?"

Jo quickly filled him in, pointing to the can. "I had to set it upright because it was still spilling kerosene everywhere. I also hosed down the porch."

"Kerosene is easy to find on the Rez," he commented. Looking around and spotting the cap in the dirt, he picked it up with a gloved hand and screwed it back onto the can. He returned to his vehicle, placed the can upright into a small plastic cooler, and jammed in a cheap drop cloth to keep it from tipping over.

"Any body secretion or foreign substances that might leave latent fingerprints on the can were probably washed away by the spilled kerosene, but maybe we'll get lucky with the top of the cap," he said. "Did you get a look at the man's face?"

She shook her head and gave him the best description she could. "It may have been Edmund Garnenez. He's been causing trouble for me and my teacher."

He nodded. "I read up on the complaints you and the *hataalii* have filed, including one about the paint that someone threw against the trading post wall. This could have been a lot worse. I'll check on Garnenez's whereabouts tonight and stop at the Ponderosa Mercantile and see if anyone there remembers who bought kerosene lately."

"Why the Mercantile? Most of the places around here carry it, including The Outpost."

"The bottom of the can still has part of the price tag—with the Ponderosa pine logo."

"I didn't catch that. Good eyes, Officer . . ."

"Atencio," he answered. "Can you think of anyone else who might have a grudge against you or the trading post? There was that nasty business just last year at your place. You think it could be connected to those events?"

Jo shook her head. "No, that's over. I can't

think of anyone who might be targeting The Outpost specifically now. We run an honest business and you couldn't ask for a better bunch of employees."

He nodded slowly. "So I've heard. My great-aunt is Esther Allison. She's always spoken highly of you."

The link didn't surprise her. Navajos always had relatives nearby. That was one advantage of the clan system. Everyone knew, or was related to, someone else nearby, and clan lineages could be traced back many generations.

"Esther's part of our trading post family," she said.

He nodded. "She feels the same way about the crew there," he said, getting back into the tribal SUV. "I'll look into this, ask around, and see what I can find. If I learn anything, I'll turn it over to the detectives."

"Thanks for your help," she said.

He looked at the rifle resting near the porch door. "You know how to shoot that?"

"I can hit a coffee can at fifty yards."

He nodded once. "Keep it close, then."

"Always do."

After he left, Jo locked up and went to her room, placing the rifle back under the bed. She wouldn't get any more sleep tonight, and she'd be paying the price for that later at work. Although she loved the dark skies and the uninterrupted sounds of nature at night, she was beginning to feel that she should move into the Stuart house behind The Outpost. The place belonged to Ben now, of course, but she had the keys and knew he wouldn't mind. Under the circumstances, he'd probably insist, but she'd ask first.

The Stuart cottage was one of Jo's favorite places. Every once in a while she'd go inside just to look around and take a breath. Even though Ben had been overseas for months, the place somehow retained his essence, including the masculine, outdoorsy scent that so defined him. Going there was the next best thing to being in his arms.

Next time they spoke she'd ask his permission to move in temporarily, but she'd have to find a way to do it without alarming him. Despite the fact that he was half a world away, Ben was attuned to even the slightest nuance in her tone.

"I miss you, Ben. Take care of yourself and come home to me," she whispered to the darkness.

It was two o'clock in the afternoon when Leigh Ann saw Ambrose pull up in front of The Outpost in his restored classic Ford pickup, painted candy-apple red. She smiled. It was impossible not to like Ambrose John. He had a grin that could stop hearts—or restart them. His hair was long, warrior style, and his body all muscle.

When he walked into the store, carrying a briefcase, he flashed a brilliant smile at Leigh Ann and Jo, who were standing close together at the front counter. "Hey, pretty ladies."

Ambrose was one of the best-looking men around. He was also gay, a fact many a woman had mourned over the years.

"Do you have a minute for me?"

"I hope you brought us some jewelry," Jo replied, nodding. "Your pieces sell at lightning speed. You're the best silversmith around."

"Yes, that's common knowledge," he said with unabashed arrogance.

Jo and Leigh Ann chuckled. "What's up, Ambrose?" Jo asked.

He stepped closer, and keeping his voice low, replied, "I've heard that both of you are having some, let's say, 'security problems' right now. So I figured I'd hang around, maybe set up a table on the porch outside, and do some finish work here. I can keep my ears open and maybe help you figure out what's going on and who's responsible."

Leigh Ann remembered how much business Ambrose had attracted the last time he'd set up shop on the premises. She looked at Jo and nodded. "I think you and Ben were in Juarez on business the last time Ambrose came here to work on his jewelry. We had record-breaking traffic that day. People would drive by, look at him, and come back to check out . . . his wares," she said with a tiny smile. "Does that sound horribly sexist, Ambrose?"

"Darling, if I hadn't wanted people to look, I wouldn't have put on a show—red headband and shirtless."

"Well, actually, you had your shirt on—just unbuttoned and opened wide," Leigh Ann said.

"Ah, you remember every detail, do you?" he said, flashing her that devastating grin.

Leigh Ann sighed loudly. "What's not to remember? You're quite an eyeful."

"Thank you, girl," he said. "So what do you say, Jo? Shall I get set up out there? All I'll need is a table, a chair, and an extension cord."

Sam had just come up from the back of the room. "I could help Mr. John," she offered.

"Great," Jo said. "Leigh Ann, I need to talk to you in my office."

"Sure," Leigh Ann replied, then watched Sam glancing around for a suitable table. "Make sure it's a sturdy one," she called out.

Sam helped Ambrose get set up, and before long, he was buffing a finished piece with a rouge cloth while she laid out the extension cord. "I saw the last pendant you made with the green turquoise, Mr. John, the one that looked like it was resting on a silver shell. It was gorgeous."

"I'm surprised you liked that piece, Samantha. I would have thought something smaller . . . maybe earrings . . . would have been more your style. And call me Ambrose or A.J. Mr. John's my father."

Sam chuckled. "I usually just wear a watch, a ring, and my silver posts. That's it. I'm not a jewelry person. I'm more of a horse person. When I'm not working with a computer, I want to be on horseback."

He smiled. "That's the kind of answer I expected."

"But my grandmother Esther loved that pendant. That one was way above my pay grade, but I'm wondering if maybe we could trade services? I could configure software for you to keep track of your business—everything from the status of merchandise under consignment, to business expenditures and taxable income. Does that sound like something you could use, Mr. . . . Ambrose?"

He set down the cloth and looked at her. "I'm interested. Keep talking."

"What kind of bookkeeping system do you have now?"

"A ledger, a number-two pencil, and a pocket calculator."

She blinked owlishly. "You're not serious."

"Sure am."

"Wow," she said softly. "Haven't seen anything like that in, well, never."

"You're making me feel like a dinosaur," he said, and laughed.

"I can make things a lot easier for you," Sam said, "especially around tax time. You don't have a laptop, do you?"

"Sure do. It's the latest, with all kinds of software."

"Great. I'll teach you how to enter things onto an electronic spreadsheet."

"Okay. How about you design the system *and* keep my books until, say, January? In exchange, I'll make a pendant for Esther—but it won't be exactly the same as the one you saw. All my jewelry is one of a kind."

"Deal, but I'll have to get the bookkeeping software set up at night and on weekends. If that's okay with you, just leave your laptop here for me at the trading post and put the paperwork in a shoe box, paper bag, or whatever."

"Will do."

"One more thing. Could you have the pendant ready in two months? I'd like to give it to my *shimasáni* on her birthday, July thirty-first."

"That'll have to depend on the availability of the right stone. I'm picky. You want green turquoise? I've got some Manassa green from Colorado, with a great golden matrix."

Sam nodded. "Sounds beautiful. It's one of her favorite shades."

"All right, then. I'll see what I can do. In the meantime, write down the name of any software you want me to buy."

"If you've got a top-of-the-line laptop, you probably have what you need already, but I'll have a list of essentials for you by the time you leave today."

She went inside, and a few minutes later came back with some cold mineral water for him. Sam placed it on the table beside him and hung around, watching him work.

"What's on your mind?" Ambrose asked, looking up after he'd finished setting a stone into the bezel of a small pendant.

She opened her mouth to speak. "No, forget it. It's none of my business."

"Go on. It's okay."

"When you first came into the store, you seemed all friendly and relaxed, but your expression changed when you looked at Jo. For a second or two you looked . . . worried. I don't think anyone else noticed, but I see things like that because in my work, like yours, details are everything. I know you and Ben are close friends, so I wondered. Is something wrong?"

"You read people pretty well, kid," Ambrose said.

Sam shrugged. "I'm right, aren't I?"

"I spoke to Ben the other day and found out he'll be going into a hot spot. That's what he trained for, but I got the feeling he thought he might not make it back out this time."

He paused. "That's just my gut talking, so keep it under wraps."

She nodded. "I think Jo sensed the same thing."

"Why do you say that?"

"She's been checking her email and Skype almost every hour. I'm guessing she's going out of her mind waiting to hear from Ben again. It's what I'd do, too, if my—" She stopped talking. "Anyway, you get the idea."

"Yeah, but now I'm curious," he said, giving her a disarming smile. "Who's the guy you've set *your* sights on?"

"Me? No one. I was speaking hypothetically."

"Aw, come on. I haven't had anyone to share secrets with since my partner moved out and I'm almost sure I'm going through withdrawal. Spill it."

Sam laughed. "Yeah, I know how that goes. My best friend's in college now, and she's too busy to even email most days. We used to tell each other *everything*."

"See that? We can create balance for each other and that'll bring harmony. All we've got to do is start talking. So who's the lucky guy?"

"It's Jack Colburn, but he doesn't even know

I'm alive. He treats me like his kid sister," she said, and rolled her eyes.

"I've met the guy, cowboy and ex-soldier, right? He's what, ten years older than you?"

"More. I'm twenty-one, he's thirty-two, and *way* out of my league. . . ."

"Why do you say that? You could catch any guy's eye."

"Yeah, except Jack's," she muttered.

"And he's not gay?"

She smiled. "Nope."

"Here I thought I'd have a shot at him."

Sam laughed. "Forget it. I got there first. What about you? Anyone new on the horizon?"

Ambrose shook his head. "I've met some people online, but I don't make friends quickly."

"You? But everyone loves you!"

He smiled. "I've got lots of acquaintances, but close friends? Those, I can count on one hand."

"I'll give you the same advice my *shimasání* gave me: Stop assuming you know what everyone's thinking."

He had to laugh. "That's the first time anyone ever said that to me."

"Yeah, I get it. You're all muscle and toughness, but when it comes to meeting people, you're insecure. You don't trust anyone's motives."

"And you'd know all this—how?" he pressed, a ghost of a smile tugging at the corners of his mouth.

"My *shimasání* again. She told me that you wouldn't deal with anyone except Ben's dad or Jo before all the bad things happened. Then Ben came back into the picture, and not just as an old friend but as a part-owner. That's when you finally allowed yourself to become part of the trading post family."

"That's true enough, but the reality is I've got to be careful. Some people hate gays."

"There's always more than enough hatred to go around. Some kids gave me a hard time back in high school because I worked harder and could outthink them. I was the geek no one wanted to take to the prom."

"It can sting to be the outsider," he said, nodding. "People, especially kids, can be so cruel."

"Oh, yeah." Sam sighed. "I better go put that folding sign out by the street, to let everyone know you're here today."

"Go ahead," Ambrose said. As Sam turned away, he added, "Oh, one more thing. I went to school with Jack, and he was always the quiet type, the 'still waters run deep' kind. Don't assume he's not interested just 'cause he's not saying anything."

"You really think so?"

"Yeah, Jack isn't easy to read. In high school, I never considered him a friend—until one day four guys jumped me and Ben after a game. We were down on the ground, but they wouldn't let up. Jack jumped in and threw them all off us. He even bounced one guy we called 'Brick'— for obvious reasons—right off the wall."

She smiled. "That sounds like something Jack would do. It's hard to get him riled, but if he thinks he's in the right there's no stopping him."

He smiled. "You're totally crazy about him."

"Yeah, I guess," she said and sighed. "Buy me a macadamia double mocha cappuccino sometime, Ambrose. I'll tell you about my lack of a love life, and you can tell me about yours."

He laughed. "You've got yourself a deal, Sam."

While Sam took care of the sign, Ambrose got ready to put on his show. He tied on his red headband, unbuttoned his shirt, and rolled up his sleeves. People would soon be stopping by to watch him work and to talk. Gossip was rampant in small towns, so with a little luck, by the end of the day, he'd have a better handle on what was happening to Jo and Leigh Ann.

Twelve

It was close to six when Jo came out onto the porch, a wide smile on her face. "It's been a long time since we've had that much drop-in traffic. You worked magic, Ambrose."

"Everyone loves a show, particularly the tourists, and this time of year they pass right by here on their way to the national tribal pow-wow in Albuquerque. That's a huge draw."

"You could make some good money selling stuff there," Jo said.

"Maybe, but I haven't wanted to travel to the city lately. It's a long trip and I don't want that much time alone to think."

"Yeah, I hear that," she said.

"What's going on, Jo? When I took a restroom break, I noticed the rifle in your office. And I saw that tribal cop stop by."

"He wanted to ask me about last night," Jo explained, then filled him in on what had happened at her house and why she was now traveling to work with a rifle handy.

"Look, sweetheart, I live less than twenty minutes from your place. If you're in trouble, call me."

"Ben mentioned that you promised to keep an eye on us here, but you don't really have to do that."

"You're wrong, Jo, I do. Ben and I are friends and that means something to both of us. If our situations were reversed, I know I could count on him to help me—no matter how tough it got. I have no intention of letting him down, so use speed dial. I can get there faster than most cops and I'm a good man to have beside you in a fight."

"I have no doubt of that," she said.

"Good. Now I'm going to talk to Leigh Ann. I think she needs a friend, too."

Jo nodded slowly. "She's investigating some stuff related to her late husband and getting in way over her head. She's proud, too much so if you ask me, but sometimes pride's the only thing a person has left."

"Yeah, and we both know what that's like, don't we?" He looked back at the table. "I finished three pieces this afternoon and Samantha put them on display. I know there was a lot of interest, but did any of them actually sell?"

"All of them," Jo said with a grin. "I can cut you a check before you leave."

"Good enough. Let me get my tools and torch packed up, then I'll grab another mineral water and talk to Leigh Ann while I wait."

"I'll send someone to help."

Jo went back inside, and a minute later, Leigh Ann came out. "I sure wish you'd stop by more often," she said.

"For my wares?" he said, teasing her as he buttoned up his shirt.

"Yeah—all of them," Leigh Ann answered, laughing.

"So, tell me, Leigh Ann, what's happening with you lately? I ran into Rachel at the Bullfrog," he said, lowering his voice. "She said you're now packing a .38 for protection?"

"Rachel has a big mouth."

"No, sweetheart, I'm just easy to talk to, or haven't you noticed? Women know they don't have anything to worry about around me."

"But they can still dream, huh?"

"All they want. It's free," he said with an irrepressible grin. "It's a great ego boost, too."

She smiled.

"Rachel hinted that you were having problems, and that the law had been paying visits. You going to tell me what's up?"

"The short version," she said, and briefly explained about Kurt's stash and the subsequent events.

"That sucks, darlin'."

"Yeah, major league. But it is what it is. That's why I've started carrying a .38."

"How long has it been since you fired a revolver?"

"I don't know . . . high school? Kurt was a rifleman and that's what we'd always shoot at the range. I don't remember him having a revolver at all until the .38 turned up. To be honest, I don't even know if he got it legally."

"I didn't hear that."

"I never said it," Leigh Ann whispered, wishing she'd just learn to keep her mouth shut.

"I'm a member of the Zia Shooting Range—this side of Farmington. Why don't we go over there and practice?"

"I don't know . . . I was planning to run some errands," she said. Target practice was something she and Kurt had done together and she really didn't want to stir up old memories.

"If you're going to be carrying that .38 around, Leigh Ann, loading, unloading, and firing it has to be second nature to you or you're likely to shoot yourself."

"No, I grew up around guns. I shot in competition a few times back in high school, too. Sight picture, trigger control, all that is practically instinctive to me," she countered, "but you make a good argument. I need to fire this particular revolver and get much better acquainted with it."

"Let's go get in some practice." Seeing Jo listening, he added, "You should come, too, darling. Bring that rifle of yours."

She considered it and nodded. "All right. I can use a confidence builder. Once the last of the customers leave, we'll lock up and head on over."

Several minutes later, Leigh Ann crossed the room to lock the front door and set the alarm. As she did, she saw John and Melvin pulling into a parking spot.

"Whoever's out there, ask them to come back tomorrow," Jo called from the back of the store. "We're closed."

"It's John and Melvin," Leigh Ann answered.

"Were you expecting them?" Jo asked.

"No, I wasn't." The men walked up onto the porch and Leigh Ann let them in.

"Hey, Leigh Ann, Jo," Melvin said, looking in their direction.

"Okay, no way you caught a whiff of my perfume, or even my hair spray. By now both have faded away," Leigh Ann said, smiling.

"True, but there's still enough light for me to tell you two apart. Your height, hairstyle, scent, posture; they're all clues in sorting out the mystery. You work with what you've got. We all do the same thing to one extent or another."

"I see keys in hand, so I'm guessing everyone here's about to leave, Melvin," John said, "so we should shove off, too. I'm already late."

"Since you're in a hurry, John, would you like me to give Melvin a ride somewhere?" Leigh Ann asked, guessing what had prompted the visit and eager to enjoy some more time with Melvin.

"John's got a date tonight," Melvin said, "and we took too long running errands."

"We were about to go with Ambrose to the shooting range and take in some target practice," Leigh Ann said, "but I can hold off on that and take you home or wherever you need to go."

"No, don't bother. Getting some target practice in is a real good idea, all things considered," Melvin said. "If you let me come along, and someone can give me a ride home afterwards, I'll be happy to buy everyone dinner."

Knowing Melvin needed to get his swamp cooler fixed, Leigh Ann decided to decline. "I have some things I need to do later tonight, so let me take you home once we're finished, okay?"

"I've got plans, too," Jo said. "I've got to catch up on some paperwork."

"Well, I can give you a ride to the range and then back to your place, bro," Ambrose said. "That should entitle me to a Navajo taco, chips, and salsa."

Melvin laughed. "You got it, Ambrose," he said, then added, "John, we're good here. Go ahead and take off to meet your lady friend."

After John left, Leigh Ann started to take Melvin's arm so she could lead him outside, but Ambrose stepped in and put his hand on Melvin's shoulder. "Hey, buddy, do you still have a thing for classic cars?"

"Sure. I just enjoy them in a different way. Engine sounds, acceleration, four on the floor, the room of a bench instead of sunken-down seats. They're all good."

"Then you're in for a treat. I just restored the interior and there's acres of legroom," he said, taking Melvin to his truck.

Leigh Ann watched them, lost in thought. She had a feeling Ambrose wanted to talk to Melvin about something specific. Wondering what it could be, she walked to her Jeep.

Melvin climbed into the passenger's side of Ambrose's truck with ease, thanks to the running board.

"I like your truck already. The bench seats and back are comfortable, and the leather has that new smell."

"I oil the hell out of it," Ambrose said.

"So what's on your mind. My gut tells me it's something important."

"Yeah, it is. I promised Ben I'd keep an eye on the trading post family, but I've got my hands full with Jo. I was hoping you'd stick closer to Leigh Ann until we can get a better handle on whatever's going down."

"Something else has happened, hasn't it?" Melvin asked.

"Yeah. Somebody tried to set fire to Jo's house late last night. Thankfully the noise woke her and she was able to run the guy off. Tribal cops are investigating."

"I'll stay close to Leigh Ann, but I need you to do something for me. Keep a sharp eye on how she handles and fires that revolver. She talks a good game, but if she's a bigger danger to herself than an attacker could be, I'm going to try to convince her to lock it up somewhere."

"All right. Let's see how it goes," Ambrose said.

"I wish she'd stay with me and let the detectives do their jobs, but that's not going to happen."

"You've asked her to move in?"

"No, we're not there in our relationship yet," Melvin answered, "but even if we were, she wouldn't do it. She's hell-bent on finding her own answers. My going to her place won't help either. I'm not familiar with the layout. I'd be . . . a liability," he said, spitting out the word.

"Somehow I doubt it. Your other senses help make up for what you can't see, and in a dark room, you're an equal."

"To a degree, yes," Melvin said, "but what I lost to that drunk driver still puts me at a disadvantage. I know my limitations—that's how I overcome them."

"Our biggest problem is that we're fighting an unseen enemy."

"And that's where the playing field levels," Melvin said with a grin.

Once they'd all reached the shooting range—a collection of firing locations and small buildings surrounded by a massive fifteen-foot-high earthen berm—Leigh Ann bought a box of ammunition for her .38 at the clubhouse.

From there Ambrose led them to the rifle range, a row of wooden tables along a firing line about fifty yards away. Jo carried her rifle, and in her jacket pocket was the nearly full box of shells she'd had in her car.

As they walked toward the site, Ambrose described what they'd be facing. "The target stands downrange are spaced at one hundred, three hundred, and five hundred yards. You think you can handle the hundred? I've got some fifty-foot bull's-eye pistol targets in my truck. They'll do for practice."

"It should be a nice challenge with my rifle. Sure," Jo replied.

They went to their assigned table—actually one of ten shooter's bench rests along the firing line. The club wasn't crowded and soon a cease-fire was announced over the loudspeaker, which allowed Ambrose to set up their targets.

"I think I know what's on your mind, Ambrose," Jo said when he returned to the firing line. "You want to be able to tell Ben that I can handle the rifle and safely defend myself. He was a sniper for his first deployment, so he'd worry about that."

Leigh Ann squinted. "That sucker's way out there, Jo. It's nothing more than a little black dot.

And you've got open sights. We didn't bring a spotting scope, so how can we tell if you're even close?"

"Ten-power binoculars," Ambrose said, bringing them out of his pocket. "I can see the bullet holes from here—if you manage to punch the paper, that is."

"Just stand back and watch the target," Jo said, sitting down and taking her position at the bench rest as the range officer announced the range was 'hot.'

They stepped back to the observer's position and Ambrose watched as she levered a round into the chamber of the Winchester Model 1894, took careful aim and squeezed off a round. Carefully feeding in another round, she took a second shot, then set the rifle down on the wooden bench and looked at Ambrose. "Well?"

Ambrose lowered the binoculars. "One's dead center, in the ten. Can't find where the other round hit."

"Look again," Jo said calmly.

"There's one hole, darling."

"Keep looking."

Ambrose lifted the binoculars to his eyes again, then whistled low. "Twins. They're next to each other, almost touching. I thought it was just one big hole."

"Even when shooting offhand, I generally hit what I aim for," Jo said quietly, "and I sight in this rifle once a year. Before my dad took ill, we went deer hunting every season. Never came home empty-handed, either."

"I didn't know you liked to go hunting," Ambrose said. "Maybe you and I—"

She held up a hand. "That's history now. All things considered, I prefer to bring home my meat nicely wrapped in butcher paper."

Ambrose laughed. "I understand. For the past few years, except for paper targets, all I've been shooting are sheet-metal critters, where you have to tip them over to score points." He glanced at Leigh Ann. "Now that we've established Jo doesn't need the practice, what do you say we move over to the handgun range?"

"That's what I'm here for," Leigh Ann said, suddenly more conscious of the weight of the revolver and the box of bullets in her purse.

They walked away from the rifle range and a few minutes later arrived at their new stations in the section reserved for pistols.

Ambrose was carrying a hard plastic case that contained his shooting paraphernalia and he sat it down on his bench, which was adjacent to Leigh Ann's. "There are target stands set up at twenty-five, fifty, seventy-five, and a hundred yards. I've got all kinds of range-approved targets here to choose from, everything from bull's-eyes to paper practice silhouettes of chickens, pigs, turkeys, and rams. What do you want to shoot at, Leigh Ann?"

She hesitated, placing her purse on her shooting bench and bringing out the new ammo.

"How about if we work our way up to the harder targets? We begin at twenty-five yards with the chicken silhouettes, then switch to fifty with the pigs?" He smiled. "And we can compete, if you want."

She nodded. "I'm game. What do you have in mind?"

"We get five shots at each distance, starting with the chickens, and score one point each time we're in the black. We'll also use the same weapon—your revolver—since it wouldn't be fair for me to use my Colt 1911 competition .45," he said. "The one who accumulates the most points win."

"Wait a sec. It's not a fair match. You've won championships—" Jo began.

"No, it's okay," Leigh Ann said. "Let's see how it goes. At least we'll be using the same pistol and ammunition. If I win, you help me clean out my attic, Ambrose. Deal?"

"Yeah, you've got it. And if I win?"

"I'll wash and wax your truck two Sundays in a row."

"Done," Ambrose said, bringing out the targets. They were the only shooters now, so a cease-fire was already in effect.

Melvin moved closer to her as Ambrose went downrange to set up the targets. "You walked right into that," he said. "Last year Ambrose won the state championship in metallic silhouette competition, beating an ATF agent in a shoot-off."

"I used to be pretty good, too. . . ."

A few minutes later, once the range was hot, Leigh Ann began to load the .38. A familiar voice greeted her. She turned her head and saw Wayne Hurley standing on the access path, Pierre Boone beside him.

"I didn't know you were into handgun shooting, Leigh Ann," Wayne said, greeting her with a smile.

"I'm just here to see if I still remember . . ."

Pierre Boone spoke up next. "Fancy meeting you here!"

She shrugged, uneasy now. The good news, at least, was that she was the one who was armed. All they were carrying were shopping bags with the range logo on them. The bad news was that it seemed a little coincidental. Had Wayne and Pierre followed them here?

"Mind if we watch for a few minutes?" Wayne asked.

"Go right ahead," she replied. It would let them know she was ready and able to defend herself if necessary. Hopefully everything she'd learned way back as a member of the junior NRA would come flooding back to her.

Melvin and Jo were standing farther down the path, remaining behind the firing line at the designated distance for observers. Ambrose, meanwhile, ignored the newcomers and opened up the box with his supplies.

They were tied after the first round and Ambrose gave Leigh Ann a more respectful look. "You're a natural. Nine out of ten for both of us. So what do you say we complicate things a little more and up the difficulty factor?"

She nodded and glanced back at the box. "How about pistol competition, fifty-yard slow fire? High score wins."

"Uh-oh, I think I've been hustled," Ambrose said.

"Maybe," she said, smiling. There was already a cease-fire, so he picked up two targets and used a staple gun to fasten them in place.

Since she'd chosen the range and targets, Ambrose went first, firing double action, which was more difficult because without cocking the hammer first, the trigger pull was heavier.

Equipped with his binoculars, she announced that he'd grouped all six shots in the center of the black circle in an area roughly the size of a fist.

"Think you can top that?" he baited her with a grin.

"Don't know," Leigh Ann said honestly, setting down the binoculars.

She fired carefully, cocking back the hammer then firing single action, which gave her more of a light, hair-trigger pull. It was slow, non-combat mode, but she maintained accuracy.

After the cease-fire, Ambrose retrieved the targets, brought them over into the shade, and Jo tallied up the points. "So far you two are still tied."

"Really?" Leigh Ann said, surprised. Out of the corner of her eye she noticed the guarded look Pierre and Wayne exchanged.

"Okay, let's go again, but we'll finish up with a different kind of target," Ambrose said, bringing out police silhouettes.

"Ugh," Leigh Ann said.

"Problem?" Ambrose said.

"Don't you have any more of the competition targets? Black dots are fine, but I hate the people-shaped ones. To me, those have a dark side that makes it less of a game. You get points for shooting in the head or heart area. The more deadly, the better. Ick."

Wayne laughed loudly and said, "It's okay, hon. You just don't have the killer instinct."

Pierre came up to the shooter's bench and patted her on the back. "You done good, girl. This kind of competition just isn't your thing. I remember Kurt saying that you wouldn't even play first-person shooter video games with him."

"That's true, but I *can* shoot. If it came down to it, I would defend myself."

Pierre shook his head. "I think you'd hesitate, Leigh Ann. You'd lose—just like you're about to do today," he added quietly.

She suppressed a shudder. His voice had reminded her of the sound made by a rattler poised to strike. If he'd meant to creep her out, he'd succeeded. She was relieved when he stepped back to the path.

"If you want, we'll aim for the torso instead of the head," Ambrose said.

"Good idea." It was time to prove her skills. Taking a position at the firing line, she shot six times. When they tallied the results, her rounds were mostly clustered around the X at the center of the target. Two, however, had gone in the circle outside that, still in the torso, but earning her nine points each instead of ten.

"Nice, Leigh Ann," Wayne said. "You've got a score of fifty-eight—almost perfect."

Ambrose took his position on the firing line. When his target was checked, all six shots were in a tight cluster in the ten circle, making his score a sixty.

He joined her seconds later, handing back the .38, barrel up for safety, plus the six shell casings.

Pierre came up and patted her on the shoulder as she placed the weapon back in her purse. "Good try, Leigh Ann."

She wasn't sure if it was her imagination or

not, but she could have sworn she'd heard a sneer winding through his words.

"See you later, all. Wayne and I need to take off now," Pierre said.

"I'm going to give you a pass on the truck," Ambrose whispered. "You were at a disadvantage with those two watching over your shoulder, sending bad vibes."

"Nah, a bet's a bet," she said and managed a smile.

"How about a compromise? I'll help you with the attic and you cook dinner for me *and* Melvin tonight?"

She smiled and gave Ambrose a quick hug. "You're all muscle, but inside you're an old softie."

He laughed. "Don't ever let anyone hear you say that."

"Like it's a secret?" Jo teased, coming up.

Ambrose laughed.

"I'm going back to the trading post," Jo said. "I want to email Ben and tell him about tonight, do some work, then head home."

"Remember that you can call me—day or night," Ambrose added.

"You're on my speed dial now," Jo said, and waved good-bye.

Two hours later, Ambrose climbed down from the attic, covered in dust. "The truss beam is braced now, sandwiched between those one-by-sixes I found in your shed. I used long wood screws to attach the supports so they should hold just fine. I also dug out the buckshot and filled the holes with wood putty."

"Thanks, Ambrose. Dinner's almost done," Leigh Ann said as Rachel set the table.

"It smells wonderful!" Ambrose said.

"Texas chili," Leigh Ann said and smiled. "I made homemade tortillas to go with it."

"She gave me a taste of the chili," Melvin said. "It's incredibly good. It has just the right amount of bite in it."

"With or without beans?" Ambrose asked.

"Get serious, guy. Real Texas chili doesn't have beans! That's almost heresy!" Leigh Ann said.

He laughed. "Just testing."

"We've got German beer, too," Rachel said.

Leigh Ann crossed to the stove and stirred the cast-iron pot. "Whoa, I made enough here for an army. If we don't get someone else to help us eat all this up, Rache, we'll be eating leftovers for a week."

"Too bad Ben isn't around, he eats enough for three people," Ambrose pointed out.

"Well, we can't feed him, but what about Jo? She's having a real tough time of it lately, and could use a little more company. I gave her a call a while ago and she's still at the trading post, hoping to get a call from her sweetie. Why

221

don't we put all this in the Jeep and take it over? We can eat there, do some brainstorming, and see what we can do about our situations."

"I like that idea," Ambrose said.

"Let me give her a call and let her know we're coming," Leigh Ann said.

Jo answered on the first ring, which told Leigh Ann just how worried her boss and friend was about Ben. "It's just me again, hon," she said and told her about their plans.

"Sam's here, too, working on the computers. If there's going to be enough for her, too, then come on over," Jo said.

"Jo, there's more than enough in that Dutch oven for all of us twice over," she said, laughing. "I always make extra."

"Then by all means, get moving. Neither of us has eaten yet, and we'd love sharing your dinner."

They set out less than five minutes later. By then it was close to eight and the sun had dropped over the horizon.

"I'm still worried about Jo," Leigh Ann told Melvin, who'd chosen to ride with her to the trading post. "She's really going through a tough time. Waiting and not knowing creates a hell all its own."

"I know," he said, shifting the plastic container with the tortillas and honey he was holding on his lap. On the floorboard was a small cooler containing plates, bowls, and utensils. "That's

222

why you wanted to take all this over there—comfort food, right? That's the heart of this meal?"

"Yeah," she said, and glanced in her rearview mirror at Ambrose and Rachel, who were following in his red pickup. Rachel had custody of the large Dutch oven filled with chili. "I think Jo will enjoy it and she needs friends around her right now."

"I've known Jo for many years and she's stronger than you think. If she takes a hard enough hit, she may go down, but she'll always get back up."

"I agree that she's a tough cookie, but we all have our limits. Even you."

He reached out and touched her arm gently. "I'm fine, and you need to stop worrying so much."

That simple touch sent an intoxicating warmth through Leigh Ann. She needed Melvin, he brought something into her life she'd never had before—tenderness and gentleness.

"Jo has her tribe, her clan, and the teachings of our people to sustain her. In that respect, she may be better equipped to deal with hard times than you are. You tough it out—but she has a support system in place. Of course you have one, too, but it's harder for you to accept it. There are people, like me, who'd be beside you every step of the way if you'd allow it."

In the privacy of the Jeep, she was acutely

aware of everything about him. She felt alive and filled with a curious sense of expectation . . . or maybe it was hope. She wanted things to work out for her and Melvin, but there were still obstacles in the way, and not just the assaults on her following the discovery of Kurt's legacy. If only she could get him to break down his own barriers and let her in.

With a burst of determination, she shut the door on those thoughts. She had to stay focused, now more than ever. "Relying on others is hard for me. I'm not used to it and the one time I did, it was a disaster."

"Kurt?"

She nodded. "I should have known better, but I was young and tired of always having to be the strong one at home. I wanted to marry my hero, the man who promised I'd never have to worry about anything because he'd always take care of me," she said, and added, "Rachel and I went through really hard times back in Texas."

"You never told me about that," he said.

"Even now, looking back is difficult," she said. "Dad was far from perfect, but Mom loved him and so did we. Then one day he decided he wasn't cut out for family life. He just split. Mom was never the same after that. She did her best by us though, and worked as long as she could, even after she got sick. I was only twelve and Rachel, eleven, but we took care of her."

She took a deep breath. "Mom's disability check didn't go far, so we got whatever little jobs we could get to keep food on the table."

"Nobody helped you out?"

"Our town was dirt poor, but neighbors helped us fix up the house and drove us places when we needed it. As for my relatives . . . not so much. They all had a million excuses," she said, then jutting out her jaw, recaptured her determination. "The mess I'm facing now comes from my own bad choices, and I have to clean things up. It's time for me to stop looking for someone to come to my rescue. I've got to be my own hero."

"I understand where you're coming from. After what you've been through it's hard for you to trust, and accept help from a friend. Pride, and the fear that it'll make you dependent on someone else, sometimes gets in your way. Like they say, it takes one to know one."

Leigh Ann glanced at him, then back at the road, realizing he'd given her another clue to what was holding him back. They were two souls wounded by life and looking for redemption . . . or maybe a miracle.

Nothing else was forthcoming, though, and if her ability to read his expression meant anything, he was brooding. A long silence settled over them, and lasted until they arrived at The Outpost.

Thirteen

They all sat around the large table in the break room, eating Leigh Ann's Texas chili and tortillas and drinking bottles of iced tea Jo provided from the cold drink cooler.

"This is really good," Jo said, finishing her second helping.

"The Dutch oven kept it warm, though it's spicy enough to provide its own heat," Leigh Ann said.

Sam smiled. "This is really first class. It's better than anything I've tasted in the cafés around here. Care to trade for the recipe?"

"You've got one to share?" Leigh Ann asked, surprised. Samantha didn't strike her as a cook.

"Nah, most of what I eat comes with instructions that say, 'peel back to vent,' but I found this really cool, free app for smartphones. It's a flashlight that uses the LED in your phone. It really works. It doesn't draw that much from your battery either, providing you only use it for a few minutes. I could load it onto your phone using the trading post Wi-Fi and save you data charges."

Sam glanced at Jo and added, "You might want it, too, boss, since you're here late so much of the time."

"Speaking for myself," Leigh Ann said, "you've got yourself a deal. It sounds useful, and for free, well, you can't beat that."

Sam downloaded the app and showed Jo and Leigh Ann how to use it as they all finished eating.

Once everyone was done Leigh Ann stood. "What do you say we do a bit of brainstorming while we rinse off dishes and get everything put away?" Leigh Ann asked. "I need some help figuring a few things out."

"What's up?" Jo asked.

Leigh Ann told them what she'd found on Kurt's flash drive, the spreadsheet printouts, what she knew about his partners, and her missing rifle.

"I'm no detective, but if you'll let me look through that flash drive, I may be able to find any hidden or encrypted files. I'll work on it on my own time, of course," Sam added, looking at Jo.

"Fine by me," Jo said, "but Leigh Ann, why are you so sure Kurt's partners murdered him? You said the police checked the men's weapons and determined that the bullets fired from their rifles didn't match the one that killed your husband."

"Here's what I think: They stole my rifle from the house prior to the murder, then used it to shoot Kurt. I know from the times I visited him there that he tended to leave his keys in his jacket or desk at work. Total Supply makes and sells copies of keys—the machine is in the back by the locks. Wayne or Pierre could have grabbed the keys while he was out of the office long enough to make a quick copy of the house key. All they had to do was wait until we were both out of the house, come in, and grab the weapon."

"How would they have known where to look?" Sam asked.

"Easy. Gun owners tend to keep weapons close at hand in case of a break-in," Melvin replied. "I'm guessing you don't have a gun safe, Leigh Ann?"

"No, I don't."

"Okay, then bedrooms would be the logical places to look, in closets or under the bed. Rifles are too long to put in an ordinary drawer."

"Makes sense," Sam agreed.

Leigh Ann shrugged. "And that's where it was, under the bed. Right now, I'm guessing the only thing keeping me from being arrested is the fact that the rifle's still missing. They probably ditched it somewhere rather than risk getting caught with it. But if it turns up, even if there aren't any fingerprints on it, things are going to look bad for me. Let's face it, the police assume that I knew Kurt was cheating and embezzling money. In their eyes, I had a strong motive for shooting him."

"If the partners still had access to the rifle, they'd have found a way to frame you with it by now. So let's focus on that money," Ambrose suggested. "If Wayne and Pierre didn't get it back, which was why they kept asking you about Frank Jones, then where did it go?"

"You said that they denied that there was any missing money, so there's something else at play," Sam said. "Clearly, they didn't want the cops taking a closer look at their books and personal finances. To me that suggests they figured that losing the cash was preferable to providing a motive for killing their partner."

"Remember what my uncle said about Total Supply and those tribal contracts?" Melvin said.

"Of course," Leigh Ann replied. "John suspects Pierre and Wayne might be paying kickbacks to tribal officials in exchange for inside information on contract bids. John was pretty sure that was why the company he works for kept getting undercut each time."

"If that's true, little wonder Total Supply's trying to squelch any investigation," Sam said. "But by continuing to ask questions, Leigh Ann, you've become a dangerous liability."

"There's no turning back for me now. I can't be free of the past 'til I find answers and clear my name," Leigh Ann said.

"I'll help you," Sam said.

"So will the rest of us," Jo said. "We've got your back."

"And I'll have yours, too," Leigh Ann said. Loyalty—it couldn't be bought, and that's what made it invincible.

After everyone helped clean up and wash the dishes in the big storeroom sinks, Leigh Ann said good night to Melvin. He'd be riding with Ambrose. Soon she and Rachel headed back home.

"Your job's secure and you work with a really nice bunch of people. I envy you," Rachel said, balancing the box of dishes on her lap as Leigh Ann drove.

"They're terrific, that's true," Leigh Ann answered. "But the trading post isn't exactly prospering. When Tom Stuart ran the place business was brisk, now not so much. Part of it could be the weak economy, but we've also been losing customers to the new superstore on Farmington's west side. Tourism is still down, too, maybe because of the recession, so our drop-in traffic has slowed."

"Trading posts . . . Well, they do sound like a last-century type of thing. Maybe you need to modernize things, like setting up a coffee bar and Wi-Fi for the customers. You already have the store network."

Leigh Ann glanced at Rachel, then back at the

road. "That's a good idea. To increase business we should try to appeal to a wider customer base and bring in younger customers. I'll pass that along to Jo. Thanks. On another matter, did Charlie, your boss, give you any problems about the police visit the other day, Rache? I know you were a little worried," she added.

"No, I went to him first thing and said the cops were following up on Kurt's death, which you'd begun to suspect was not really an accident. That's all true. When he asked what triggered the new investigation, I told him you'd found some letters that suggest he'd been threatened, but I was sworn to secrecy, at least for now, and that I really shouldn't be telling him this. He was relieved, glad I wasn't in any trouble because something like that could hurt his company's reputation."

"I'm just glad the press hasn't gotten wind of this," Leigh Ann replied, taking another glance behind them.

"You keep looking in the rearview mirror. Do you think someone's following us?" Rachel asked after a moment.

"No, I'm just being extra careful. Under the circumstances it can't hurt."

Rachel nodded. "Do you think you'll ever have a normal life, Leigh Ann? You know, the two kids, picket fence, and minivan kind?"

"I don't know, Rache, but I sure hope so. I

deserve something better than what life's handed me so far."

"So reach out and take it. Melvin's there for you, and he's exactly the kind of man you want."

"I'm not sure that'll ever be in the cards, Rachel."

Although she usually only worked nights and Sundays at The Outpost since that was when the computers were free, Sam stopped by early the next morning in hopes of seeing Jack. She told Jo she'd come by to pick up Leigh Ann's flash drive, but she was sure Jo hadn't been fooled.

As she went to the break room for coffee, Sam heard the rumble of a truck pulling up. Turning around, she hurried out back and saw Jack with a load of hay, backing up to the barn. He was topping off their bales, which were second or third cuttings by now and sold fast this time of year. It was the perfect opportunity to spend a little time with Jack. He'd appreciate the help stacking the alfalfa.

She was coming down the steps of the loading dock when she heard a vehicle racing up the drive. She stopped as a familiar-looking old pickup eased into the staff parking. A moment later, Del jumped out, something tucked under one arm.

"Del, what are you doing here?" she asked. "Ditching school?"

"It's a half day for students—teacher in-service

training—so I got permission to leave campus a little early. Jo told me you were coming in today. I need your help, Sam."

"Sure, buddy. Whatcha need?" Sam asked as he came up, breathing hard.

"I've been working for weeks on a term paper for English lit. Last night the stupid computer crashed and now I can't call up the file. My teacher had already seen my outline and notes so she gave me until tomorrow. I really need that paper, Sam, it's on Stephen Crane. Can you make it come back somehow, long enough to print it out or make a secure copy?"

"Do you have a rough draft somewhere?"

"No, just my notes. I meant to copy the last version to a flash drive, but I never got around to it. I'm always on the run these days. It's not easy to go to school full time and still work nights and weekends."

"I've been there," Sam said with a sigh. "Go help Jack put away the alfalfa and I'll see what I can do."

Sam sat in the break room and powered up the laptop. From her seat at the table she had a clear view of the loafing shed, so she'd at least be able to watch Jack unload the hay. Despite the fact that his left forearm had been replaced with a prosthesis, he could buck hay as fast as any rancher she'd ever seen. She'd never seen him drop a bale.

Jack always wore an impeccable white T-shirt when working. She'd seen him without it once and had felt like a love-struck fourteen-year-old. She'd almost drooled. Jack's chest was broad and hard. The dark scars around his ribs and near the center of his stomach had only made him look even more formidable—dangerous, stronger, and incredibly masculine.

Unfortunately, he was more interested in his horses than in her. She'd tried everything, including helping teach his weekend classes, hoping he'd somehow notice her, but that hadn't happened yet.

Sam focused back on Del's laptop. There was a bad sector on his hard drive, and she was already running a recovery program to transfer data to another spot and get his system working normally again. Fortunately, his word processing software made backup files automatically, so once the bad sectors were blocked off, she'd probably be able to track down and call up the file he'd wanted.

Five minutes later, everything was accessible, but just to make sure he wouldn't lose it again she quickly copied the file to a flash drive.

"Del, come take a look," Sam called out, stepping out the back door. "I'll help Jack finish up."

Del turned, a smile on his face, and raced toward her. "Thanks," he whispered as he passed her on the steps, rushing inside.

"Hi, Sam," Jack said, glancing at her for a second before using a pair of hay hooks to lift another bale off the back of his flatbed truck. "I'm almost done, so just stand back. No sense you getting all hot and dusty."

He bucked the remaining five bales, never losing the rhythm. Since the truck was backed up so close to the barn, there was no way she could climb up without getting in his way. Sam stayed where she was, watching him. "Jo's glad you can keep us supplied. You have the best quality alfalfa around, Jack. It's always rich and leafy," she said.

"We irrigate, watch the weather, and stow our bales under loafing sheds so nothing ever gets wet and moldy. I don't use herbicides either. It's old school, like my dad taught me. I work my butt off making sure the fields are free of bindweed, Johnson grass, and other nuisance plants. That's why I charge more. The customers get something that's worth their money."

"That's why Jo likes doing business with you. Nobody has ever returned a bale or asked for a refund or credit."

"With real estate prices down I was able to buy the field to the west of my place. Business is good, so I'd like to expand," Jack said, placing the last bale on the top of the stack before removing the hay hook from the grip of his prosthesis.

"We still sell a lot of bedding, horse feed, and farm supplies here. That's steady business for us," Sam said, coming closer.

He ran an arm across his forehead. "I better get going. I've got two more deliveries and I want to finish them before it gets too much hotter."

He handed her an invoice, tipped his hat to her, then got into his truck and drove off.

She watched until he turned onto the main highway and disappeared.

"Man, you've got it bad, don't you?" Del said, coming up behind her, laptop under his arm.

"What? Jack's just a real nice guy," she said with a shrug. "I enjoy talking to him."

"Yeah, right," he said and grinned.

Uncomfortable, she changed the subject. "Did you check your files?"

"Yeah, Steve's all there. Thanks for saving my butt, Sam. I don't know what I would have done if I'd had to start all over again from my notes. It's taken me weeks to put everything together in a way that makes sense."

Sam smiled. "Come on. Let's go back inside and check the rest of your text files. You can tell me if there are others you'd like me to back up. I already copied your term paper onto a flash drive, keeping the same file name as before."

"Thanks, but maybe we should stay out here for a while, or maybe stick to the storeroom.

A couple of deputies showed up, so I grabbed the laptop and excused myself. They're in the break room now, questioning Leigh Ann. From what I overheard, they think she's been giving them false information. They were leaning on her pretty hard."

"Where did you hear about her situation?"

"Jo gave me the high points over the phone this morning while we were planning my work schedule. She was concerned that everyone who worked with her needed to be extra alert—you know, just in case. So Leigh Ann thinks maybe her husband's death was no accident?"

"Something like that, but make sure you keep this to yourself, okay? We need to be looking out for her, of course, but the less outsiders know about it, the easier it'll be getting to the truth," Sam replied.

"Gotcha."

As they stood there talking, the green-and-white SJCSD squad car drove off. Sam led them back inside, eager to find out what happened.

Leigh Ann was in the break room, pacing back and forth, visibly upset. Jo was there with her.

Leigh Ann pushed back several errant strands of hair from her face. "Kurt's partners are playing it smart. Letting the police go over their books was their way of making me look bad. Of course they've had plenty of time to massage the numbers since Kurt's death. I'm not surprised nothing matched when they compared what I gave them to the company's business records."

"Leigh Ann, don't you see it? You pushed them, and now they're pushing back," Sam said. "Your husband's partners are afraid of *you*. If this is about the kickbacks like Melvin suggested last night, you need to find out who sees those contract bids when they come in."

"That would narrow the list," Jo said with a nod, "but you'll have to move carefully. If tribal honchos are taking kickbacks, they also have a reason for making sure no one looks at Total Supply too closely."

"Sounds like you need some real evidence," Del said, sitting down at the table and opening his laptop.

"Like names and details that'll prove corruption's taking place," Sam concluded. "Leigh Ann, did you bring me that flash drive, the one with the copies of those altered files?"

Leigh Ann reached into her purse and handed it to Sam. "Here it is. It's supposedly a copy of every file on the original. What is it you're hoping to find?"

"Maybe there's an encrypted file you didn't notice, or one that's concealed with a name change so it won't look like a spreadsheet or text file. Give me a little bit of time, and I'll see what I can get for you."

Sam grabbed her own computer, which was still on the break room table, and sat down as she powered it up. After twenty minutes of intensive work, she leaned back and looked up. Her expression must have given it away.

Sam saw the look of hopeful anticipation in Leigh Ann's eyes fade. "I tried every program I had, but couldn't find any disguised or additional data files on the drive. I'm really sorry, Leigh Ann."

"It's not your fault, honey. Kurt was a rat, but he wasn't a complete fool."

"Most businesses have multiple backup systems nowadays on separate partitions on their hard drives and external drives as well. Even in the cloud. With the right software, deleted files can be accessed if they haven't been overwritten. Most business people aren't savvy enough to dig out all those and permanently delete them, so they could still be there. If the police are looking at their records they're bound to find them."

"According to what I was told, the county detectives didn't bring in any computer experts. That would have cost money. They just contacted the company's auditor and got a statement from her verifying the books were in order and that there were no irregularities. I'm afraid that's all they're going to do, too," Leigh Ann said. "At this point, they're convinced I made up the story to divert attention back to the partners. For all I know, they see me as the prime suspect in Kurt's murder." Leigh Ann's voice broke on the last word, and excusing herself quickly, she hurried to the restroom.

With a long sigh, Jo left to man the cash register, but Sam and Del remained behind.

"I wish we could help Leigh Ann," Del said.

"There may be a way—if you're willing to break a few rules."

He smiled and closed his own laptop. "How can I help?"

With Del at the wheel, they drove past Total Supply while Sam checked her laptop for Wi-Fi signals.

"Gotcha! I just got a hit on a network named Totally. Pull off the road and I'll see if I can hack into their system. All I need is a password now," Sam said, looking down at the display on her laptop.

"How about I take the next street? We might still get a good signal and they won't be able to look out and see us beside the road," Del said.

"Okay."

Fifteen seconds later, Del turned down the side street. "Still got a signal?"

"Barely. Better turn around and get closer. Park on the same side of the street and we'll inch forward along the curb until the Wi-Fi comes in strong."

Five minutes later, Del looked over at Sam, who was typing.

"Damn, I was hoping they'd use some form of their business name as a password, or an employee name. I've got a good password cracking program here, but nothing obvious works."

"Keep trying, Sam, I know you can do it."

Another two minutes went by. "I'm in! The password is '@supplytotal.' Amateurs."

"Great. Now what?"

"I'm going to search for a Frank Jones account, or any file that's the same size and date as the one on Kurt's flash drive."

"I never would have thought of that, not the Jones thing, but finding a file that's just the right size and date," Del said with a nod. "Gotta remember that."

"Better stay away from hacking, Del. It's addictive—and kinda illegal."

"Didn't hear that, Sam."

"Here's something. I've found some data files hidden in a PC health subdirectory within the operating system. I'm going to take a look at one," she whispered, her heart beating faster. "Almost there . . . oh crap."

"What?"

"It's encrypted."

"So, crack it, hacker girl."

"No way, not without NSA software. The password is fifteen characters long. It'll take years."

"So we're screwed?" Del asked.

"Yeah, we might as well go back to The Outpost."

Jo came out of her office into the hallway when Sam returned. "I thought you'd already left. You're working tonight, aren't you?"

"Yeah, but Del and I were curious, so we decided to drive by Total Supply before he went home to print out his term paper. I'm just back to pick up my car."

"Okay. I'm not going to ask exactly what you mean by curious. See you this evening," Jo said, shaking her head as she stepped back into her office.

"You're never just curious, Sam. What's going on?" Leigh Ann asked, coming into the hall from the front of the store.

Sam told her what they'd done. "We were hoping to help you out. I know you're in a tight spot."

"Sam, you shouldn't have hacked into their system! You put yourself in danger. Those two guys are bad news, girl—real killer bad news."

"You needed help and I know how to hack into anything that's not encrypted, but this . . . was beyond what I could do."

Leigh Ann hugged her. "You put yourselves on the line for me, you and Del. I won't forget that."

"They'll never know I tried to access those files, don't worry. If there's anything I can do, Leigh Ann, just say it. I want to help," Sam said.

"I know, hon, and I appreciate it."

As Sam left out the back, Jo came out of her office and joined Leigh Ann. "I overheard," she said, automatically glancing into the front room. Esther was at the register and Regina was dusting the pottery collection. "It helps knowing we have friends who'll stand by us, doesn't it?"

"Yeah, it does," she said. "Speaking of friends, how's Rudy doing?"

Jo grew somber. "He and Victoria decided to go back home again, so I paid them a visit just to make sure everything was okay. I didn't stay long, but Victoria was scared and Rudy was acting really guarded, which isn't like him at all. Neither of them would talk about it, though."

"Jo, maybe I'm to blame. My problem with Wayne and Pierre may have inadvertently spilled onto them. There *is* a tribal connection."

"Rudy has a lot of patients, but I don't know of any connection that would link the kickbacks to him."

"You're probably right," Leigh Ann said, and glancing back at the front, changed the subject. "Foot traffic here at the store is really light today."

"I've noticed," Jo said.

"Rachel came up with a good idea I've been

meaning to pass along all day." Leigh Ann told her about the coffee bar with Wi-Fi.

"Here?" Jo said, surprised. "Where?"

"I'm thinking maybe we can get rid of the drinking fountain, customer coffeepot, and the table that goes with it, and set up the brewing counter there. We already have the water supply and drain in place. We'd need to create some space for several bistro tables and chairs, probably up front by the windows. There's enough space there already, where those old wooden benches used to be. If we plan carefully, we'd have plenty of room for a coffee bar in the back, plus seating up front, via the center aisle."

Jo considered it. "It could work. We'd still have our traditional trading post, plus the kind of place that's in tune with the new generation. We're already licensed to serve sandwiches and coffee. Purchases could be made at the rear cash register, so the coffee bar only has to be big enough to prepare and serve the drinks."

"It's worth a try, particularly since it wouldn't require any major remodeling," Leigh Ann said, looking around, rearranging things in her head.

"I've been considering another idea, too. Since we can't compete with the warehouse grocery prices, or the inventory superstores offer, I thought we should expand the line of merchandise we're currently offering online, maybe do a little targeted advertising, too." Jo took a deep breath, then let it out slowly. "When Tom ran this place, things were a lot simpler."

"Maybe not," Leigh Ann said. "We've never had such a clear, behind-the-scenes look 'til now."

"I'll talk to Sam about all this. It's time we did something to attract new, younger customers— ones with money in their pockets. A coffee bar with Wi-Fi might just be the way, and we're already using wireless connections between the server and terminals."

"As far as products, we should experiment with different coffee blends and come up with our own signature brew," Leigh Ann said, now excited about the prospect.

Hearing the bells over the entrance jingle, they both glanced over and saw a tall, dark-haired Army officer in uniform walk into the trading post.

Leigh Ann's heart sank. She turned to Jo in time to see her face go deathly pale.

Fourteen

Jo was frozen to the spot. Forcing herself to move so she could buy Jo a little time, Leigh Ann met the officer. "Hello, how can we help you?" she asked, hoping he was just a drop-in customer.

"I'm First Lieutenant Michael Donahue, United States Army National Guard. I'm looking for Josephine Buck. I understand she's the owner."

"That's me," Jo said, her voice thin.

"Ma'am, I'm Mike Donahue, assigned to the 226th Military Police Battalion in Farmington." He shook her hand briefly. "May we speak in private?"

"Of course," she said with a nod, but her knees buckled as she started down the hall. Jo caught herself in time, but by then Leigh Ann was at her side. "Let me go in with you."

Jo nodded, her eyes already moist with tears.

Once inside, Leigh Ann remained beside her, standing, as Jo sat. Although she tried to give Jo an encouraging smile, Jo appeared not to notice.

With a wave of her hand, Jo offered the officer a seat. "You can speak freely. We're family here."

"You're listed as Sergeant Benjamin Stuart's PNOK, primary next of kin, and I have news the service requires us to deliver in person."

Jo's eyes were wide, brimming over with tears, but she didn't move a muscle.

Leigh Ann swallowed the lump at the back of her throat and placed her hand on Jo's shoulder.

"Sergeant Stuart's missing in action, ma'am. According to the report I was given, his medevac helicopter came under fire and was forced down in a remote location. His team was on a recovery mission, evacuating wounded soldiers."

"*Missing,* not dead or wounded?" Jo said immediately.

"Yes, ma'am. Radio contact was made with the downed chopper, then lost. The exact location of the helicopter is still unknown, but an active search is underway with air and ground units. Unfortunately the situation is fluid at this time and no more details are available. No soldier is ever left behind, ma'am. We'll find Sergeant Stuart and the other crew members."

"So there's hope . . ."

"Yes, ma'am. I'll stay in touch and provide you with updates as I receive them. In the meantime, our CAO, a casualty assistance officer, will be contacting you within a few hours to see what support or resources you might need."

"That won't be necessary. What I need is every bit of information you can gather, Lieutenant," Jo said, her voice thick.

"Understood, ma'am. I'll keep you informed

247

every step of the way. All available resources are being utilized to find Sergeant Stuart and those who were aboard the medevac helicopter. Here's a number where I can be reached anytime, day or night."

"Thank you," she managed, taking the offered card.

Leigh Ann patted her on the shoulder. "If that's all, I think Ms. Buck needs time to process this. Can I see you to the door, Lieutenant Donahue?"

Leigh Ann led the way out, and as she entered the main room saw Ambrose speaking to Esther. She cocked her head, signaling Ambrose to go see Jo.

As soon as the lieutenant left, Esther and Regina hurried over to Leigh Ann.

"What's happened?" Esther said, her hand curled around the cross at her neck.

"Is he . . ." Regina's voice trailed off as she found herself unable to finish the thought.

"The medevac helicopter Ben was in went down and a search is underway, but the officer either didn't know or wasn't sharing any more details. They probably want to keep it all under wraps for security reasons, since they're trying to find Ben and the others with him."

Esther took a shaky breath. "Then there's still hope, thank God."

"Yeah, there is, but the lieutenant wasn't

exactly upbeat about it." She glanced back at the office.

Esther exhaled loudly. "Talking to Ambrose will help. Jo trusts him and Ambrose is one of Ben's best friends. That link will give her some comfort."

"You didn't see the fear in her eyes . . . ," Leigh Ann said.

"I don't have to," Esther said. "I know what it's like to wonder and worry if the person you love will ever be there for you again."

"I'm sorry," Leigh Ann said, and gave her a hug. "We're all here for you, too. Lean on us anytime."

When Ambrose stepped inside the office, Jo was sitting perfectly still, her face pale.

"I just heard," Ambrose said.

"I'm fine," Jo said, automatically, her eyes on the wall.

"Sell that to someone who doesn't know you." He lifted her to her feet and wrapped his arms around her. She didn't pull away; instead she rested her head against his shoulder and cried silently.

"Ben's tough. He'll be all right."

"You don't understand. If he doesn't come back, I may be to blame, at least in part."

The last sentence was barely a whisper, but he heard her. "Your fault? How could you possibly have had anything to do with his helicopter going down?"

"No, not the helicopter." she said. "I know in my heart that he survived the crash, but to make it out of there he'll need to stay focused. I told him what happened to Rudy, and if he thinks I'm in danger, like I was after his dad was killed, he'll worry about me instead of watching out for himself and his men."

Ambrose tilted her chin up with one finger. "We both know Ben. If he's worried about you, or thinks you need him, he'll fight even harder to survive. What you've really done is ensure he'll do whatever it takes to come back home." He met her gaze. "You *know* I'm right."

She gave him a shaky smile.

"Ben loves you, he always has. He'll walk through hell itself if that's what it takes to make it home."

Jo nodded slowly. "No matter how tough it gets, Ben won't give up."

"Of course not. He thinks that's for pussies—his words, not mine."

She smiled hesitantly. "Yeah, that sounds like him." Jo stepped away from him, and stared out the window, lost in thought. "He's in trouble, Ambrose, but at least he's alive. I can feel it. What connects us is hard to explain, but it's a fact."

"Then hold on to that."

She nodded. "Fear's my worst enemy right now. Not knowing what's going to happen next is like a shadow I can't outrun."

"You've got to shut the door on those thoughts, Jo. Ben will come home to you—know that. In the meantime, he needs you to run the business and look out for yourself."

She took an unsteady breath. "Speaking of that, I've got to go see Rudy and find out what's going on there," she said, and explained.

"I'll go with you," Ambrose suggested.

"Right now, Leigh Ann's in more trouble than I am, Ambrose. Stick with her. She's scared."

"I gave Ben my word I'd be there for you. Leigh Ann has Rachel and Melvin."

"All right, but I need to talk to her before I go," Jo said.

"I'll go get her," Ambrose said.

Leigh Ann walked into the office a moment later, Ambrose right behind her.

"You okay, hon?" Leigh Ann asked.

Jo nodded. "Ben isn't the only one fighting enemies, Leigh Ann. We've got to cover our butts here, too, and protect the trading post. That witchcraft pouch the creep left here would have really upset some of our customers if I hadn't found it first. That's one of the reasons I'm moving into Ben's house for a while. He wanted me to do that when he left, or at least stay in the hogan. I put it off, but now I want to be here

251

in case there's another problem," she said, then added softly, "I'll feel closer to him there."

"Stay in the house, not the hogan. There's no door, just the wool blanket over the entrance," Ambrose pointed out.

"Good point. You'll be within county jurisdiction here, too, and the deputies will have a shorter response time. At your Rez home you'd have to depend on the tribal officers and they're few and far between. It's still dangerous at night, though, particularly for a woman alone," Leigh Ann said. "The closest house is what, a quarter mile away?"

"How about I move in, too, the house, not the hogan," Ambrose suggested. "I think he'd approve of us sharing his place. We could also put in a few motion-sensor lights around the outside like you have here at the trading post. If anything larger than a jackrabbit approaches the house, he'll find himself in one helluva spotlight."

"That's a great idea. We'll amp up the lighting. But you don't have to babysit," Jo said with a smile. "I can take care of myself. You've got your own life."

"Which means I can choose where I live it. I'll bring my supplies over and work in the garage. It's not like you use that space for your truck," he added with a laugh.

"What about you, Leigh Ann?" Jo asked. "Are

you sure you'll be okay at home, just you and Rachel?"

She nodded. "Rachel's going out of town for a few days. Her boss is sending her to a real estate sales conference in Albuquerque. I was planning to lock my doors and just sit tight, but when I told Melvin, he thought that was a lousy idea."

"For the record, he's right," Ambrose said.

"I wasn't thrilled with the prospect either, so Melvin and I made new plans. John's dropping him off here in a while. I'll give him a ride to one of the tribal offices so he can deliver a sculpture, and afterwards he and I will go over to my place so I can pick up a few things. I'll be staying at his house until Rachel's back," she said.

"You all know where he lives. There's nothing around for miles except critters. Melvin's hearing is super sharp, so he'll know if anything out of the ordinary is going on. I'll stay on the lookout, too, and if there's trouble, I have my .38. No one's going to hurt me or Melvin."

"Don't underestimate Melvin's ability to protect you," Ambrose said. "I taught him a few fighting moves a while back, and he's quick and strong as a bear. If he gets his hands on anyone trying to hurt you . . ."

Melvin walked slowly across the wooden porch of The Outpost carrying the heavy box containing an antelope sculpture. The work had been commissioned by the Navajo Nation Parks and Recreation Department and was going to be placed on exhibit at the Antelope Canyon Visitor's Center.

Antelope Canyon Park was way over at the northwestern tip of the Navajo Nation, south of Lake Powell. He remembered the canyon as if he'd been there yesterday, though the last time he'd visited the narrow, twisting passages and rainbow-colored sandstone, he'd been in his teens. He'd have to go again someday, with a guide, and run his hands along the curved walls, and measure nature's wonders using his remaining senses. Tribal treasures like Antelope Canyon were among the things he'd missed most after losing his sight.

Reaching out with the tip of his boot after taking exactly ten steps, he felt for the door, needing to know exactly where he was before setting down the box to reach for the handle.

"I'm here, Melvin," Leigh Ann called out. She waited until he was clear before opening the door. "Saw John dropping you off."

He felt the rush of cool air from inside the trading post. "Am I early?" he said, stepping back to his right.

"No, I'm ready to go. My Jeep is already around front. Want me to take that for you until we get down the steps?"

He knew she meant well, but if he started depending on others for the small things, he might as well give up and use a cane or a service dog. "No, just put your hand on my right shoulder and lead the way to the Jeep."

There was a slight stumble going down the steps, but Melvin hung on and didn't drop the box. Five minutes later, they were on their way, heading west on Highway 64 onto the Rez and Shiprock, their destination.

"Will I be able to see the antelope?" Leigh Ann asked in her slight twang.

He loved her West Texas accent, it had a charm and cadence all its own.

"It's going to be transported this evening by courier to the Visitor's Center at Antelope Canyon, so I'm reluctant to take it out of the packing material. But there's a photograph in my shirt pocket. Take it."

He leaned to the side and felt her fingers reaching into the pocket. She had to grope in order to keep her eyes on the road, but the brief touch felt nice and he smiled.

"Did I tickle you?" she asked, glancing over for a second.

"Nah, I'm not ticklish."

"Maybe someday I'll find out if you're lying, sugar."

She checked traffic, saw there were no vehicles within a half mile, so she brought the photo up by the steering wheel for a quick glance. After confirming it was still safe down the road, she took a second look.

After a beat, she sat the photo on her lap. "It's beautiful. The figure's graceful, but it's powerful, too. I like the way its head is cocked to the side, like it's curious. Down in Texas, we'd call this a pronghorn."

"That's another name for it. According to the experts, it's the closest any Native American animal is to the African antelope."

"Thank you, Mr. Science."

"You're welcome," he said, laughing. Leigh Ann was easy to talk to, particularly in contrast to John, who often had a beef with someone or was cranky about work.

Fifteen minutes later, as Leigh Ann slowed to a crawl and made several slow, sharp turns, he knew they were getting close to their destination.

"Hang on to the box, speed bump ahead," she said.

He reached out and held on, but she'd slowed so much the bump was almost an afterthought.

"We're here—tribal offices," she announced. "I'll come around."

He heard the *click click* of her heels as she walked around the front of the Jeep, then the door opened. "Hand me the box, Melvin, and once you're out, I'll give it back to you."

Three minutes later, they entered the cool lobby

of the Navajo Nation Shiprock Agency and Leigh Ann led him to the receptionist's desk.

"Here comes a guy in a suit," she whispered as the snap of boots on tile came from his right.

"*Yáat'ééh, Hosteen* Littlewater," a young man welcomed, coming up to Melvin. "Is this the antelope sculpture I've heard Director Nez talking about?"

"It sure is, Mr. . . . ."

"Benally. I'm Thomas Benally, Director Sorrelhorse's assistant. Mrs. Peshlakai is away from her desk at the moment. Can I lead you to Director Nez's office?"

Melvin turned toward Leigh Ann, whose outline was just to his left. "Find a comfortable seat and wait for me. I'll be back soon," he said.

"Take your time, Melvin," she answered.

A few seconds later, he felt a hand touch him briefly on his right shoulder and a gray shape appeared. "Would you like some help?" Benally asked, hesitation in his tone.

"If you'll stay close, I'll be able to follow and that'll be enough." Most Navajos disliked touching a stranger. Despite his disability, he was no different in that respect. He'd learned to shake hands a long time ago, but even that didn't come as easily to him as it did to an Anglo.

The hall was carpeted, based on the near silence of their footsteps, but Benally moved slowly.

Maybe he was a little uncertain about his role as guide.

As they passed an open door Melvin overheard a man he assumed to be Navajo, judging from his accent and tone. "Cut to the chase: How much is the contract worth to you?"

Curious, Melvin slowed down.

Benally picked up the pace instantly, however, forcing Melvin to speed up. A few seconds later Melvin heard a door slam behind them.

Ten minutes later he was back in the Jeep and Leigh Ann was navigating the side streets, heading back toward the highway.

"If the others like your sculpture as much as Mr. Benally did, you're going to have some very happy customers," she said, stopping at a traffic light.

"Director Nez unpacked the sculpture so he could see it for himself. He was so happy, he had Benally take a photo of us with the sculpture."

"Once we get out of heavy traffic remind me to return your photo," she said, stopping at the red light leading onto the main highway.

"Naw, keep it. John took several and he can print more."

"Thanks."

The light changed, and as she started to make the turn the Jeep lurched and the engine died.

Hearing the car behind them honking, she looked in the rearview mirror. It was Wayne Hurley, of all people, in his big pickup. He waved and honked again, pointing to the green light.

She waved back. "Keep your shirt on," she muttered.

Leigh Ann put the stick in neutral, switched the ignition off, then turned the key again and touched the gas lightly. The engine turned over this time, so she put it in gear, and made the turn onto the highway. As she speeded up, she gave Hurley, who was following, one last wave.

"On the road again, no sweat," she said, relief in her voice.

"Has this happened before—the engine dying when you stop in traffic?" he asked.

"Sometimes on hot days. Fortunately, it always restarts. Maybe the idle is set too low, or something."

"Have you ever considered trading in this ride for a new one, or maybe a good used model?"

"I'm barely getting by now, Melvin. Business has never gone back to where it was when Tom Stuart was alive, and expenses continue to rise. The trading post will survive this, I'm sure, but it's still in transition. I'm concerned that we all might have to take a cut in hours so nobody has to be let go."

"I had no idea. I guess things are tight for everyone right now."

"Including you?"

"I get by okay. Sometimes the unexpected comes up, like my swamp cooler breaking down, but this check will take care of those repairs and then some," he said. "One way or another, I always manage."

Hearing a familiar electronic tune, she fished her cell phone out of her shirt pocket and put it on speaker. "Hi, Rache. Are you still in town? I thought you'd be on your way to Albuquerque by now."

"I just passed through Farmington, but I thought you might want a heads-up. I stopped by the drugstore for hair spray and ran into Pierre Boone. He told me they just received the squirrel trap you ordered and he offered to bring it by. I told him you usually don't get off work until after six and I was going to be out of town for a few days," she said. "He said okay, but to let you know it had come in."

"Okay, thanks for the heads-up," Leigh Ann said. "Have fun," she said, ending the call.

They rode in silence for several more minutes before Melvin spoke again. "I'm glad you'll be staying with me."

"So you can continue working on your new sculpture?" she asked hopefully.

He smiled. "I've never stopped working on it, but it'll help to have you at home, talking to me."

"How soon will I be able to see it?"

"Not for a while. It has a ways to go before it's finished," he said, and, smiling, added, "I never realized how curious you are."

"I'm not always, but this time, yes."

They arrived at Leigh Ann's a short time later. The sky was gray, covered with a thick layer of clouds. It was getting dark fast, too, with the sun low in the sky.

"It feels cooler than it should for this time of day. It must be cloudy."

"Yeah, but I doubt we'll get any rain. It'll evaporate before it hits the ground—at least that's what the weatherman said." She went around and took his arm. "Come on in. I'll get you something to drink while I pack up a few things."

"A drink's not necessary. Just get your clothes and whatever else you'll need."

"You don't want to hang around here any longer than we have to, do you?" she said, leading him up the sidewalk.

"I'll feel safer at my place where I know my way around."

She opened the door and flicked on the lights, but nothing happened. "The power's off," she said after a beat.

"Does that happen often?"

"Maybe three or four times a year. The entire neighborhood has the same problem. The power goes off for no discernible reason, and comes back whenever it feels like it. I think it's because our area was developed without much planning, at least when it comes to utilities. Yet here we are, with the two biggest generating stations in the state within, what, fifteen miles?"

She led him to the chair in the living room, but before she could move away, he grasped her arm and placed one finger over his lips.

He pointed upstairs.

Leigh Ann heard nothing at first, then after several seconds heard what sounded like padded footsteps.

"I've got a gun, and I know how to use it," she yelled, retrieving the .38 from her purse. "Get out of my house *now!*"

There was silence for a moment, then she heard a window open upstairs.

Leigh Ann stepped in front of Melvin and pointed the gun toward the stairs. If the burglar wanted to climb out a window, that was just fine with her, but if he came down here, she'd blow him to kingdom come.

A heartbeat later, she heard running footsteps across the roof, then the rustling of bushes out back and a thump. That was followed by the sound of a squealing hinge, and a slam. After that, all she heard was the pounding of her heart.

Melvin reached out and put his hand on her shoulder.

"That last noise was the back gate," she managed.

"Hopefully he's long gone," Melvin replied.

She stepped to the front door and pulled it open, holding the pistol barrel up.

"Wait another minute," Melvin said. "Listen. There, an engine revving."

Leigh Ann looked down the street and saw the taillights of a vehicle speeding away. "I'm going out back to check the breakers. Stay here."

"We need to stick together in case he wasn't alone. I'm going with you," Melvin said.

She took his arm, and, using the flashlight app on her phone, walked out the French patio doors to the panel at the back of the house beside the electrical mast. "Someone switched off the master breaker."

"Switch it back on, then let's go inside," he said. "After you call the police, take a look around, and see what's missing—if anything."

"You don't think this was an ordinary break-in?"

"Do you?" he countered.

"No, not really," she admitted after a beat.

"Tell me something. Are you carrying that revolver around with you full time now?"

"I keep it in my purse."

"Are you sure that's a good idea?"

"I don't think I've got a choice, Melvin. The gun . . . well, it equalizes the odds against me."

"A .38 revolver has no safety."

"Yeah, that's true enough, but you have to squeeze the trigger to shoot. If I don't—it won't. I'm familiar with guns, Melvin, remember?"

"The real danger is that you'll hesitate to shoot another person. If that happens, it'll only take a second for your enemy to rip the gun out of your hand and use it against you."

"That won't happen," she said firmly.

"Why not?"

"I'm through being a victim. By the time he takes it from me, the gun will be empty, and he'll have at least six holes in him."

He nodded. "Okay, then."

Leigh Ann reached for the doorknob. "What I can't figure out is how he got in."

"Was this door locked?"

"Yes. I had to unlock it to go out back."

"And the front door?" he asked, moving past her into the kitchen.

"I used the key to get in."

Once inside the house, she flipped on the back patio lights and kitchen light switches at the same time. "The lights work now."

"Is there a third door, maybe leading from the garage to the backyard?" he asked.

"No, but there's a garage window, let me go take a quick look at that." She hurried, then a moment later, returned. "It's intact, and locked.

Whoever it was must have picked one of the locks."

"You changed the house locks after your keys were stolen from the Jeep, right?" Melvin asked.

"Yes, but come to think of it, it's possible the burglar got in the same way he got out—through an upstairs window."

"Do you normally leave those open?" Melvin asked.

"The second story can get really hot during the day, so I crack the windows. Since they face the back of the house, I figured it would be okay," Leigh Ann said. "Guess I was wrong."

"Is there a tree high enough to reach the roof nearby?"

"Yeah, which is probably how he got down."

"Let's go upstairs and check things out," Melvin said.

Pistol still in hand, Leigh Ann led the way to the second story, then down the hall to her bedroom. Inside, she flipped on the light switch and saw the window was wide open. The screen had been pulled off and dropped onto the roof. The curtain rod was dangling loose on one side, the drapes on the floor.

"The window's wide open," she said, describing everything, including the fact that all her dresser drawers had been emptied and their contents tossed across the carpet.

Leigh Ann set down the pistol, then

automatically started scooping up her clothing and dropping them back into the drawers. Then she stopped and began to make a big pile in the center of the room instead. They'd have to go through the hottest wash cycle possible before they ever touched her skin again.

"Are you okay?" he asked.

"Yeah, I'm just putting my scattered clothing into a pile so I can wash everything," she said, then by way of explanation, added, "He touched them."

"I understand."

"We'll have to stop at the superstore before going to your house. I want to buy some new underwear," she said. "Right now I better check out the rest of my room."

She looked under the bed and saw that the shotgun was still there and the rifle case hadn't been touched. She went to the closet next, but couldn't find anything that even appeared to have been moved. The shelf held her shoes, all stored in plastic boxes, and everything else was on hangers.

With Melvin next to her, she proceeded to go through each room in the house. Soon she determined that the only other place that had been searched was her office. "He sure made a mess," she said.

"Describe it to me," Melvin said.

"He opened all the desk drawers and dumped

everything on the carpet. I keep my utility bills in an accordion file next to the wall and those have been scattered all over the area rug."

"Anything else?" he asked, standing in the doorway.

"My old desktop computer is on, so maybe he made a copy of some of my files," she said, sitting behind the desk.

"What do you keep there?"

"Not much. I use the computer to keep track of my monthly bills and help me stay on budget. I also have my Internet provider loaded into it, but there's nothing earth shattering in there. It doesn't have my bank account numbers or anything like that."

"You still haven't called the police. Maybe you should do that now," Melvin said.

"They won't be able to do much because we can't give them a description of the intruder. They probably won't take prints either. Nothing appears to have been taken, not even the shotgun."

"You've still got to try, Leigh Ann."

"All right, I'll call," she said, though she suspected it would be a waste of time.

After returning her pistol to her purse downstairs, she went over to the kitchen area and offered Melvin, who'd followed her, a glass of iced tea. "The dispatcher said because it's not an emergency it'll take a while."

As they sat down at the dining table, a thick silence settled between them. "I feel as if I'm stuck between a rock and a hard place," Leigh Ann said, choking up now. "Everything I do seems to endanger other people—you, Rachel, Jo and the trading post."

"You don't know that's true, Leigh Ann," he said, reaching for her hand and finding it.

His touch soothed and excited her all at once and she tried to focus on that instead of the fear. "All I ever wanted was a quiet, ordinary life. After Kurt died and I found a job I loved, I thought I'd finally get my chance. I guess I was wrong."

"You don't know that. Don't try to predict the future," he said.

"What if I end up getting arrested for a crime I never committed?" She paused. "You know, I've always tried to be the good girl—good ol' dependable Leigh Ann, the one who always plays by the rules. Maybe it's time I made my own rules."

"That's a better idea. In a situation like this, not doing what others expect will give you the advantage."

"That sounds like another reason for me to stay at your place."

"Yeah, exactly," he said, and smiled. "In fact, you *and* Rachel should both move in with me until this matter is resolved."

"I appreciate the offer, but I can't take you up on it. I'll stay with you until Rachel's back, but once my sister's home I've got to finish what I've started."

"Just remember to stay cool and fight smarter, not harder."

She was about to answer when she heard a loud knock. "Sheriff's department. This is Deputy Mills. You reported a break-in, ma'am?"

Leigh Ann stood to let him in.

"Leigh Ann," Melvin whispered. "Tell him what he needs to know, but don't volunteer information. Remember: your rules, not theirs."

"Right," she said with a nod as she went to open the door.

Fifteen

After the officer left, Leigh Ann took a deep breath and began to pace around the living room. "Now do you see why I didn't want to call them? He wrote up a report, mostly for insurance purposes, and that's it. When the detectives investigating Kurt's death hear about this, they'll assume I set the whole thing up."

"They're free to come up with as many theories as they want. You can't stop that from happening," he said. "Just stay focused on finding the truth and shut out everything else. That's the only way you'll win."

"You're a good friend," she said, stepping into his open arms. All she'd meant to do was give him a hug, but his body felt so good against hers. In his arms there was safety . . . and danger.

As he held her tightly against him, her heart began to race. For a brief moment she was tempted to throw caution to the winds and let nature take its course, but if she did, she'd just make things worse.

"Let's go," she said, moving away reluctantly. "We've got a long drive ahead."

After stopping at the superstore outside Farmington so she could buy some inexpensive clothes, they continued toward Melvin's place. A few miles from their destination, about halfway up a graveled road and miles from the closest neighbor, she braked at a stop sign.

Immediately after she started up again, they both heard a loud *pop* and the steering started to pull to the right.

"I think we punctured a tire," she said, compensating with the steering wheel as she came to a stop again. "Let me get out and take a look."

Leigh Ann glanced around. It was dark here in the middle of nowhere, though there was a glow in the sky from the city to the east. Leaving the engine and the headlights on, she walked around to check the right front tire.

"I've got a flat, Melvin," she called back. "There's a big board filled with nails stuck to the tire."

As she brought out the jack and lug wrench, Melvin got out, and felt his way along the side of the Jeep toward the sound of her voice.

Leigh Ann looked over at him just as he froze in midstride and began turning his head to the side.

"Get back in the Jeep," he whispered harshly. "Drive on the rim if necessary, but let's move. Hurry. Leave the tools."

She looked around with the flashlight, probing into the waist-high sagebrush. "Huh? It's okay. There's no one around."

"Yes, there is," he said. "Give me the lug wrench."

Leigh Ann did as he asked, then looked around again with the flashlight. "I don't see anyone."

"Behind you."

As she turned to look, two men rose from behind the brush just off the road and out of the glow of the headlights. They were wearing masks and camouflage uniforms of some kind. The gleam of knife blades in their hands captured her attention instantly.

"Melvin, knives!"

Both men rushed Melvin, but he swung the lug wrench with deadly accuracy against the first man, catching him with a glancing blow on the arm. He tucked his left shoulder down and stiff-armed the second man in the chest, sending him stumbling backward. Both attackers backed off a few steps.

Leigh Ann, now behind Melvin, reached inside the Jeep through the open window for her purse and pulled out her gun. "Don't move or I'll shoot you full of holes!" she said, stepping past Melvin for a clear line of sight.

The men spun around and ran off into the brush.

Leigh Ann fired once at their legs, barely missing the slower of the two. As she took aim again they both vanished into the dark.

"Leigh Ann, stay low and keep your back to

the Jeep. Save your bullets and call the sheriff's department."

She stepped back to where he was and crouched beside him, her revolver out and ready. It took a little longer calling 911 with only one shaky hand, but no way she was putting down her revolver until the deputies arrived. She was scared, tired, and most of all, confused.

"They targeted *you,* Melvin, not me. Why?" she said, her voice low.

"Maybe they saw me as the bigger threat, the one they needed to neutralize first," he answered. "That was until you brought out the pistol."

"It's obvious now that the board filled with nails was put there to set us up for an ambush. But why? What did they think we had?"

"Maybe they were looking for whatever it was they failed to find at your house earlier," Melvin said.

"Could have been Wayne and Pierre?"

"The men I fought off weren't both Anglo."

"How do you know that?"

"When I hit one with the lug wrench, he grunted, then said '*shicho*' in perfect Navajo."

"What's it mean?"

"*Shichó* with accent over the *o* just means 'my' as in yours, mine, and so on. But without the accent, the high tone, it means male genitalia."

"Oh."

"As I said, he was Navajo. And there was

something about the voice—I've heard it before . . . somewhere," he said. "Don't worry, it'll come to me. We'll figure it out once we're at my place. For the moment, though, we have to stay alert and wait for the sheriff."

So they both came at Mr. Littlehorse?" the young deputy verified, looking at Leigh Ann, who nodded. He glanced at Melvin, and noting his expressionless eyes, added, "Are you completely blind?"

"Not a hundred percent, no, but at night I can't even make out shapes unless the object is bathed in enough light to present a silhouette," Melvin answered.

"And you're sure the attackers wore gloves?" he asked Leigh Ann.

"I'm sure."

"I can second that," Melvin said. "I took a grazing punch and felt hide, not knuckles, against the side of my face. I could also smell the leather. The gloves were probably new."

Leigh Ann watched a second deputy put the knife into a bag, then write something on the paper. "Can you trace that without fingerprints?"

"We'll try, but this is a very common, inexpensive hunting knife, the kind that's for sale at every sporting goods store and Walmart across the country," he said, his gaze on the other officers working the area.

"Is there any way to track these men down now?" she asked.

"We found where their vehicle was parked, so we'll be taking tire impressions. Boot prints will also give us each man's approximate height and weight. We may even be able to identify the brand they wore. Of course, if Mr. Littlewater can recall whose voice he heard and come up with the name of his Navajo assailant, we'll bring the suspect in for questioning."

The deputy helped Leigh Ann change the flat, while the other officers collected the evidence, including the tire and nail-studded board.

After another half hour, Leigh Ann and Melvin were back in the Jeep heading to his home.

"I'm surprised they didn't take your .38," Melvin said after a while. "You still have it, right?"

"Yeah, I told him I keep it in plain view while driving at night—which is legal—and that I'd fired it at the men once. The deputy who checked the cylinder confirmed that, then wrote down the revolver's serial number and put the weapon back on my car seat. If I'd hit one of the men, or there was blood anywhere, I'm sure the cops would have taken it. The deputy said I'd done the right thing defending myself. He even gave me a little advice about aiming a pistol in low-light conditions."

"Think they'll run the serial number?"

"Guess I'll find out in a day or two," Leigh Ann replied, slowing for a rough spot in the road. "I just hope it wasn't stolen."

"Keep a close eye on your rearview mirror. We don't want to run into anyone else tonight," Melvin warned.

Leigh Ann noted the tension in his shoulders. "Melvin, I'm truly sorry I got you into this mess."

He smiled. "Are you kidding me? I finally got a chance to show what I can do and try out some of those moves Ambrose taught me. No regrets here."

"You're being polite," she said.

"No, I'm not. I like you, Leigh Ann, more than I should," he said, his voice low and deep. "Tonight I finally got the chance to show you that I'm more than a blind sculptor."

She reached out to him and took his hand. "I never doubted that for a moment."

He moved his hand and clasped hers firmly. "A reminder now and then can't hurt."

They arrived at Melvin's house a short time later. She grabbed the small suitcase she'd brought, along with the plastic shopping bag containing her new clothes, and then went around to help Melvin. This time of night his footsteps were usually less steady, but at least here he was on his home turf.

"When did Ambrose teach you to fight?" she

said, making conversation as they walked toward his porch, his arm around hers.

"He came to me years ago after I got attacked by a drunk while waiting for a ride. I'd told myself that I'd never let my blindness become an insurmountable obstacle, but getting my butt kicked destroyed my confidence. For the first time, I felt vulnerable. It wasn't a good feeling."

As they stepped inside, she turned on the lights.

"Would you like something cold to drink?" he asked.

"That sounds good," she said. She thought he might mean having a beer, but decided not to ask. As usual, there was the half empty bottle of whiskey sitting there in the living room. She'd been curious since the first day she'd seen it, wondering just how much he drank, or if he drank at all.

"You're been in my house several times, so I'm sure you've noticed that bottle of quality single-malt scotch over by my chair. It's real smooth, with a faint smoky taste. Would you like a couple of glugs over some ice cubes?"

"That sound terrific," she said. "Let me get the glasses and fix it. You want yours on the rocks too?"

"No scotch for me, thanks. I haven't taken a drink in years. I keep the bottle there as a reminder that I'm in control of my own destiny and that life's all about choices."

"That's what's wrong with *my* life. I'm not in control—of anything," she admitted, selecting a small juice glass from the rack beside the sink. "I've spent far too long going with the flow. It was easier in a lot of ways, you know? Then I woke up. Now . . ."

"Don't let it get you down, Leigh Ann. You'll find the answers you need soon enough," he said, walking over to where she was standing beside the refrigerator.

She stepped back as he came closer.

"You don't have to put distance between us. Nothing's going to happen."

"Sometimes I want it to," she admitted in a soft voice, opening the refrigerator and bringing out some ice cubes from the tray beneath the icemaker to place in her glass.

She brushed past him, crossing over to the living room area and that bottle of scotch.

He turned in her direction. "You and I aren't trusting people, and we both have things we may never talk to one another about, but if you think about it, there's balance in that."

As she poured herself a drink, she was surprised to see her hands were shaking. Had she been alone, she might have just broken down and cried. Everything she wanted was right in front of her—and completely out of her reach.

"Bring your drink and come into the study with

me so I can work on that sculpture. That'll help me unwind."

"I don't see the sheepskin rug," she said, following him into that room and looking down at the floor. "Would you like me to get it for you?"

"It's not necessary, not anymore, just sit wherever you like. At the beginning it was a matter of getting the right feel for the sculpture through your pose, proximity, and the sound of your voice. That helped me create an image in my mind, but I have that now," he said, moving behind the table he'd set up there, then reaching back to the melamine-covered shelf behind him.

He moved his hands carefully, feeling his way, then grabbed hold of a plastic-covered object and turned, easing it down onto the table, still covered.

Leigh Ann leaned forward in the chair, straining to get a glimpse of what was beneath the black cover, but she couldn't even determine its shape.

"Help yourself to another shot from the bottle anytime you want," he said.

"Thanks, but I'm good. I'm still nursing this one," she said.

"There's something else in your voice," he said, then after mulling it over, added, "Leigh Ann, are you uncomfortable staying here alone with me?"

"No, but I'm worried about you. I've pulled you into a huge mess and I don't know how to get you out."

"I don't want out. When I've got too much time to think about myself, it pulls me down," he said, intensity giving his words an edge. "Helping you . . . pushes back the darkness."

She sat up a little straighter. "That darkness isn't something you can outrun by proving you can take care of yourself, is it?"

"No," he answered.

In the subsequent silence, Leigh Ann watched his focus shift to the sculpture. He'd uncovered it, but she couldn't make sense of the object, which was still undefined, at least in her eyes.

He was a lot more interesting to look at anyway. Concentration was etched on his features. As her gaze rested on him, she wished she could have brought something positive into his life, not just danger.

"You're safe here. Are you upset?"

"Why would you think that? I haven't made a sound," she said, her voice unsteady.

"You also haven't said a word. That's not like you."

She wiped her tears away with the back of her hand, then stood and reached for the box of tissues at one end of the table. "I'm just angry. When I started all this with the box from the attic, I told myself it was the right thing to do, that I had to settle the past before I could put it behind me. Now I realize that what was really driving me was pride. I wanted to prove to myself that I was tough enough to face up to whatever Kurt had done, and deal with it."

He covered the figure, gently put it back on the shelf, and felt his way around the perimeter of the table, stepping close to her. "We all make mistakes. We're human," he said, taking her hands in his.

"I made some stupid moves. Now I've exposed everyone around me to danger and turned everything into a giant mess."

"Progress doesn't always travel in a straight line. You'll find some answers, then maybe lose ground when you uncover more questions. Eventually you'll move forward again. That's the way things go," he said, pulling her into his arms and stroking her hair tenderly.

She nuzzled into him, her face buried into the hollow of his neck. His strong arms felt so good all she wanted was to surrender. She'd always dreamed of a man who'd brave the fires of hell for her, whose courage was matched by a steadfast heart. Melvin was all that and more. Yet something told her to hold back. "Nothing is ever simple is it?" she responded, walking back into the living room.

He followed, found her hand again, and led her to his couch. They sat down together, leaned back against the cushions, then he pulled her toward him, her back against his chest, his arms around her. "You're amazing, Leigh Ann. What first drew me to you was the sound of your voice. Just beyond that pleasant friendliness was caution. You'd pull back instantly the second things went from personable to personal. That's when I knew there was a lot more to you than what you allowed people to see."

"When I started working at the trading post, I was scared to death of failing—of being told I wasn't good enough."

"I understand exactly how you felt. It was that way for me, too, at one time. I wondered if I really was a good sculptor, or if people were buying my art out of sympathy because I was blind. That doubt forced me to work harder and reach deeper to bring my sculpture to life."

"How could you ever have doubted your skill? Your work touches everyone, and amazingly enough, each person sees some-thing different in your creations."

"For a long time I doubted everything, me most of all," he said. "The worst part was hearing pity in people's voices."

She shifted around in his arms, resting her head on his shoulder, and looked up at him. "I've been there, and you're right, it does get under your skin. Everyone knew Kurt had been fooling around—everyone, that is, except me."

"The past makes us who we are, but it doesn't determine what we'll become," he said. "Of course that's a lesson that takes a while to learn. For a long time I was hurting, life had screwed me, and I wanted to lash out at someone or something. Since I couldn't, I took it out on myself."

Still leaning against him, she reached for his hand and wound her fingers through his. Maybe this was part of his secret, what was keeping him awake at night. "So you drank to make it stop eating at you."

"Something like that. My memories of the accident never stopped haunting me. My failure . . ." He grew quiet.

"I don't understand. You were hit by a drunk driver. How did *you* fail?"

"Not how—who." He sat up straighter and as she shifted, he stood and stepped away.

"Talk to me, Melvin. Let me help," she said, going to his side and placing her hand on his arm.

"You can't. No one can."

She led him back to the couch, but they remained standing. "You've told me about the importance of balance in any relationship. If you help me, yet refuse to accept my help, you're undermining our friendship."

He nodded slowly. "You're right. To walk in beauty, harmony and balance are needed." He considered it for several moments. "It's also possible that talking this through with someone like you, who'll at least keep an open mind, may help. Uncle John's advice is to just step away and let go of the past, but I can't."

He began to pace again. "I can't sit down to talk about this. I've got to move."

"Then go ahead," she said, returning to the couch and giving him the space he needed. Her heart was beating overtime now. Melvin was finally opening up to her, and that could change everything between them, for good and bad.

"The night of the accident the driver behind me was all over the road," he said, "so I gave him as much room as possible, hoping he'd pass me and be done with it. When he cut in front and hit me, my truck flew off the highway and into the irrigation canal. So did he. I lucked out—my truck landed right side up. His car was upside down. The impact knocked me out at first, but the cold water rushing in shocked me awake. I managed to kick the air bag away, climbed out the open window, and made it to the cab roof.

"My head was bloody and hurt. When I realized that the current was pushing my pickup toward his car, I was sure I'd get thrown into the wreckage and get pinned underneath."

"What about the other driver?"

"Never saw him," Melvin said and shook his

head. "But on the opposite bank there was a girl, maybe nine or ten. She was up to her knees in the water, reaching out and calling to me. I was getting ready to jump off the roof of my pickup when it hit something under the water and threw me in the current. I hit my head again and got sucked under. I must have blacked out after that, because I can't remember anything else until I woke up in the hospital.

"The sheriff's deputy told me they pulled me out of one of those siphons on a side canal," he concluded in whisper.

"What happened to the little girl? I don't remember ever hearing about her until now."

"I don't know. I told the first person I spoke to after I woke up about her, and the police searched, but she was never found, dead oralive. The police eventually concluded I'd imagined it, but I know she was really there. I remember her clearly, because she's the last thing I ever saw."

Leigh Ann went to Melvin and put her arms around him. "I'm so very sorry you had to go through that hell."

He'd never know how badly she'd wished she could go back in time and rewrite history—for her, for him. "I finally understand why you can't let this go. You need to know what happened to her. That's the only way you'll ever be able to make your peace with this. So let's look into it together," she suggested. "We'll figure out who she was and what she was doing there. Let me help you."

"I appreciate the offer," he said, brushing a kiss on her forehead. "But if the police couldn't do it, I don't see how we're going to be able to find answers either."

"We won't give up 'til we have them." She'd move heaven and earth if that's what it took for him to find closure. Later tonight, when she got home, she'd find out the name of that other driver—the one who'd caused all this. It was somewhere on the Internet, she knew that for sure.

Meanwhile, she was grateful for what Melvin had shared with her. "Thank you for telling me about this and for trusting me."

He held her for a while, then reached down and kissed her.

Her mouth opened under his tender pressure, and for a few moments his barely leashed passion and roughness wove a spell around her. She felt powerfully feminine and vibrantly alive.

Hearing an annoying sound in the background, she tried to shut it out, but it persisted. Leigh Ann realized the irritating tune was coming from her phone.

He eased his hold reluctantly. "Is that Rachel's ring tone? Maybe she canceled her trip."

"No, that's not hers. It's similar though, and that means it's my cousin," she said, wishing Dale's timing had been better.

She took her cell phone from her purse. "Hey, Dale, what's going on?"

"I heard about the break-in at your place and what happened afterwards with those men who ambushed you. Good thing you were carrying that .38."

"Yeah, for sure. Now tell me, do the detectives think we made all that up?"

"No, in fact, it looks like they're finally starting to take your story seriously. They've decided to try and locate the employee who was at the storage place the day Kurt's locker was emptied. Detective McGraw will probably pay you another visit tomorrow."

"I've already had my fill of Detective McGraw," Leigh Ann replied.

"He's a tough cop, Leigh Ann, but he's fair."

"I hope you're right. Thanks for the heads-up," she said, then quickly added, "Dale, while I've got you on the line, I need a favor."

A few minutes later she hung up. Finding Melvin in the kitchen, she told him what Dale had said.

"That's all good news. It's about time they started believing you."

"Yeah, I think so, too." Looking at the can of soup he'd brought out, she continued, "Since I'm staying here, why don't you let me earn my keep by fixing the meals?"

"There's not much for you to work with," he

warned. "I've got soup, some ready-to-eat meals in the freezer, and hot dogs."

She opened the freezer. "There are little markers on the frozen dinners. Is that Braille?"

"More like my own shorthand—like with the bills in my wallet."

She looked in the cupboards, found some spaghetti and a jar of spaghetti sauce. "I can fix what Rache and I call 'cowboy Italian.' I'll make spaghetti, put little chunks of boiled hot dogs in it, then add just a touch of green chile," she said, taking the lid off the jar of flame-roasted green chiles and sniffing it to make sure it was okay.

"That sounds . . . interesting."

"It's pretty decent—half comfort food, half adventure," she said, laughing.

"Let me turn on the evening news while we get stuff ready," he said, then joined her at the counter. "What can I do to help?"

"Just sit down and keep me company. I think the fewer cooks the better the results, especially when knives and fire are involved."

"All right then," he said, chuckling, and sat down at the table to listen to the broadcast.

"The litany of misery, that's what my uncle used to call the news," she said, making conversation.

He laughed. "Yeah, but it's good to be informed. Weather, traffic, medicine, contaminated food . . ."

"Yeah, I hear you. It's not what you know that can hurt you. It's what you don't know."

The top local news came from the station's lead investigative reporter, who was interviewing a high-profile Navajo department head.

As the man spoke, Melvin sat up straighter. "That man—who is he?" he asked, listening closely.

Leigh Ann finished chopping the hot dogs and looked at the television. "The caption says he's Lewis Sorrelhorse, director of Range and Livestock Management."

He listened for a moment longer. "I heard his voice today at the tribal office, asking how much a contract was worth. He might also be the guy who attacked me with the knife."

"I saw Wayne as we were leaving the tribal government building today. Remember when the engine died at the stoplight?"

"Yeah. Was he just driving by?"

"No, he was the guy behind us who honked. He saw me, too, 'cause when I looked back at him, he waved," she said. "Maybe he went there to meet Sorrelhorse."

"Sorrelhorse is a big gun. He's been employed by the tribe for years."

"I've heard or seen that name somewhere else recently, too," Leigh Ann said as she finished preparations for dinner.

"On the news?"

"I can't remember offhand, but the name rings a bell," she said. "Hm. Let me think."

Silence stretched out as she concentrated, trying to remember.

They ate dinner quietly and as Leigh Ann began clearing the table, she smiled. "I've got it. I know where I saw that name. It was in the little notebook I found with Kurt's things. I turned it over to the detectives."

"You think you'll be asked about it tomorrow, when the one in charge of the case comes to talk to you? McGraw, was it?"

"Yeah, but I'm not going to volunteer any more information. I'll answer his questions and that's it."

"Good plan," he said. "Once we're done cleaning up here, I'd like to go back and work on the sculpture some more. Are you up to it?"

"Sure," she said. "I'm so curious! I won't ask you about it directly, but tell me this much: Are you happy with the way it's turning out so far?"

"No, something's missing, but I don't know what that is yet. I need to spend more time with the figures. It'll come to me."

"Before we get started," she said, looking through the doorway at her overnight bag, "where do you want me to sleep tonight?"

"In my arms," he said without skipping a beat.

She felt a shiver touch her spine, but refused

to react in any way he'd detect. "Neither one of us is ready for that."

"If one of us isn't, then we can't," he said with a nod. "So take the spare room. Come on, I'll show you the way."

He walked with her down the hall and motioned to his left. "In there. I keep fresh sheets on the bed for the times John shows up late at night unannounced."

She brought her bags inside and looked around. The room was simply furnished, with a bed, a wardrobe, and a chest of drawers. The bed was covered with a plain white bedspread, but a vivid color just below piqued her curiosity and she pulled the spread back. "The sheets are hot pink!" she said. "Is there something I don't know about John?"

He laughed. "Only that he can be a pain in the butt when he shows up after having one too many. I put those there because pink was his ex-wife's favorite color. Since then I've noticed he doesn't drop by here in the evening as often anymore," he added with a grin.

"Fortunately for you, I love the color," she said. "Actually it's one of my favorites." She looked back at him. "Is it time to work on your sculpture?"

"If you're ready, I am."

"Lead the way," she said, knowing that he was the master of his domain.

Sixteen

Jo sat alone in her office. Ambrose had moved in last night and after hearing him snore like a freight train for hours, she'd seriously considered taking her rifle and blanket and going out to sleep in the medicine hogan.

Common sense prevailed, however. Instead, she'd turned on her MP3 player, put in her earbuds, and kept it playing the rest of the night. Today, she'd make a point of finding more relaxing music that would allow her to drift off to sleep a little easier. All she'd had on the player now were fast-moving songs that helped her keep pace when she went for runs in the mornings.

Jo sipped yesterday's leftover coffee and stared at the computer. There was still no word from Ben or the U.S. Army via the local National Guard unit, and the waiting was tearing her apart. She was afraid to even glance at news reports from Afghanistan.

Hearing a knock at the back door, she went to answer it. She'd kept all the doors locked since it wasn't business hours and she'd wanted time alone to think.

"Who's there?" Jo called out, looking through the peephole.

"It's me," Ambrose answered. "I heard you

leave, but I wasn't quite ready to get up," he said, smiling as she let him in. "Now that I'm here, I thought you could treat me to a good cup of coffee and maybe a bear claw, the ones that you get from Mrs. Yazzie?"

She smiled. "Good choice. Unfortunately she won't deliver for another hour, but I think there's a day-old one still in the cooler. I saved it for Leigh Ann and then forgot to give it to her."

"Thanks. I'll find what I need, then brew up some fresh coffee in the break room," he said.

Five minutes later, she heard another knock at the back door and rolled her eyes. "It's not even seven!"

Ambrose went with her. It was Sam, holding two breakfast sacks from a fast-food restaurant in Shiprock. "My grandmother's coming in early, too, and she asked me to pick up breakfast." She looked at Ambrose and smiled. "There's plenty for everyone, I bought extra."

Jo smiled. "What's this all about?"

"My grandmother knows things have been tough for you lately, so she suggested we all get together for breakfast just to remind ourselves that we're not alone. We can't help the military find Ben, but we can take care of things here."

Jo nodded. "I like that. Thanks for the support."

Ambrose answered the door after that, greeting Leigh Ann, Esther, and finally Regina.

As Regina joined them in the break room, Jo

noted how tired she looked. "Is everything okay?" Jo asked softly as they met by the coffeepot.

"Yes—and no. Pete's been making noises about wanting to play a bigger role in the baby's life. He doesn't really—the baby drove Pete crazy when he was home—but he's using that against me. He wants me to worry about him trying to get custody or worse, maybe just take her when I'm here at work."

She took a deep breath. "So my uncle's living with us now—Mom's brother. Leroy's a former marine and Pete's afraid of him. They've had a few run-ins in the past."

"I'm glad your family's there for you," Jo said. "Looks like we all need a little extra help."

When they returned to the table, Jo decided to tell everyone her new plans for the trading post. "Leigh Ann gave me an idea, via Rachel, and I've been doing a lot of thinking about adding a coffee counter with Wi-Fi. Yesterday, after seeing an ad in the online *Daily Times*, I called a coffee house in Farmington that's remodeling and bought last year's espresso machine model, the sink and counter that supports it, and some bistro tables and chairs. I also arranged for them to deliver everything to our door. The owner is going to call and let me know when they're on their way so I can coordinate things with the plumber."

"How are we going to move that counter and sink over by the water fountain?" Esther asked. "I'm a clerk, not a dockworker."

Jo laughed. "We can have the delivery people set it on one of those wheeled dollies from the storeroom, then just roll it to where it's going to go. It only weighs about a hundred pounds, at least the counter and sink, but it's bulky, of course. The plumber will take care of disconnecting the fountain and installing everything."

"That'll do," Esther replied.

"Sam, now the ball's in your court," Jo said, turning to her. "We need an Internet connection for our customers. How complicated is that going to be?"

"We already have Wi-Fi, so getting things up and running won't be a problem. I'll call the IT guy if I need help," Sam responded.

"Good," Jo said.

"We also need to figure out what we'll be serving," Regina said. "To cater both to locals and passing tourists, we'll need great fresh-brewed regular coffee in addition to espresso, cappuccinos, and so on. It would be great if we could come up with something that's unique to us—a hook."

"Just remember that the coffee bar's main function is to generate interest in the merchandise the trading post offers," Jo said.

"Well, with the coffee bar in the back and the seating up front by the windows, our customers will get a clear look at the interior going back and forth," Leigh Ann added.

"So maybe some of the high-end displays need to be relocated toward the front," Jo said. "No better way to show the drop-in customers, especially tourists, the best of what we have to offer while they're seated at the tables."

Hearing another knock on the back door, Jo glanced around the room. "We're all here, so who's that?"

"Jack?" Sam said hopefully, garnering curious stares and a couple of smiles.

"I'll get it," Ambrose said.

A moment later, Jo heard a familiar voice and Rudy Brownhat stepped into the break room.

"I came by, hoping we could talk before your people started your workday," he said, addressing Jo, "but I see I'm already too late."

"No, it's all right, uncle, we're just finishing up a staff breakfast. Let's go into my office. We can talk there," she said just as another knock sounded.

Jo rolled her eyes and looked at her teacher. "Go ahead and I'll join you in a moment."

Ambrose returned with Detective McGraw, who immediately focused on Leigh Ann.

"Mrs. Vance, I'd like a few minutes of your time," he said. "In private."

"We'll leave so you can talk in here," Jo said, giving Leigh Ann a nod. Glancing at the others, she added, "We'll try meeting later today, or maybe tomorrow, depending on how things go."

As everyone left the break room to Leigh Ann and the detective, Jo filled an empty mug with coffee and stepped into her office. Rudy's expression was somber and that worried her. "Is everything all right, uncle?"

"Yes, I'm just tired. The effects of the poison will linger for another week," he said.

"Would you like some coffee?" she said, holding out the mug.

He nodded, taking the cup. "Is there any sugar? I need an energy boost right now."

Jo reached into her desk drawer, searched for a second, then brought out two packets of sugar. "I keep a stash in here," she said, handing him the packets and a stirrer still wrapped in plastic. "Are you sure you're okay?"

He nodded, adding the sugar, then stirring it for a few seconds. "I came because there's something I need to tell you," he said, taking a sip of coffee. "The wife of one of my patients picked me up this morning and drove me to see her husband. Her neighbor is the boyfriend of the woman you and I treated, the one who passed away."

Jo felt her body tense. Garnenez, the boyfriend, had been a problem all along.

Rudy continued. "I asked her about him and learned something surprising. After he threatened me, he went to a Cortez bar and got drunk. He ended up scuffling with the police officer who tried to escort him out and was arrested. He spent that night and all day Saturday in the Montezuma County Jail."

"So he couldn't have been the one who tampered with your tea jar Friday night," Jo said slowly as the impact of what he'd said sank in. "Then who is after us? Do you have any idea?"

"Not for sure, no, but I know where to start looking. Months ago, one of my patients came to me and requested a Sing. He was unhappy and many things in his life were out of balance. He told me that he knew a tribal official who was rigging bids, cheating companies like the one he worked for, and the tribe, too. He had no proof, but he was convinced he was right," Rudy said.

"The only place harmony could be restored is within the man. The situation is beyond your control. You're a *hataalii*, not a policeman," Jo said.

"Sometimes restoring balance is just a matter of waiting for the right moment to present itself," Rudy said. "Nine days ago I was invited to attend a wedding. The head of Range and Livestock Management for our tribe—the same department my patient had mentioned in connection with the crooked official—was there. I made a point of talking to him. I told him what I'd heard about the corruption, not mentioning the source, and asked if he knew anything about that."

"Seems reasonable," she said with nod.

"I thought so, too," Rudy said. "But unfortunately, he assumed I was accusing *him* of breaking the law. He told me that kind of talk would cost me dearly. If I tried to damage his reputation, he'd destroy mine. He said that the recent death of one of our patients would make it easier for him to create the kind of fear that would ruin me among the Traditionalists. It could also capture the attention of those who practice evil and make me their enemy as well. I'd lose my patients and face new dangers."

Jo inhaled sharply. She knew precisely what that meant. If word spread that Rudy had killed a patient in order to gain the dark powers of a skinwalker—a Navajo witch—Rudy's reputation would never recover. He'd also face retaliation from skinwalkers because he'd drawn unwanted attention to their practices. That would explain the foul medicine bag hung on the doorknob, and maybe even the paint.

"My guess is that he carried out those threats almost immediately, a preemptive strike, so to speak. He was smart enough to make it look like your patient's boyfriend was responsible for your problems," Jo said.

Rudy nodded. "That makes sense. That young

man is in the tribal official's clan. I bet he was at that wedding, and that's when he was told about his fiancé's blessing. The official knew the young man had a hot temper and would probably seek me out."

"It wasn't a perfect plan. The official didn't know the fiancé would end up in jail when he did, or doesn't think we'd find out," Jo replied, nodding her head. "Who is this man? I need to know where the danger is coming from."

"Remember that I have no way of proving any of this," he warned, then seeing her nod, continued. "The tribal official is Lewis Sorrelhorse. At the wedding, I'd tried to convince him I wouldn't bring up the subject again, but he obviously wasn't convinced. I've been so focused on the young man, I'd forgotten about Sorrelhorse 'til last night."

"What happened?"

"I don't know if you saw the news, but Sorrelhorse is at the center of a new controversy about travel vouchers and double billing the tribe. Yesterday Sorrelhorse sent his assistant over to threaten me, a man named Benally," Rudy explained. "He accused me of giving Sorrelhorse's name to the press since my wife's brother's nephew works for the TV station. I assured him I hadn't said anything, but I don't think he believed me. After Benally made threats I grabbed my rifle and threw him out of my home. Sorrelhorse is trying to quiet us, one way or the other."

There was a loud bang outside and they both jumped at the noise.

"Fire!" someone yelled from the front of the store.

Jo leaped out of her chair and grabbed the closest fire extinguisher off the wall. "Call the fire department," she told Rudy, and rushed out of her office.

"What's going on?" Sam asked, coming out of the storeroom.

"Mr. Brownhat's pickup caught fire," Leigh Ann said, running toward a second extinguisher.

Jo rushed outside and saw the billowing smoke coming from the wheel well of Rudy's pickup. She raced over, quickly pulling the safety pin on the extinguisher. She could only see a trace of flames in the tire well, but that was clearly the source.

Jo got down on her knees and began spraying the driver's side front tire and the area inside the fender, trying to find the most effective angle to extinguish the fire. The scent of gasoline was strong and the stringy black smoke from the burning tire was so pungent she started to gag. She rose to a crouching position, wondering if she might need to back off if the fire got more intense.

Detective McGraw came up behind her, holding

another extinguisher. "Don't get any closer," he warned, adding spray from his tank to her efforts.

"No, no, no! I have ceremonial items in my truck, things I can't replace! I have to get them out of there," Rudy yelled, running down the porch steps.

"Stay back, sir," Detective McGraw ordered, glancing back. "If the fuel system catches fire, there could be an explosion."

Leigh Ann stepped up and held out an extinguisher twice the size of the one McGraw had been holding. "Detective, here. This CO_2 one might do the trick."

The detective sat his tank down on the gravel, took the one she offered, and began spraying a fog of carbon dioxide up into the gap between the engine and the melting tire.

Jo continued to spray the tire, which had collapsed down onto the rim in a mass of bubbling goo. There was a whoosh and a sheet of flames shot out from behind the metal wheel. Jo jumped back, and the detective moved in, spraying the new spot with a cloud of white mist. "Brake fluid. Smell it?"

"Careful," Leigh Ann warned as the detective continued spraying underneath around the front brakes.

Jo nodded and inched around the front of the vehicle, ending up beside Leigh Ann as they both searched for any new source of flames.

Rudy, who'd been standing back, suddenly leaped into action. He raced around the tailgate of his pickup and grabbed the passenger side door handle.

"No!" Leigh Ann yelled, but Mr. Brownhat had already opened the door and was reaching inside. She raced over. "Get back! If the gas tank catches fire . . ."

"I've got to save the ceremonial items in these two boxes," he said, handing her a cardboard box, then reaching for the second. "What's in them can't be replaced!"

She took the box and hurried with him to the porch, where they placed both boxes on the floor against the wall.

"Got all the important stuff," he said, nodding. "Thanks." He joined Jo down in the parking lot and together they watched as the flames finally went out and the smoke disappeared. All that remained was the acrid scent of melted rubber. Detective McGraw stepped back. In the distance a siren was wailing.

"Not a total loss," Jo said, coming up to the porch to join Leigh Ann. "Good thing we keep a fire extinguisher in every room."

"You saved what's important," Rudy said, shaking McGraw's hand, then Jo and Leigh Ann's next.

"Unfortunately, you're not driving home in that truck, uncle," Jo observed.

"How'd the fire start?" Sam asked from the edge of the porch. The smoke had dwindled to a trickle, but there was a big puddle of nasty black tire residue on the gravel.

Detective McGraw, still holding the CO_2 extinguisher, squatted down to look underneath the engine. "This was no accident. Somebody splashed gasoline onto the tire and threw a match." He pointed toward the remains of a wooden match resting in the puddle of gooey rubber.

"Just our luck that you drive an unmarked car, Detective. A patrol cruiser might have deterred the attack," Jo said, glancing around as the fire truck approached.

"Yeah, I hear you," McGraw said, then turned around. "Do any of you have any idea who's behind this?"

Rudy looked down at the ground, then after a long beat, looked back up. "I might."

"I could add a name or two to the list," Leigh Ann muttered, "particularly if this was meant as a warning."

"As soon as the fire department is done here, we'll put up a sign stating we won't be opening until ten, lock the doors, and meet in the break room," Jo said.

Thirty minutes later they were all gathered in the break room. Leigh Ann noticed that Regina's hands were shaking as she poured coffee for everyone from the staff pot, which was located on a small filing cabinet.

Detective McGraw, seated at the head of the table, glanced around the room. "I've read the incident reports about what's been happening to you in the last few weeks. Now I want to hear any details or ideas you might have, anything that you didn't bother telling the police. Who wants to start?"

"All we have are guesses," Leigh Ann said. "Like the fire, for instance. None of us saw whoever did that to Rudy's truck, but we have our suspicions."

"Some of you have made dangerous enemies recently. Let's focus on that," McGraw said.

Jo nodded and looked at Rudy. It wasn't her place to tell her teacher's story.

Rudy took a deep breath. "This is difficult for me," he said at last. "As a *hataalii*, people confide in me, and breaking that trust in any way has consequences."

"If you have knowledge of a crime, and you don't come forward, you become an accessory," the detective warned.

Rudy spoke slowly, choosing his words. "A patient came to me with great concerns about his job and the possibility of corruption within our tribal government. I began looking into the matter on my own. I wanted to restore balance to my patient and our tribe. Eventually, I met the director of Range and Livestock Management at a wedding, but when I spoke to him, the man instantly went on the offensive. He even threatened me. I had no proof of anything, so I kept quiet, but recently he sent his assistant to remind me again."

"Uh-oh," Leigh Ann said softly.

The detective looked at her. "Is there a problem?"

Leigh Ann bit her bottom lip, aware of what she was doing. "I think I'm seeing a connection between Rudy's and Jo's problems, and mine."

"What's your connection to tribal politics?" McGraw asked.

"Personally, none, but my late husband Kurt was involved with a tribal official named Lewis Sorrelhorse, the same person Rudy spoke about. I don't know what their association was, but Sorrelhorse's name appeared in my husband's notebook, the one I found and turned in to your department."

"Do any of you have proof that Sorrelhorse is behind what's been happening?" McGraw asked.

Leigh Ann told him what Melvin had heard and how he'd identified Sorrelhorse's voice on TV.

"Was he one hundred percent certain of that ID?" the detective asked her.

"Yeah, and Melvin's hearing is nothing short of remarkable. If he says that's who he heard, you can count on it."

"I'll examine the notebook you turned in a little closer," McGraw said, then looked from face to face. "So you all agree that there's a commonality—well, a possible commonality—to all that's happened?"

"In my mind, the link is there—Sorrelhorse, the owners of Total Supply, the death of my husband, and the troubles Jo, Rudy, Melvin, and I have had," Leigh Ann said. "Those are way too many connections to believe this is all just coincidence."

Jo nodded. "I agree completely. So what now?" she asked the detective.

"This new information is a great lead, but it's not evidence. I'll have to do some more digging and get some help from the Navajo police, too." He looked around the table. "In the meantime, I strongly suggest that you all watch each other's backs. Don't get caught off guard or go out alone. Since we don't know for certain who's behind all this, trust no one outside this room and keep quiet about your suspicions."

Leigh Ann accompanied McGraw to the building's front door so she could let him out and lock up again once he left. When she came back to the break room, she found the others sitting in silence.

"The real question," she said, "is what should we do next?"

"I have to return to my medicine hogan. I

have other patients coming," Rudy said, standing.

"Uncle," Jo said, "your truck's out of commission, and you'll need to have it towed to a garage. Take my pickup for the time being." She held out her keys.

"Thanks, but that's not necessary. All I need is a ride home. My wife's cousin has a second car. I'll borrow hers until my truck's fixed," he said. "If I can use your phone, I'll call my mechanic in Shiprock and have him come to get my pickup."

"All right," Jo said. "Leigh Ann, could you take care of things here until I get back? I'll have my cell phone, so if the army contacts me—email, phone call, or whatever—let me know."

"Jo, why don't you stay here and let me give Mr. Brownhat a ride?" Leigh Ann asked. Jo seemed to be a bundle of nervous energy waiting for word on Ben. She'd be better off here in case news did come.

"Is that all right with you, uncle?" Jo asked Rudy. He nodded.

While Rudy spoke to his mechanic, Leigh Ann loaded his boxes into her Jeep. When she came back for her purse, Jo intercepted her in the hall. "Don't travel out there alone, not after all that's been happening. Take Sam with you."

Sam, who'd been standing a few feet away, cleared her throat. "I was hoping to set up the Wi-Fi today," she said.

"Then I'll go with Leigh Ann," Regina said.

"Guys, I have a better idea," Leigh Ann said. "Regina will be needed here to help Esther get the fabric display set up. So how about this—I'll take Rudy home and before I head back, I'll top and pick up Melvin, if that'll work for him. I promised I'd give him a ride later anyway so he could run some errands," she said. "I'll ask if he minds staying here until I get off work. There are some things I'd like to talk to him about."

Leigh Ann hoped to get the opportunity to talk to Melvin about her latest discovery. Last night, she'd stayed up late searching the Internet and found a report of the accident in the online edition of the Farmington newspaper. There was an image of Melvin, already a known photographer, but no photo of the drunk driver, who was listed as "Ronald Jonas."

She'd remembered hearing about the incident at the time, but that was years before she'd met Melvin, so she hadn't read any details or thought any more about it at the time. Now she'd been able to identify the man's parents—his next of kin—and had found a listing that had included their address, hopefully still current.

"Okay," Jo said. "We can open up now. During the times when we're not busy with customers, we can start moving things around here to make room for the coffee bar and to relocate some of the merchandise. If we're lucky, we can rearrange things without needing to close."

Seventeen

Leigh Ann had just arrived at Melvin's home when her cell phone rang. Seeing it was Jo, she answered quickly, hoping there'd been news about Ben, but the second Leigh Ann heard Jo's expressionless tone, that hope faded.

"Where are you right now?" Jo asked.

"At Melvin's," she said. "I'll be back at the trading post in thirty or forty minutes."

"No, don't bother. That's why I'm calling. I just got a call and the coffee bar and tables are going to be delivered within the next few hours. Once the stuff arrives, we're closing for the day, assuming the plumber can get here. I'm also checking to see who, if anyone beyond a certified plumber, needs to approve the hookup. It's new to me; Tom always handled that stuff. To complicate things even more, Sam had a problem with the router that'll provide the Wi-Fi. She's going to be putting in long hours today."

"How long will the trading post be closed?"

"Hopefully, just for the rest of today," Jo said.

After they exchanged good-byes and disconnected, Leigh Ann saw that Melvin had come to the door. She got out of the Jeep quickly and followed him inside.

"I'm curious," he said as they walked through the house. "Does it seem rude to you that I go ahead of you whenever possible?"

"No, I never even thought about it. I just figured you knew where you were going. That is, until you bump into something," she teased.

"Very funny. At least I do that less in my own home. You know, it's always been second nature to me to go first. Anglo culture has the man step back politely so the woman can go ahead of him. Navajos do the opposite, and I've got to say, it makes a lot more sense to me. If there's trouble, the man would face it first."

She smiled. "An alternate take on chivalry and manners. I've got to say, I like the Navajo way better."

"The temperature is always coolest in this room," he said, once they reached the den. "That's why I work in here."

The sculpture was on the table, covered with a black plastic bag. "I guess you don't need me to sit for you anymore?" she asked, disappointed.

"Actually, I do, but only to capture the mood, your spirit if that explains it better. When you're happy, or sad, or worried, all that comes out in your voice, and that helps me add defining touches to the figure. It's almost finished."

"Can I take just a quick little peek?" she asked. "I'm dying here!"

He laughed. "No, not yet. Soon, I promise." He

locked the turntable in place to keep it from moving, then put away the sculpture. "I've been working on this for hours, so I'm ready for a break. You came just at the right time. Would you like something cold to drink?" he asked, heading to the kitchen.

"Yeah, I'd love it. It's already hot out there today," she said.

"So tell me, what brings you over this early?" he asked, pouring iced tea into two glasses.

She told him what had happened at the trading post and about the likely connection between Sorrelhorse, Total Supply, and Kurt's shooting.

"What you know, or at least suspect, could end up putting all three men in prison. If they're guilty, you've just given them even more reason to get you out of the way for good. Do you realize that?"

"Yes, but I'm through being scared," she said. "Fear's a strange thing. It can't sustain itself. After a while, it loosens its hold on you because you're too tired to give it the energy it demands."

"I hear you, but you'll still have to stay alert, Leigh Ann."

"I will," she said, then after taking a sip of her iced tea, continued. "Now it's my turn to help you, but first, there's something I need to know. Are you prepared to look into what happened the night of your accident? I mean, really ready— no matter what answers you find?"

"Yeah, I am. I'm tired of second-guessing myself, and wondering if I could have done something more."

"Okay then," she said, telling him what she'd managed to find on the Internet about Ronald Jonas and his family.

"What do you think we could learn from his parents?"

"I'm not sure, but it's a place to start."

"All right. Let's go," he said, finishing his drink. "You asked me if I was ready to face things squarely, and I am, but what about you? While looking into this you may learn things about me you wished you'd never known. You've been curious but cautious lately, and I suspect that my uncle John has mentioned I've been moody and have had trouble sleeping."

"Maybe, but do you think I'll suddenly hate you and walk away because you're going through some issues? That's not going to happen," she answered. "I'm on your side, Melvin, just as you're on mine in dealing with Kurt's murder and the backlash from that."

"You're right, Leigh Ann. We've got each other's back, and nothing can change that."

As she looked at Melvin, she knew her future lay with him, and that she was making the right choice. When you got right down to it, you could only live life in the present, and that made moments too precious to waste. Once they were clear of the roadblocks in their way right now, she'd be free to go with her heart.

Less than a half hour later they arrived at the Waterflow home of Mr. and Mrs. Carl Jonas, the parents of Ronald Jonas, the forty-year-old who'd caused Melvin's accident.

As Leigh Ann parked beside the mailbox identified with the Jonas name, she took a deep breath, noting the carefully tended lawn and bed of roses beneath what looked like the living room window. A small green garden wheel-barrow containing pulled weeds and a leaf rake was sitting beside the narrow sidewalk. Centered along the wall was the covered porch, where two empty wicker chairs stood side by side.

The house was smaller and probably older than others along the street in this development, but was clearly well maintained. "This is it," she told Melvin. "There's a curb here, so the step down, then up might be tricky. I'll come around."

Several seconds later, as they walked up the sidewalk, Leigh Ann noticed a tall, thin man, who appeared to be in his seventies, standing inside at the window beside the curtains. No matter what they learned, she couldn't help but feel sorry for a mother and father who'd lost their child in such a sudden and violent manner. Like Melvin, they also had to live with what Ronald had done.

As they stepped up onto the porch, the man opened the front door. "Can I help you?" he called out, then stiffened the instant he saw them up close. Leigh Ann got the distinct impression that he recognized Melvin.

She could see through the small entryway into the living room, where an elderly woman in a flowered housedress was sitting on a large sofa, staring blankly at the television.

Melvin quickly introduced himself and got right to the point. "Mr. Jonas, I need to ask you some questions about the night of the accident, five years ago."

He shook his head. "There's nothing more I want to say. It's over. My son made a mistake, and he paid for his sins." Mr. Jonas turned to glance at a large photograph on the wall trimmed with black ribbon.

Leigh Ann looked at the photo of Ronald Jonas, did a double take and gasped, her stomach sinking as she realized for the first time just who he had been.

"You okay?" Melvin whispered, squeezing her hand.

She nodded, struggling to calm her racing heart. "I'm fine. Go ahead."

Melvin spoke. "I'm so sorry for your loss, sir, but that night I also lost something. My sight," he added gently.

"I'm sorry for what you've gone through, Mr.

Littlewater, but my son lost a lot more—his life. That's all the revenge you'll get."

"Sir, I'm not interested in revenge or apologies," Melvin said, his voice calm and low. "We didn't come to upset you or your wife, either. I'm just trying to put some things together, details I can't seem to remember clearly."

"Like what?" he asked hesitantly.

"Before my sight faded away, I know I saw a young girl, maybe nine or ten years old, at the site of the accident."

The man's face paled, and he took a step back. "No more! Go away. My wife and I have been through enough since that night. After our son's death my Hazel had a stroke. She's never been the same. There's nothing more I can tell you, so please leave."

"Sir, if you could just tell me one thing," Melvin pressed. "Did your son have anyone with him in his car that night?"

Mr. Jonas visually sagged, then he sucked in a shaky breath. "Get off my property right now or I'll call the police," he snapped, then slammed the door shut.

Trying to focus on what was most important right now, Leigh Ann held on to Melvin's hand as they walked back down the sidewalk. "Something's not right here," Leigh Ann said. "His reaction was way over the top. He's hiding something."

"You mean how he paused after I asked if his son had someone with him that night?"

"Yes, and he reacted visibly, too."

"What did you see?" Melvin asked.

"Anger at first, then fear," she said.

"Anger, for stirring up memories. I get that, but what is he worried about? Nothing more can hurt his son."

"I think we need to find out," she replied, helping him into the Jeep.

"How?"

"Let me think about it a moment," she said, switching on the ignition. She drove to the end of the block, then abruptly decided to go back and circle the neighborhood. Her head was still swimming in the knowledge that there was a connection between her and Ronald Jonas. Until now he'd only been the faceless drunk who'd almost killed the man she loved.

It was something she now had to make up for, and the only way she knew to do that was to help Melvin in his own quest for the truth.

"We're going back to that house?"

"No, but I think we should try to talk to a few of the Jonases' neighbors. The houses here are close together and it reminds me of one of the neighborhoods Rache and I lived in as kids. Everyone knew everyone else's business. I have a feeling it's the same here."

She looked around and saw that a home two

doors down from the Jonas residence had a sign in its front yard, announcing a neighborhood association meeting to be held there later that night.

"This is a good bet," she said, explaining her discovery to Melvin as she pulled up to the curb. "People involved in neighborhood watches usually know what's going on with their neighbors."

They climbed out of the Jeep and walked up the sidewalk together, as before. Leigh Ann knocked on the door and placed her hand over Melvin's where it rested on her arm. Never before had the urge to hang on to him been so strong.

An attractive redheaded woman in her early thirties answered the door. Leigh Ann introduced herself and Melvin, then added, "Can we talk to you a minute about Ronald Jonas?"

The woman nodded and gave her name as Mrs. Naomi Ortega. "Come in," she said, ushering them into her living room. Leigh Ann and Melvin took seats on the couch and Mrs. Ortega made herself comfortable in a nearby chair.

"Ronald's accident happened five years ago; why is it important now?" she asked in a gentle voice, looking at Leigh Ann, then Melvin.

Melvin said, "What happened to me can't be undone, but I need closure. I believe someone else was there at the accident site that night, a young girl."

"I remember hearing about that possibility back then. If I recall, the police searched the entire area, especially downstream along the canal. They never found evidence that suggested any-one else was present or had witnessed the accident. There were tracks everywhere, of course. Dozens of people stopped after the accident," Mrs. Ortega said. "Maybe you were confused because of your injuries?"

Leigh Ann could tell that she meant no disrespect, and from Melvin's calm response, she sus-pected that he felt the same. "It's true that no one reported a missing child, but the girl might have been a runaway from out of the area," he said.

Mrs. Ortega took a deep breath. "This is still a touchy subject around here. The fact is, Ronald Jonas was a registered pedophile. When the courts allowed him to move in with his parents, a few of the men from our neighborhood asso-ciation got together and paid the Jonas family a visit. Carl and Hazel insisted that their son was innocent and had been wrongly convicted, but no one was buying that. Ronnie was told plainly that if any neighborhood kids turned up missing or were harmed in any way, people would go looking for him first."

"Did Ronnie stay out of trouble after that?"

Leigh Ann asked. Her sympathy for the man's death had never been great, but now it was even less so.

The woman shook her head. "About six months afterwards, some of the kids reported a guy hanging around the elementary school a few blocks down. Ronnie had pulled up beside two girls walking home and asked them if they needed a ride. My stepdaughter was one of those girls, and once her dad realized who Leta was talking about, he and some other men paid Ronald a visit."

"What happened?" Leigh Ann asked.

"Ronald claimed that he'd only offered to give Leta a ride home because he knew she lived almost next door, but I was told that not even his parents bought that excuse. The men told Ronald that someone would be watching him, and if anything like that happened again, he'd face neighborhood justice."

"What about your stepdaughter?" Melvin asked.

"Leta's in high school now, living with her mother, and doing just fine. I heard of a second incident involving Ronald sometime later, but it wasn't in our neighborhood."

"What happened?" Leigh Ann asked.

"Ronald got drunk on Halloween and tried to get a ten-year-old into his car. Her mother was following the trick-or-treaters and managed to stop her daughter in time. The girl's father and two of his friends beat the hell out of Ronald a few days later. Ronald never reported it to the police and hid out in his parents' house for weeks. Next I heard he was planning to move out. Then he got into that accident with you," she said, looking at Melvin.

"Did any other kids go missing around that time?" Melvin asked.

"No. That's the first thing our neighborhood watch team looked into. I'm sure the police, who knew Ronald's background, double checked everything, too."

"Maybe so," Melvin answered, sounding unconvinced.

"We really appreciate your help," Leigh Ann said, standing. Melvin also got to his feet.

"No problem. I just didn't want you to go up and down the street trying to push for answers. There's still a lot of ill will about Ronald around here. People resent the fact that the Jonas couple didn't keep Ronald on a shorter leash from day one."

"Odd that the parents didn't move out afterwards," Leigh Ann said. "You'd think they'd want to get away from the memories, the accusations, and all."

"After Mrs. Jonas's stroke, they just kept to themselves," Mrs. Ortega said, showing them out.

As they walked back to Leigh Ann's Jeep, she reluctantly brought up the question now on her mind. "Is it at all possible that you hallucinated? Maybe you saw an angel?"

"That's your Christian upbringing. I'm not of your faith so I very much doubt I'd see an angel. I also have no reason to believe I was hallucinating, but I just don't know," he said. "What I remember of that night are mostly flashes of images."

"There's one more thing we can do. Sam knows all kinds of ways to search on the Internet. I mean well, but half the time I just get lost or don't use the right key words. Let's ask her to look into it and let us know if she finds any mention of a missing girl in the Four Corners area on or around that date."

"Good idea. I'll be happy to pay her for her time," Melvin said with a nod as he climbed into the Jeep. "For now, what do you say we go home and I get some more work done on that sculpture? Or do you want to talk about your strange reaction when we met Mr. Jonas? I heard you gasp, like you were startled by something. I felt you shaking."

"It was such an emotional situation, being there. I'm fine now," she lied, climbing behind the wheel. She'd eventually have to talk to Melvin about what she'd discovered from that photo, but that could change everything.

Right now, she'd rather have his company, no matter what the price might be later on.

"Are you sure about that?" he asked as she started the engine. "Your voice sounds . . . strained."

"No, I'm okay. I'm just anxious for you to finish your project," she said, pulling out into the street. A distraction like this was certainly the best way right now to clear her head until she could reevaluate her situation. "So tell me, is the figure coming out the way you want?"

"Yeah, it's almost done. The work has been intense, though, and that kind of focus comes at a price. By giving it everything, I've lost my objectivity—it's now personal. Although my goal was for each person to see a part of themselves in the sculpture, there's no guarantee that'll happen," he said. "I took a risk. Eventually I'll find out if I've succeeded or failed."

"Do you regret having done it?"

"Not at all. I've stayed in my comfort zone for too long. It was time for *Darkness Girl* to be born."

"*Darkness Girl* . . . ," she said slowly, savoring it. "I like the name you gave her. What made you choose something like that?"

"She's one of the intermediaries *hataaliis* include in our sacred sand paintings from time to time, and she fits in with the duality of this sculpture. The clay is two-toned, light and dark. In many ways she symbolizes the sighted world

323

and mine, though the sighted will be the ones to judge it.

"I have to wait and see if my vision has the power to touch them, or if they'll just see this piece as an okay attempt at human form by an animal sculptor." His voice turned bitter for a moment. "Human beings like pigeonholing everything and that's how people see me as an artist. I want to prove that I'm capable of much more, but a closed mind is one of the hardest obstacles to overcome."

"If you think it's good, that's all that should really matter. You shouldn't measure its worth based on another person's opinion," she said.

"As true as that may be, it doesn't work that way in the arts. We need the world's reaction to be favorable if we hope to survive. God protect us from the critics."

"The more you care—about anything—the more vulnerable you become. Rejection, no matter what form it takes, cuts deeply."

"Is that part of the reason you work so hard and put in such long hours at the trading post? Are you afraid it'll somehow be taken from you?"

"Partly, yes, but it's more than that," she answered. "I want to do a fabulous job and show Jo that her faith in me is justified. She gave me my chance, and all things considered, I get far more out of my job there than anyone realizes.

The way everyone cares about each other fills an empty spot inside me. I don't make a fortune, but I'm valued."

"So it's perfect for you?"

"I'd like more responsibility, and maybe the chance to become a full-time buyer, but I'm exactly where I need to be, particularly right now."

"Because you'll have friends around you while you settle your past?"

She nodded. "Detective McGraw is finally looking in the right direction, but I plan to go to Total Supply tomorrow during my lunch hour and talk to Wayne. Maybe I can prod him into saying or doing something that'll give me some more answers. He's the weakest link."

"You shouldn't go alone," Melvin said.

"I'll be okay. It'll be broad daylight and during business hours." *And I'll have the .38 in my purse,* she thought.

"Will you call me after you leave there?"

"Sure." A special warmth spread through her. It was nice to know that Melvin really cared, that the attraction between them wasn't just hormones and wishes. She could count on one hand the number of people who'd ever worried about her. The thought of losing him over something she'd done five years ago suddenly chilled her heart, and she had to calm herself a moment before she could speak again. "As soon as I'm done, I'll get in touch and let you know what happened."

Eighteen

The next morning Leigh Ann arrived at the trading post early, passing new signs that announced the café. As she was climbing out of her Jeep, she saw Jo walking over from the house in the adjoining lot. The somber expression on Jo's face told her there'd been no news about Ben. Leigh Ann's heart fell but she managed a smile. "Good morning. How are the plans for the coffee bar going?"

"The hookup and coffee bar installation took barely two hours, and while that was going on the staff and I were able to get everything else relocated and set up. Larry, the plumber, said we didn't need a county inspection and that our electrical hookups were already up to code."

"So the signs I saw outside are for real?"

"Yeah, we're good to go. Sam was also able to straighten out the Internet issues and test it out. We should be fully operational today. We actually reopened from five to six last night to serve some of our regular customers who'd stopped by. We even learned how to use the espresso machine. I've got to say, I liked the reactions we got from those we served."

"What did you have to brew?" Leigh Ann

asked, surprised. "Last I heard Esther was still researching various blends."

"We had some espresso, which was okay, but it was Sam who made our day. She mixed a little bit of milk, coffee, and caramel flavoring and topped it with a huge serving of whipped cream. She called it The Outpost Blast. One customer liked it so much she brought extras to take to her evening shift coworkers."

"What kind of coffee did Sam use? Our breakroom brew?"

"No, it was one that Esther had on her short list—that Santa Fe blend with piñon. It was too strong just for black coffee, but once you blended in the milk and cream, it was perfect."

"That's great! And you said the Wi-Fi works?" Leigh Ann asked as they climbed the steps leading up to the back door.

Jo smiled. "Perfectly. You can access the Internet from every spot inside the trading post—even the front porch and loading dock. Sam stayed late, playing with it, and even did some research for you and Melvin off the books. How's that going for you, anyway?"

Leigh Ann followed Jo inside to the office area and updated her on their search for the mysterious young girl from Melvin's accident.

"How sure are you that the girl was real if nobody else saw her?"

"Melvin's convinced of it," Leigh Ann replied.

Once inside the main room, Leigh Ann looked around and whistled low. "Wow, adding the bar and tables and repositioning some of the merchandise changes the entire feel of the place," she said. "I love that touch, too," she said, pointing to the chalkboard listing the coffees available.

"I honestly wasn't sure how our regulars would react," Jo said, "but from the tiny sample last night, so far, so good. I think we might get more passing tourists dropping by, too, though only time will tell. There were several who came in yesterday during our brief reopening and two were really captivated by Melvin's display. One wants to commission a horse sculpture, the other a mountain lion."

"That's great. Do you think they'll be in the area long enough to come back and cut a deal?" Leigh Ann asked, knowing Melvin would be pleased.

"Yes, they left their cell phone numbers so they could call and confirm sometime today. They're willing to meet his terms, half up front and the other half upon delivery. I quoted them Melvin's highest figure, the price he thought we'd never get. They never even blinked! Both men are sales reps on vacation, but they work this area. They'll be coming back in another four weeks and could pick up the sculptures if Melvin agrees and the pieces are ready. I've already got their credit card numbers and will run them through once Melvin gives me the okay."

"I'll talk to him. He told us before that he was willing to work on more than one thing at a time if the projects weren't overly large or complex."

"Let me know," Jo said.

Leigh Ann returned to the break room, planning to make a fresh pot of coffee—their usual blend. After all, the new drinks weren't free for staff, so she expected her coworkers would favor the familiar coffee.

As she plugged in the pot and pushed the brew button, Sam came in.

Leigh Ann smiled. "You're here early."

"I had second thoughts and decided to set up a separate router for the coffee bar Wi-Fi. That'll make our regular network more secure. Jo doesn't pay me by the hour, I'm a contract worker, like you, so she doesn't mind if I switch my time around."

"I heard you fixed some mean coffee yesterday."

Sam smiled. "It's a recipe I came up with for myself months ago. I couldn't afford to buy the four-dollar brews at the fancy coffee shop, so I created something I thought was even better."

"Jo said that you did some research for Melvin and me last night," Leigh Ann mentioned. "Did you find out if any girls the right age were reported missing around the time of Melvin's accident?"

"I used several search engines, but there were no Amber Alerts issued or reports of runaways that coincided or were close to the date of Melvin's accident," Sam said. She hesitantly added, "I did find one thing. . . ."

"What?" Leigh Ann asked. Seeing the worried look on Sam's face, she added, "You can tell me anything. Don't feel you have to hold back."

"It's a detail about Melvin's first accident. I'd gone back quite a ways before I stumbled on it, and you probably already know about this, but . . ."

"*First* accident? You've lost me," Leigh Ann said.

"When Melvin was fifteen, he and his family were in a bad car accident," Sam said, then paused as Jo came into the room. When both Leigh Ann and Jo nodded, the younger woman continued. "According to the reports, Melvin's dad was driving. It was pitch black outside, and as the car rounded a curve they came across two deer crossing the highway. His father swerved instinctively, lost control, and rolled the car. It went through a fence before it came to a stop," Sam said. "His parents both survived, though they were badly injured. Melvin only had a few cuts and bruises, but his twin sister, who'd been sitting right beside him, was impaled by one of the metal fence posts. She died."

Leigh Ann stared at her in horror. "Melvin never said a word to me about any of this," she managed at last. "Are you sure you've got the right family?"

"I found it in the *Diné Times*, the reservation newspaper. Melvin's last name showed up in his sister's obituary."

"I had no idea," Leigh Ann said, sitting down, knowing that this tragedy had probably made his recent accident just that much more difficult to handle.

"Maybe Melvin just doesn't want to talk about the dead," Sam said, "especially when it's someone who was that close."

Jo nodded. "That's a valid reason, but this could go beyond not wanting to call his sister's *chindi*. This kind of incident opens itself to some other very bad interpretations."

Sam looked at Jo. "Yeah, I've heard about that. It's the main reason I wasn't sure I should even bring it up."

"Guys, I need to know," Leigh Ann said. "What's the problem?"

Sam excused herself, then Jo asked Leigh Ann to follow her into her office. After she closed the door, both women sat down. "Skinwalkers, Navajo witches, are very different from the modern Wiccan witches you have probably heard of."

Leigh Ann nodded and Jo went on. "Skinwalkers are feared and despised. One of the ways a Navajo skinwalker is said to gain his powers is by taking the life of a relative."

"But it was clearly an accident, and Melvin wasn't even driving," Leigh Ann said.

"What might have fueled some whispers among traditional Navajos was the fact that Melvin came through almost unscathed."

"He got lucky," Leigh Ann said defensively.

"Some beliefs are hard to brush aside," Jo said softly.

Leigh Ann nodded and swallowed hard. "He never told me." She shouldn't have been disappointed, she already knew he was a man of secrets, but her heart felt as heavy as a rock.

"Sometimes things are just too painful to talk about, Leigh Ann. Don't assume that a lack of trust is the reason he never spoke about it," Jo said, as if reading her mind.

Leigh Ann didn't answer. Melvin and she were allies, but ones with pasts shrouded in long shadows. He was heavily burdened with guilt and other issues, and now, as of yesterday, she had a new secret that could tear them apart. Once he knew that secret, would Melvin be able to live with it, or would it break them apart for good?

The sandwich sign announcing the coffee bar might have done the trick, since Leigh Ann noticed an increase in walk-in traffic throughout the morning. Although several people came in just for coffee or an espresso, a good percentage made an additional purchase. Three people asked about Melvin's sculptures and took one of the fliers Samantha had printed up.

It was a little past eleven when Jo approached Leigh Ann, who was working the front register. "The next time you talk to Melvin, find out how he feels about letting the trading post place a regular monthly order for say, two small sculptures—he picks the subject. We buy them outright and resell them here. He'd have a certain amount of money coming in regularly, instead of having to wait for a commission, and I think we can easily sell two pieces a month based on recent history."

"I'll ask," Leigh Ann said. "It's time for my lunch. I've got the early time slot today."

"Go. I'll take over here."

Leigh Ann's cell phone rang as she headed for her Jeep, intent on driving to Total Supply. Recognizing Melvin's ring tone, she fished it out of her pocket and answered, promising herself she wouldn't ask him about that first accident. "Hi, Melvin."

"Are you on your way to Total Supply?" he asked.

"I'm just leaving the trading post now."

"You sound tense," he said.

She muttered a soft curse. Her mood had given her away. "I'm okay, just thinking ahead."

"Be careful what you say," he said. "Are you sure it wouldn't be better if I came along?"

"No, unless I'm alone, Wayne will tense up and I won't learn anything. I'm going to appeal to him from the standpoint of someone who knows what it's like to get swept into something and suddenly find you're in way over your head."

He didn't answer right away. "That might work," he said at last. "But I still wish you'd take someone as backup. Isn't Ambrose there? He's staying with Jo, right?"

"Don't worry, I can handle this. I know what I'm doing," she said, trying to sound confident.

"It's hard to predict what others will do, Leigh Ann, even the ones we know best."

He couldn't possibly know why she'd reacted like she did after seeing Ronald Jonas's photo, but what if he suspected she knew about his twin's death? He'd given Sam permission to dig into his past. Maybe he hoped it would all come out. Either way, she'd promised herself she wouldn't bring it up. She'd wait for him to broach the subject first.

"I'll call you later, okay?" she said.

As she placed the phone back inside her shirt pocket, her thoughts remained on Melvin. Sooner or later, she'd have to tell him about her newly discovered connection with Ronald Jonas, and the role she'd played in the accident that had claimed his sight. He'd spoken of the price attached to failure, and how vulnerable that fear could make you feel. She understood that now, but to do the right thing, she'd have to risk it all.

Somewhere along the way, she'd fallen in love with him, hard, which meant she couldn't let any secrets form a wall between them. She knew from her own marriage how deception and betrayal could destroy lives.

Leigh Ann saw Pierre walking through the Total Supply back lot as she pulled up. She hung back, hoping he was heading for his vehicle. Catching Wayne alone would give her a slight advantage. He was never as guarded when Pierre wasn't there. Leigh Ann parked behind a large, extended cab truck and watched Pierre climb into a new-looking silver SUV. Moments later, he drove out of the parking area, heading east toward Farmington.

She breathed a sigh of relief. So far, luck was on her side. She went inside, glanced around, and through a large glass partition saw Wayne at his desk. There was only one salesperson on the floor and he was with a customer, looking at some metal fence hardware. Leigh Ann went around the counter and straight to Wayne's office.

He looked up when she knocked and gave her

a tentative smile. "Hi, Leigh Ann. You're here about the squirrel trap? I'm afraid the one that arrived turned out to be damaged. We didn't notice until you'd already been contacted. I'm sorry for the delay. I ordered a replacement and we should have it in a few more days. I'll call you when it comes in, okay?"

"Thanks," Leigh Ann said. "Do you have a moment? I need to talk to you about Kurt."

His expression went from harried to somber and he cleared his throat. "I see," he managed, his voice sounding strained. "Have a seat. Do you want something to drink?" he asked, clearing his throat again while going to a small fridge in the corner. "Water? Soda?"

"No, I'm good," Leigh Ann said. She waited for him to sit down again, noting that he'd looked around the room first, as if checking to see who might be listening. "Wayne, I know what's going on. Navajo officials are being paid kickbacks for making sure tribal contracts are awarded to Total Supply. I have reason to believe this has been going on for some time, and that Kurt took part, too."

"What? Where did you get a wild story like that?" he asked, glancing toward the clerk tending to the customer.

His tone conveyed fear, not surprise. Wayne was a bad actor, which spurred her to press on.

"Kurt kept a list of tribal officials, probably

336

those who were involved, or else potential targets. Lewis Sorrelhorse's name was at the top. I've got a reliable witness who overheard Sorrelhorse talking to someone from Total Supply about how much a new contract might be worth."

Wayne turned pale.

"That someone was you, Wayne. Remember, you even honked your horn and waved to me when we were both leaving the tribal offices."

"Leigh Ann, you have no idea what you're getting into," he whispered. "Walk away from this. It has nothing to do with you."

"It has everything to do with me. The cops think *I* had something to do with Kurt's death, that I was his partner in crime. I'm innocent and I'm going to do whatever it takes to prove it."

"Leigh Ann, go back to work, or go home. So far you've been lucky, but don't keep pushing. Actions have consequences."

"I'm not backing off. Kurt's murder and the kickbacks are connected and I'm going to find out how."

Hearing Pierre's voice outside, Wayne tensed up even more. "I can't talk to you about this," he said, almost in desperation.

"Then maybe I should ask Pierre," she said, wishing he'd stayed away longer. She was sure Wayne would have told her more if given the time.

"Listen to me good, Leigh Ann. Pierre's

convinced that you've got the money Kurt stole from us and, to him, you're already a liability. Stop causing trouble and lay low. That's your only chance. I can't protect you any longer."

Hearing the door opening up front, Wayne changed the subject instantly. "The replacement trap is being shipped priority, and I'll check to make sure it's in good working condition this time before we give you a call."

"Hey, you two," Pierre greeted, coming into the office, holding what looked like a stack of mail in his hand. "What's going on?"

"Leigh Ann dropped by to check on that squirrel trap, the one we had to reorder."

Someone called Pierre's name, and he turned to see a man in the back holding a clipboard. Pierre waved. "That's Ralph from the feedlot. I've got to go again. Good to see you, Leigh Ann."

As Pierre walked off, Leigh Ann met Wayne's gaze. "Wayne, you're a good man. After Kurt passed away you made sure I was handling it. You even helped me with the life insurance forms and made me a good offer on Kurt's share of the business. There's no way I'm going to believe you're a willing part of whatever's going on over here. I think that you're caught up in something that's spinning out of control. Help me set things right. Don't let Pierre pull you down with him."

"Leigh Ann, there are some powerful people involved, the kind who are very bad enemies."

"To stop the ones who are already coming after me, I need to know what's going on. This isn't about calling the police—this is about staying alive. Help me, please?"

Wayne stared at his desk, lost in thought. "Okay," he finally responded, resignation in his tone. "We should talk, but not here." He looked at a big wall clock. "Meet me in twenty minutes over by the old red barn off of Orchard Road, the one with the roof that's caving in. It's south of the highway, this side of Waterflow."

"Just past the casino billboard?"

"Yeah, that one. Park beside the barn and I'll meet you there on my lunch break. And don't tell anyone where you're going."

Leigh Ann gave Pierre—who was outside next to a truckload of water troughs—a cheery wave as she crossed the parking lot. By the time she got into the Jeep, her hands were shaking. She hugged her purse close, the weight of the .38 revolver making her feel less vulnerable. She was close to finding answers, she could feel it, but danger was also closing in fast.

She drove for a few minutes before she pulled off the highway to call Melvin. She quickly filled him in on what had happened. "I'm on my way to meet Wayne now."

"I don't like this, Leigh Ann. It has a bad smell."

"No, I understand Wayne. He's just scared. Talking to me for more than a minute or two would have flagged Pierre for sure."

"Wayne's hip deep in this and you know it. I'm betting he was the man who cleared out Kurt's storage locker."

"Wayne's involved, no doubt about that, but I also think he'd like to find a way out."

"And you're willing to bet your life on that? At least call your cousin Dale."

"He's turned everything over to McGraw, and the police still don't trust me, not completely anyway. I have to see this through. This might be my only chance to uncover the truth."

"I guess I'll see you when you get back to the trading post. You can tell me about it then," Melvin said.

"You're at The Outpost now?"

"Yeah. I finished the sculpture and John gave me a ride in. Jo called to talk business but it was easier to cover everything face-to-face. It also allowed me to sign my new agreement with The Outpost immediately."

"All right then. I shouldn't be long. See you later."

"Be very careful."

Less than ten minutes later she pulled up by the barn. Wayne was nowhere in sight, but he'd said to give him twenty minutes. She sat back to wait, making sure her phone was nestled safely in her shirt pocket, set to record.

Before long, Wayne's red pickup came up the dirt road. Once he parked in the shade next to Leigh Ann's Jeep, she climbed out and walked up to his open driver's side window, purse in hand, the .38 within reach, if necessary. Her phone was recording now.

"All right, Wayne. I'm here. Now what's going on?"

"You have no idea what you're stirring up, Leigh Ann," he blurted out in anger. "Kurt set up a phony vendor, Frank Jones, and was bleeding our company. When Pierre noticed there was no inventory from Jones, he gave the vendor a call and discovered that the number was out of service. An Internet aerial map search for the listed business address showed a vacant lot.

"Kurt was handling the account exclusively, sending company checks to a mail service address. It didn't take a genius to figure out what was going on," Wayne added bitterly.

"Did Pierre confront Kurt?" she asked.

"Not at first." Wayne took a nervous look down the highway in both directions, then climbed out of the pickup and stood with her beside the Jeep, arms across his chest. "He staked out the UPS store and saw Kurt picking up the checks. Pierre had him then, but he and I talked about it and decided to confront Kurt during our hunting trip. A private meeting on neutral ground sounded like a good idea. All we were

341

planning to do was force Kurt to pay back the money, but things got crazy."

"What happened?" Leigh Ann asked, grateful for having brought the revolver with her. If Wayne admitted to murder, she'd become an instant loose end and she doubted he'd let her just walk away. Maybe she should have followed Melvin's advice after all and brought backup.

"Listen to me, Leigh Ann," he whispered harshly, not answering her question. "Bad things are going to keep happening to you and your friends, including that blind guy, unless you come up with the money Kurt stole. Then you need to back off. Sell your house. Do whatever it takes. Pierre's patience has run out."

"Pierre and Sorrelhorse were the ones who attacked Melvin and me a few nights ago, right?"

He started nodding, caught himself, then put his shaking hands into his pants pockets. "I've already said too much. I won't hurt you, but I can't speak for Pierre or the tribal people who've been taking money under the table. Pierre's the one who shot Kurt with the rifle he swiped from your house."

"But you were the one who cleaned out Kurt's storage compartment, aren't you? I don't have the missing money, so tell me. Did you decide to keep it for yourself and tell Pierre it wasn't there?"

He shook his head and took a quick look back down the road. "No way."

"Okay, I believe you, but even if you didn't keep the money, that possibility is bound to occur to Pierre, too, if it hasn't already. What if he decides that you and Kurt were working together and ripped him off?"

"He knows I wouldn't do that. You're the one who's in danger. Get the money fast, any way you can. I'll try to stall Pierre a little longer. I think he'll back off if he knows you're not going to be a problem. He—"

Suddenly there was a thump, and Wayne's chest erupted in an explosion of blood. He gasped as she heard a gun go off somewhere down the road.

"Wayne!" A bullet hole appeared in the Jeep and a second gunshot blast followed, a split second behind the impact. She dove to the ground, hiding behind the tire and trying to fight the choking terror that gripped her as she looked down the road for the shooter. Remembering the .38, she reached into her purse and brought it out, trying to figure out where to aim.

Wayne slowly sagged to his knees and fell to the ground. Leigh Ann was splashed with something wet and warm—his blood, she realized with a shock. Trying not to scream, she rolled to her left, scrambling to get farther under the Jeep.

On her back now, she switched the pistol from her right hand to the left and groped for the cell phone in her pocket. She needed to call for help, not record the sounds of her own death.

A horn began blaring frantically from the direction of the highway. A heartbeat later, the whine of a bullet passed overheard, coming from the same direction. Looking, she saw a bright red pickup racing toward the barn. Ambrose John was at the wheel and he had one hand out the driver's side window. Leigh Ann heard another bang and realized he was shooting at someone, the person who'd shot Wayne.

The gunfire continued from both directions as Leigh Ann scrunched down, trying to be as small as possible. After three futile attempts, she managed to quit shaking enough to stop the recording and call 911.

Nineteen

Detective McGraw walked over from his vehicle, notebook in hand, and joined Leigh Ann as the crime scene team continued to search the area. "We've located the sniper's position and are gathering evidence there. According to Mr. John, who broke up the attack, the shooter was using his vehicle door as a rest for a rifle. The footprints and tire tracks back that up, and we have a description of the vehicle, a new-looking silver SUV. But there are still things we need to know."

"I've told you everything I can remember about what happened," she said. "You've also got the recording I made of my conversation with Wayne Hurley. You copied it to your own phone, correct?"

"Yes, and thanks. However, we'll need actual physical evidence and witness testimony in order to make an arrest," McGraw said. "What you've gotten by going all cowboy on us is a lot of hearsay evidence."

"But you also have another murder victim, plus a recording that should point you directly to his killer. In addition to that, the vehicle Ambrose saw is probably the SUV owned by Pierre Boone. If I'd brought a witness or the police along to this meeting, you think Wayne would have said anything besides hi and good-bye?"

"It was still a risky thing to do, and you could have ended up dead, along with your friends."

"I doubt that," Ambrose said, coming up. "I was closing in. If he hadn't jumped into his SUV and raced away, I would have taken him out."

"There's a good chance that you wounded him," McGraw said. "We found drops of blood on the ground beside the shell casings from the sniper's rifle."

"He was hunched over, sighting down the barrel, so I didn't have a good sight picture," Ambrose said with no particular inflection in his voice. "Still, I'm guessing there's a hole or two in that door."

"Copy that. You have a concealed carry permit, and this Colt .45 is your registered weapon. You might want to call the department tomorrow and see when they'll be able to release it to you."

Ambrose nodded.

"If we're free to go, I have to get back to work," Leigh Ann said.

McGraw nodded. "There's a bullet hole in your Jeep, so you'll have to leave it behind for now. We'll need to process it for evidence, too."

"How long before I get it back? It's my only transportation."

"It shouldn't be long, maybe by the end of today if you're lucky."

• • •

Leigh Ann rode back with Ambrose and Melvin. "Thanks for checking up on me, guys, and for driving away that gunman, Ambrose," she said, her purse on her lap. "You saved my life."

"I understand why you felt you had to do this," Melvin said, "but there's a reason why even cops take backup."

"I didn't expect anyone to start shooting," she said.

"Precisely my point," Melvin answered.

Ambrose, who'd been quiet for a while, finally spoke. "I get you, Leigh Ann. I know exactly why you came alone. Your back was against the wall and you needed to prove something to yourself, no matter what anyone else thought."

She looked over at him, the raw undertone in his words immediately capturing her attention.

"Back in high school, I was the weird gay guy, the pussy no one except Ben would hang out with. After graduation Ben left for the army and got his shit together, but I was still at loose ends. At the time, the military wasn't an option for me.

"Around then, my uncle got diagnosed with cancer and asked me to help him finish a few pieces of Navajo jewelry he'd presold."

"So that's how you got started!" Leigh Ann said.

"I learned all I could from him, but for a long time I resisted making my own pieces. I'd just

347

worked on his designs. Eventually, my uncle passed on and left his tools and supplies to me—along with a letter. In it, he said he understood I was tired of being judged, but that for the first time I was being given an even chance. My pieces would be valued on their own merit. The only question that remained was whether or not I had the balls to go for it."

"You really didn't know how good your own designs were?" she asked, surprised.

"No, I was pretty clueless. All of my life I'd been the guy who didn't fit in anywhere. For all I knew, people would see my designs the same way. That's why I went to Santa Fe to sell my pieces instead of Gallup or Farmington. I figured if I failed, it was far enough away I wouldn't have to hear about it constantly, and it wouldn't matter as much." He smiled. "Of course, I sold everything the first day, even with all the competition."

"Way to go!" Melvin said.

Ambrose smiled at Leigh Ann. "Meeting Wayne wasn't just about clearing your name, was it, Leigh Ann?"

She gave him a thin smile. "No, it wasn't," she admitted.

Leigh Ann reached for Melvin's hand. "Melvin, you've been there for me every step of the way, and I appreciate it, but I needed to face my enemies without hiding behind someone else. I had to prove that my fears couldn't control me," she added. "Wayne Hurley was the one who paid the price."

"If you saw him as the weak link, you can bet Pierre did too," Ambrose said. "He followed Wayne today because he didn't trust him. Wayne's days were already numbered."

"Maybe so," she admitted. "But I'll never go solo like this again. Things can go wrong in the blink of an eye."

Leigh Ann was at the back register talking to a customer who was purchasing groceries when her cousin Dale walked in wearing his sheriff's department uniform: a khaki shirt and green trousers with the usual handgun and cuffs. Surprised, she smiled and waved at him. "Be with you in a minute."

Dale waited until Leigh Ann was finished, then joined her. "Can we talk in private?"

Jo, who'd seen Dale enter the trading post, caught Leigh Ann's attention and nodded toward the back. "Take my office."

Leigh Ann led the way down the short hall and waved him to one of the chairs as she leaned back against Jo's desk. "I wasn't expecting to see you, cuz. Are you working with McGraw now?"

"Not officially," he said. "I came because I wanted to make damned sure you never pull another stunt like the one you did today. I know you want to clear your name, but getting zipped up in a body bag isn't going to help you much."

She forced herself not to cringe. "Have they talked to Pierre Boone yet?"

"No. According to a clerk at Total Supply, Boone said he had to catch up to Wayne so he could sign some papers, then left. He never came back and he's turned off his cell phone. We're attempting to locate him now. If anything turns up, I'll let you know. Until then, be very careful and avoid being alone."

"What about Sorrelhorse? How's he involved?"

"Tribal police detectives are talking to him, but until some concrete evidence pops up, law enforcement is still just fishing."

"Melvin's sure it was him," she said.

"A voice ID alone doesn't hold up well in court, Leigh Ann."

"He's blind, but incredibly attuned to his surroundings. His testimony is reliable."

"I have no reason to question his honesty, but he's been wrong before. I read some of the old accident reports, even going back to the childhood auto accident when his sister was killed. After the second wreck, years later, he reported having seen a young girl on the scene. No one was ever found, and there were too many footprints to prove one way or the other. The shrinks think he may have just gotten the two incidents confused, the result of confusion and head trauma. Besides, we need more than what he heard. Voices are easy to mimic, and we deal in facts."

Leigh Ann walked Dale to the door. As they stepped out onto the porch, his cell phone rang. Dale looked at the display. "Tribal police, I've got to take this. Hang on a second, Leigh Ann."

She nodded, then turned away to give him some privacy. The call didn't take long, and when she turned to face him, he was smiling.

"Some good news," he said. "The tribal police have arrested Sorrelhorse. The DNA taken from the blood on the tire iron that Melvin used to knock away the attacker's knife has been tracked back to Sorrelhorse's assistant, a man named Benally. Benally asked for a deal with the DA and turned his boss in for taking bribes and kickbacks. According to Benally, Sorrelhorse reviewed every contract offer that came in and was tipping off Total Supply so they could undercut everyone else."

"Finally!" she said smiling. "That's great."

"There's more: Benally confessed to throwing the paint and planting some witchcraft objects at the trading post. He also claimed that Sorrelhorse was the one who poisoned Rudy Brownhat," Dale added.

"I'm guessing Pierre was one of the guys with the baseball bats and knives," she said.

"I agree, which means you've still got to watch your back, Leigh Ann. We've got hard evidence now, but this is far from over," Dale warned.

When she went back inside, Melvin came in to join her. "I was in the break room, but you must have left the office door open because I heard most of your conversation, including what your cousin told you about my twin sister. How did you find out about her?"

"When Sam did her Internet search to see if any girls had been reported missing around the time of your accident, she found an old newspaper account of what happened to your family. I was waiting for you to tell me when the time was right."

He nodded slowly. "I took my sister's death very hard. She and I were as opposite as two people could be, but we were still as close as, well, twins. What made things even worse were the rumors that started circulating about me," he said.

"Melvin, I'm so sorry," she said, taking his hand gently with both of hers.

"Leigh Ann, there's one thing you've got to believe," he said, his fingers intertwining with hers. "I know what the psychiatrist concluded, but the girl I saw the night Ronald Jonas ran me off the road wasn't my imagined sister. Her age, size, and weight were different. My sister was fifteen when she died. The girl I saw was a lot younger."

"Do you remember anything specific that might help us find her?"

Melvin smiled. "You believe me."

"Yes, I do."

He pulled her into his arms. "Thank you."

She sighed, enjoying that moment of closeness. His chest felt hard, yet welcoming, and his arms were strong but gentle. Melvin was a maze of contradictions, but she was hopelessly in love with him. He was special in every way. A blind artist who saw with his soul, he could create a masterpiece with his hands, or make her melt with a fleeting touch. He could be gentle when she needed it, or passionate and rough. He could take control or relinquish it with equal ease.

"I love you, Leigh Ann, and my love doesn't come with demands, nor does it require anything from you in return. It just is."

She placed her fingertips over his mouth. "It's because I love you, too, that I won't hold you to this. Remember that."

"Leigh Ann, I know you have something you're keeping from me, and that it has to do with our visit with the Jonas family. Your reaction when we were with the father gave yourself away. Trust me and tell me what it is. Let's work through this together."

"I *will* tell you, but I'm not ready yet," she said, stepping back.

"You want to look at the sculpture I've finished. When you do, you'll be able to see yourself as I see you. Will you honor the balance and tell me then?" he asked.

She swallowed hard. "All right."

"You don't have to be afraid," he said, his voice steady and sure.

He was wrong. Some things were impossible to forgive. "For now, let's keep looking for the little girl you saw. Are you okay with that?"

"You bet."

Leigh Ann glanced back one more time. Regina was manning the cash register and Esther was serving someone at the coffee bar, so no help was needed out front. "Let's go into the break room for a few minutes, have something cold to drink, and work on this."

"All right," he said, reaching out and letting her take his hand.

When they reached the doorway, Leigh Ann saw Jo and Ambrose inside. They were discussing the details of a permanent sign that would promote the new additions to The Outpost.

Leigh Ann stopped. "Melvin, let's postpone our brainstorming session for now and just grab a drink."

"No problem, come on in. We're almost through," Jo said, standing.

"Jo, could you stick around for a moment longer?" Melvin asked. "You're an apprentice *hataalii*, so I was hoping you could help me with something. I need to fill in some gaps, details that

354

happened the night of the accident that cost me my sight. Do you know a way to restore memory?"

"There are several ways," she said. "I'd start with a special pollen blessing and ask you to meditate on Long-Life Boy and Happiness Girl. Together, they stand for the continuance of happiness. They represent contentment and peace that lasts. I'd work with the Plant People, too, and compel them to help you."

"I'd like to hire you and get this done as soon as possible," Melvin said.

Jo hesitated. "I'm only an apprentice. You need my teacher. If you're interested, speak to him, but do it soon. He has many patients and a busy schedule."

Melvin shook his head. "This is very personal, and I don't want anyone else involved, Jo. Will you do this for me?"

Jo considered it. "It would have to be a brief blessing, not a ceremony," she said at last.

"Can we do it today?" Melvin asked.

She took a minute to think it through. "We could do it after work, if you want," Jo said, and seeing him nod, continued. "I'll start gathering the things I'll need and place them in the hogan." She left immediately and Leigh Ann heard her go into her office.

"Will that work?" Leigh Ann whispered to Ambrose.

"Growing up on the Rez, I saw many things I

couldn't explain," Ambrose said. "If anyone can help Melvin, it'll be Jo."

Melvin gave Leigh Ann's arm a squeeze. "I'm not a Traditionalist, but like Ambrose, I've learned that the things we can't explain are often the most effective."

After the trading post closed for the day they gathered behind Ben's home in the newly constructed log hogan he'd funded. Leigh Ann had only been in it once, at Jo's invitation, and then it was just to look around.

Jo sat in the rear, on the west side of the hogan along with Melvin, her patient. Leigh Ann and Ambrose sat at the south and north, respectively. According to Jo, these positions were based upon tradition.

To begin, Jo offered Melvin a cup of specially brewed herbal tea. "The Holy People gave the Diné special plants, ones we could turn to for help. The Plant People are there for us and they'll help us accomplish what we have to do now. I've used a very special medicine, *Tádídíín dootłizh nitsaaígíí*, what's known as large blue pollen."

As Melvin drank, Jo closed her eyes in silent prayer. "I want you to repeat everything I say, word for word," she told Melvin, then turned over the basket in front of her and began using it as a drum.

As her Song rose in the air, Leigh Ann remained perfectly still. The monotone chant held a mesmerizing quality that seemed to resonate with power and the richness of traditions she didn't understand.

The haunting quality of Jo's Sing drew her in, and she felt herself relaxing. Its soothing nature wove itself around her, pushing away everything except the harmony the Song brought as a gift to those present.

Jo handed Melvin a special pouch. "In this bag are a rock crystal and some sacred pollen. During creation, a crystal was placed in the mouth of every person so that everything he or she said would come true. Pollen is a symbol of well-being, so in this case, the crystal acts as your prayer, the pollen as the blessing of harmony."

"Thank you," Melvin said, holding on to the pouch.

"I want you to meditate on Happiness Girl and Long-Life Boy. One of the many things they represent is achievement of a goal—success."

They sat in silence. After several minutes, Melvin's breathing became more rhythmic.

"Shut out all other sounds and listen only to my voice," Jo said. "Think about that night. What do you see in your mind?"

"The glare of headlights, then the car, upside down, bobbing in the water, its wheels still turning."

"Concentrate only on the sounds around you. What do you hear?" Jo asked.

"Water rushing by, bubbling, and a voice . . . calling to me."

"A man's voice? A woman's?" Jo asked.

"No, a girl's. It's a high-pitched sound above the rushing water."

"What's she saying?"

"Hurry, uncle, swim. I'll pull you out."

"Now focus on her and tell me about her."

"She's standing in ankle-deep water, reaching out to me with one hand."

"Her hair, is it long or short?" Jo asked, her voice calm, soothing.

"Long, down to her waist, and black. She's Navajo."

A small noise caught Leigh Ann's attention and she looked over at Ambrose. He was writing something on a small pad.

"Is her hair loose?" Jo asked.

"No, it's braided, on one side. My right side, her left."

"Is she wearing glasses?" Jo continued.

"Yes, dark frames."

"Is she thin, medium, or heavy set?" Jo asked.

"Slender—straight up and down," Melvin answered, his voice calm. "Lanky."

"Tell me what she wearing," Jo said.

"Jeans and a light-colored T-shirt. There's something drawn across it. It's long and slender and pointed on one end." He remained silent for a moment. "It's a blue feather."

Melvin used one hand to wipe the perspiration off his forehead and expelled his breath in a hiss. "The images are gone. Now there's only gray."

"We are finished," Jo said. "The blessing has been given and it is done. Now all is well."

As Jo brought the blessing to a close, Melvin tried to hand the medicine pouch back to her, but Jo declined.

"It's for you to keep. It's part of the blessing."

While Leigh Ann, Melvin, and Ambrose returned to the trading post, Jo remained behind to gather up the items she'd used and to restore order.

Sam, who'd arrived in the interim to work on software, greeted them with a smile and went to the café counter to fix herself an Outpost Blast.

Leigh Ann looked at Ambrose. "What were you writing back there?"

"I wasn't writing. I was sketching the girl based on Melvin's description." He turned the pad so she could see the image.

"That was a good idea," Melvin said. "It's all fading away again for me."

"I made some mocha cappuccinos for all of you," Sam said, coming to join them. "They're on me."

They sat down, and once Jo joined them,

Ambrose passed around his sketch so they could all study it.

"The T-shirt looks familiar," Jo said, mulling it over.

Sam took a look. "That's the logo of Cottonwood Elementary School, a private school over in Waterflow. Their mascot is the piñon jay," Sam said. "My oldest sister's niece is a first-grader there."

"That's the closest community to where the accident occurred," Melvin said.

Ambrose studied his sketch with a critical eye. "It's a pretty generic image—thin Navajo girl with the characteristic high cheekbones, dark eyes, and the rest. It's the glasses and braid down one side that may open up some possibilities."

"But kids change and that was what she looked like five years ago," Melvin said.

"We know the school the girl attended back then, so if we can access some old yearbooks from that time period, we might get a hit," Leigh Ann said.

"It's useless to try and find anything like that online," Sam said. "Yearbooks with photos of underage children tend not to show up until those people become adults. It protects the kids."

"We'll figure something out," Melvin said. "Look how far we've come. Jo?" he added, looking toward the place where he'd last heard her voice.

"I'm here," she answered.

"Thank you. What you did for me . . ."

"Was only a favor for a friend," she said.

Leigh Ann watched them and smiled. The trading post was the glue that held them together. As long as it stood, none of them would ever have to fight alone.

Jo opened the back door slowly, wondering why everyone had come in so early this morning. It was barely six thirty and the staff parking area was full of cars. Even Ambrose had skipped breakfast to hurry over from the house. As she crossed the storeroom, she heard laughter in the break room.

"We hear you, boss," Leigh Ann called out. "Come and join us. Regina brought fried pies, I made coffee, and Ambrose is about to sing."

"Just a sec," Jo replied, hurrying into her office and moving the computer mouse to wake up the screen. No emails. There was still no word on Ben.

Leaving her purse, she walked into the break room, deciding not to let her mood ruin the day. "I didn't know Ambrose could sing," she said, glancing at Leigh Ann, Melvin, Regina, and Ambrose, who were seated around the big table, pastry and coffee in front of each of them.

They all laughed at her comment, especially Ambrose. "I can't, but I'm so hungry I was ready to do anything to get you in here. We're having a small celebration this morning. With Sorrel-horse in jail and Pierre Boone on the run, things are definitely looking up."

Regina offered Jo a plate with a golden fried pie. "Peach?"

"My favorite, thanks," Jo said, taking a seat. "So what is this really, a bribe? You all want a raise?"

"Yeah, and I don't even work here," Melvin replied, eliciting laughter.

Esther came down the hall carrying a heavy tote bag.

"More goodies?" Jo asked, taking a cup of coffee offered by Leigh Ann, who was seated closest to the coffeepot.

"Of a sort. Sorry I'm late, people, but it took me longer than expected to get what I needed." Esther took several school yearbooks from her bag. "Sam told me what you all learned last night. Since my neighbor's kids all went to Cottonwood Elementary when they were young, I was sure I could borrow some yearbooks.

"I borrowed ones dating as far back as seven years," she continued. "If the girl you saw that night attended that school, Melvin, she'll be in one of these. This may take some time, but it'll be easier than going to the school and trying to wade through their red tape."

"That's great, Esther. We'll look through these

during our breaks today and compile a list of names that might fit Ambrose's sketch," Leigh Ann said.

"I'll leave them all here in the corner," Esther said, setting down the bag. "Now I'm going to try one of Regina's fried pies. Any apple ones left?"

"Sure," Regina said. "I saved one for you."

Ambrose stood and pulled back an empty chair. "Sit over here, Esther. Join me, or I'll sing."

Leigh Ann unlocked the front door for business, greeting three customers already waiting on the porch. Two of them headed directly for the coffee bar, where Esther was waiting to serve them, and the third grabbed a shopping cart.

Ambrose and Melvin had joined forces and were setting up at a table where their artistic skills could be seen and discussed by anyone who came inside.

Jo was at the front register, so Leigh Ann decided to sneak into the break room and take a quick look through the yearbook that coincided with the time of Melvin's accident.

She started with the oldest children, the fifth-graders. Leigh Ann looked at two classes and found five girls wearing glasses, but the only two who had slender faces weren't Navajo. One was black, the other was white, what locals called an Anglo. She flipped to the fourth-graders. Two had glasses, but they were light-colored frames and only one had long hair.

Leigh Ann wrote down her name anyway, and decided to look at the group photos in the front more closely, hoping to spot a girl with a braid. As she leafed through the pages, she found a listing for "late comers." Among the photos there was one of a girl who fit Melvin's description almost perfectly—the hair, the braid, and the slender build. She was also a fifth-grader.

"Got you," Leigh Ann said, quickly writing the girl's name on a sticky note.

"Meaning our mystery girl?" Ambrose said, stepping into the room.

"Look at the photo, then your sketch," Leigh Ann said, pointing at the images. Ambrose did and smiled.

"Irene Largo. Hopefully, she still lives in the area."

"The Largo name sounds familiar to me, but I'm not sure why," Leigh Ann said.

"If she goes to Kirtland Central now, maybe Del knows her," Ambrose said.

"I'll ask when he comes in," she said.

Ambrose poured two cups of coffee. "When I take Melvin his cup, you want me to tell him you've got a hit?"

"Yeah, but remind him that all we've really got is a possibility. By the end of today, we may have found other girls who also fit the sketch," Leigh Ann said.

"Good point."

Hearing the office phone ring, Leigh Ann hurried down the hall to answer it. Jo, coming from the opposite direction, got to it first. "Hello. The Outpost. Josephine Buck speaking."

Leigh Ann stood, wondering if this was *The Call*. Then she remembered that in the case of death or serious injury the army delivered that news in person.

"Yes, Lieutenant, this is Jo Buck," Jo said quickly, her voice somber. "Have you heard anything more about Ben? I mean, Sergeant Stuart."

Unable to hear the other side of the conversation, Leigh Ann held her breath and watched Jo.

"Yes, I understand. Do you have any idea when we'll know?" Jo asked, her voice shaky. "All right, then."

Jo listened for a while longer, looked up and saw Leigh Ann, then with tears in her eyes managed a shrug. "No, no thanks. I'm staying right here where I can keep busy. You can reach me at the trading post, or on my cell. Call when you get news. Yes . . . Bye."

As Jo hung up, her shoulders sagged.

"Here, darling, let me hang on to you for a while," Leigh Ann said, giving Jo a hug. She heard footsteps and turned to see Esther, Melvin, and Ambrose crowding into the doorway. Regina was right behind them.

Jo stood up straight and stepped back, wiping away her tears. "It's not necessarily bad news. The downed helicopter has been located, and appears to have crash-landed safely despite being damaged. The crew apparently abandoned the aircraft and sought cover. A rescue unit is on the ground and an operation is underway to neutralize enemy snipers before they bring in any more choppers. There's evidence from a surveillance drone that the crash survivors may have established a defensive perimeter around a cave, but other than that no more information is available."

"Any idea when you'll know?" Ambrose asked.

Jo shook her head. "Several hours, maybe longer. The lieutenant said I could come and wait in his office at the Federal Building in Farmington, but I told him I'd rather be here working with you guys."

"With family," Esther said with a nod, and reached out to squeeze her hand. "We've been praying for Ben, and for you, and we're not going to stop now."

"Thank you." She looked from face to face, managed a smile, then looked out into the hall. "Who's managing the store? Let's get to work, people."

Twenty

It was close to 7:00 P.M. when Leigh Ann drove up a narrow but paved street in a small housing development just east of Kirtland Central High School, along old Highway 64.

"Okay, we're here. The house number matches, so this is where Irene Largo lives, according to Del. I knew that name sounded familiar. Del dated one of the Largo girls a while back," Leigh Ann said, pulling into the driveway of a modest stucco home with a metal roof and decorative window shutters. A light blue minivan was parked close to the door, and, as she stopped, someone parted a window curtain and looked out.

While Leigh Ann walked around to help Melvin out, the front door of the house opened and a Navajo woman in her mid-thirties came out onto the concrete stoop. "May I help you?" she asked, reaching out to grab a small child trying to squeeze past.

"Back inside, sweetie," the woman said to the child. "Irene, could you take Amy?"

"Coming." It was the voice of a teenage girl. Hearing it, Leigh Ann gave Melvin's hand a squeeze as he stepped out of the Jeep.

"Mrs. Largo? I'm Leigh Ann Vance, and this is my friend, Melvin Littlewater. We're the people

Del Hudson called you about. Could we speak to you and your daughter Irene for a few minutes?"

Leigh Ann heard a gasp and turned to see a tall, slender Navajo girl with long black hair standing on the porch, her arms wrapped around the little one. She was staring at Melvin like she'd seen a ghost.

"Mom, it's him! He's the man I saw on top of the truck in the canal that night."

Five minutes later, Melvin and Leigh Ann were seated on a love seat facing the sofa where Irene and her mom sat. In the middle was the little girl, who was clutching a stuffed dog and staring at the strangers.

"It was after dinner and dark outside, and I was walking home from Kathy's house, remember, Mom?" Irene said.

The woman nodded. "My old Chevy wouldn't start, so I was waiting for Irene's father to come home so we could go pick her up," Mrs. Largo explained, then looked at her daughter, and added, "You should have stayed at Kathy's, like I told you."

"I know, but I had that project to finish before I went to bed, and I'd walked along the ditch tons of times before," Irene said.

"Never in the dark, alone, with no flashlight or cell phone," her mother added.

"Okay, now I know better. Anyway, I was

walking down the ditch bank and a truck drove past me on the highway. Then a car raced by, passing the truck like it was standing still. But the guy in the car cut back too soon and crashed right into the truck, knocking it off the road and into the canal. The guy in the car also lost control, flipped, and it went over the guardrail. It ended up in the canal, upside down and pinned up against one of those big floodgates. It was weird, because the headlights on the car were still on. I could see the truck floating down the ditch, too, about to smash into the car."

Leigh Ann could see Irene's hands shaking. She could tell that Melvin's shoulders were rigid and tense. Leigh Ann put her hand on his arm, silently supporting him.

"That was you in the truck, right, Mr. Littlewater?"

"Yes. At least I wasn't upside down," Melvin said.

"I was running toward the accident when I saw you climb out the window and up onto the roof of the truck's cab," Irene said. "I tried to wade in, but the sides of the ditch were too steep."

"You almost fell in," he said.

"I wanted to help but I couldn't reach you," she said, choking back a sob.

"It's okay Irene, you did everything you could. You were only what, ten or eleven?" Melvin said gently.

"She was eleven," Mrs. Largo responded. "And when she couldn't find help, she turned around and ran home."

"I could hear cars stopping to see what was going on, but because the headlights on the car that was in the water had gone out, I was afraid no one would spot you and you'd drown. I thought if I could get home in a hurry, Mom and Dad could do something."

"When Irene ran up the driveway, my husband and I were already in our pickup, about to go looking for her," Mrs. Largo said. "Irene jumped in, soaked to her knees, and told us about the accident. On the way there I called 911. I was told that the deputies and emergency personnel were already on the scene. Traffic was backed up ahead, so we turned around and came back home."

Melvin nodded. "You never told the sheriff's department that Irene had been there."

"No, it was already over, and we wanted to keep her out of it. Later, we read in the newspaper that the driver of the car had drowned and that you, Mr. Littlewater, had survived but were blind."

"I had nightmares about that accident for a long time," Irene said in a shaky voice.

Mrs. Largo nodded. "She'd wake up screaming and crying. It took her almost a year to get back to normal."

"I'm glad you made it and that you're okay, well, except for . . ." Irene stopped. "I'm sorry. That was really stupid."

"Don't feel bad. I'm okay, and although I lost my sight, being blind has made me aware of things I might never have noticed otherwise." Melvin squeezed Leigh Ann's hand. "We should go now."

Leigh Ann drove in silence, looking over at Melvin from time to time. He hadn't said a word since they'd left the Largo home. She had been silent as well, not wanting to interrupt his thoughts. Now he had closure, but she wasn't sure if that had brought him the peace he'd wanted.

"Are you okay?" she asked at last.

"Yes, for the first time in years, I am. Thank you for helping me close this door once and for all. Now I can finally move on."

"My turn's coming soon, too, I feel it. Once the police find Pierre, I'll be able to breathe again."

"Then it'll be our turn."

She couldn't imagine life without Melvin. He completed her in ways no one ever had. If only she'd told him the other day when she'd finally learned about her role in his accident.

"Where are we off to now?" he asked, breaking into her thoughts.

"Before we head back to your place I want to make a stop at my house. I need to pick up a few more tops and slacks," she said. "Don't worry, I'll be quick."

"Just remember to stay alert. The danger's not over yet."

Melvin was at the dining table, drinking one of Rachel's diet Cokes, when Leigh Ann came down the stairs with a small overnight case containing fresh clothing. "Let me change purses, then I'll be ready to go. I want my largest tote. It'll hold the .38 better, and until Pierre's caught, I want it handy."

"My guess is he's on his way to Mexico by now, but you can't afford to get complacent."

As she put the contents of her purse into her tote, she picked up her keys, then realizing she still had two spares for the old locks, decided to take them off the key chain.

"Sounds like you've got quite a collection of keys," Melvin commented. "I only have one—my house key."

"I usually carry the Outpost keys, the key to the Jeep, one to Rachel's car, your house key, and mine. The only important key I don't carry is the one that belonged to Kurt. That one's in the kitchen drawer with the flatware. No one would look there for it. I still haven't been able to figure out what it's for, but eventually I'm sure I will."

"It doesn't fit the metal box you found in the attic, the one that almost got you shot?" Melvin asked, putting down his Coke.

"No. It was inside that box, though."

"Describe the key to me."

"It's small, about an inch and a half long, too small for a house lock or a car. It's also brass, not steel or aluminum, and had the number zero fifty-five on it."

"Is it stamped, like a trunk key?"

"No. I know the kind you mean, but this is more upscale. Here, feel it," she said, taking it out of the drawer and putting it in his hand.

"Hmmm. This is for a more expensive lock, maybe a drawer in a nice desk, or to a cabinet. It hasn't been used much because the notches are sharp. The lock is more complex, with the notches differently spaced from each other and there are three grooves, all in different places, two on one side, one on the other," he said, handing it back to her. "Where did you try this key?"

"I tried it on everything I could think of here in the house, and a couple of places in the garage, but got nowhere. The locks out there are all the same kind, and this one is obviously for a different type."

"Did Kurt spend a lot of time in the garage?"

"Oh, yeah," she said. "There's a ring of keys just for his stuff out there, with numbers he etched on them that indicate which lock they fit. I keep it with the kitchen utensils. There's no number fifty-five out there either. They range from one to twenty."

"This must fit something you haven't tried yet, then," Melvin said. "Is it a fancy garage with lots of storage cabinets?"

"Yeah, it is. He practically lived out there."

"Then the missing cash may be hidden there somewhere, too. Why don't we try to find another lock?"

"I've already checked, but okay," she said, reaching for the garage key ring in the drawer with the spatula and other big utensils. "A treasure hunt is always more fun with a friend."

"Arrgh, twice as much fun. You've got a pirate with a patch over both eyes," Melvin said. They both laughed freely for the first time in days.

Taking his hand, Leigh Ann led Melvin into the two-car garage, which was extra roomy today with no vehicles inside. She began to flip switches to turn on the lights, explaining as she did. "There's an overhead fluorescent fixture out here, plus Kurt installed lamps over the wide counter that runs the length of the north wall. I sold his big table saw, drill press, and lathe when I needed money for some of the bills, but the garage is still full of man toys. Right now the counter holds power tools, like saws, drills, and a leaf blower. There's also a pegboard with hand tools hung on various hooks."

"Where are the cabinets in reference to the counter?" he asked. "Above or below?"

"Both, and they all have locks," she said. "Rachel and I looked inside those already."

"Did you open everything you found inside there?"

"Mostly, yes, but there were a few toolboxes and containers we didn't bother with for one reason or another. Also, we were afraid of spiders."

"Let's go through everything now—again."

"What about spiders?"

"Shine the light in first, and put on some gloves, just to be safe," he suggested.

She did, but all she found in the top cabinets were small tools, nails and screws, and containers holding sandpaper, steel wool, paintbrushes, rollers, and other hardware items. Leigh Ann narrated as she went, so Melvin knew what was going on. Then she started on the bottom cabinets, working right to left.

"The first cabinet has no lock. Inside, all I can see are gallon paint cans, stacked two high. Kurt would always save leftover paint, planning to use it for touch-ups or second or third coats."

"Start looking in the cabinets themselves. Is there anything that doesn't seem to belong, or looks like a recent repair?"

She aimed the flashlight around the cabinet interior. "There's a raised back panel and, hold on, I think I see a place for a key on the inside corner. Then again, it might just be a small rodent hole; I can't get a clear enough aim with the flashlight. I'd need to get these paint cans out of the way first."

"Hand them to me and I'll set them aside," Melvin said.

Leigh Ann got down on her knees and removed the cans one at a time. Melvin took them and within a few minutes they'd set all twelve paint cans onto the garage floor.

"There *is* a locked panel set into the back of the cabinet," Leigh Ann said, excited now. "Melvin, let me give you the flashlight, I'll tell you where to aim it, and we'll see if the key fits."

After a few seconds of guiding his hand, the light was positioned on the metal keyhole.

"Perfect, now don't move," she said.

Leigh Ann inserted the key and pulled open the hinged door. "Crap! After all this, it's empty. Not even a cobweb," she said, looking closely, then closing it back up again.

"Guess somebody got to it first," Melvin said.

"I've had it. That money's meant to stay lost," she said. "Let's go get dinner. Are you hungry?"

"Yeah, starved," he said, stepping back. His foot bumped against one of the paint cans.

"Let's put these back first. Hand them to me one by one, okay?" she asked.

"Good idea," he said, handing her the can he'd kicked. Leigh Ann slid it back inside the cabinet and reached for the next can.

Melvin was holding the second paint can with

a funny look on his face. "This can is awfully light, and I felt something shift inside this when I picked it up. There's something solid in there, but liquid paint flows and dried paint shouldn't be moving at all. You'd better check it out."

"Let me get something to pry the lid off with." She hurried over to the pegboard, grabbed a screwdriver, then returned and opened the can.

"Green everywhere," she said in an awed whisper, "and I don't mean paint."

"Greenbacks, maybe?"

"More cash than I've ever seen in my life. It's in tight rolls of twenties, fifties, and even hundreds. This is it, Melvin, the mother lode."

"We'd better check out the rest of the cans," he said. "More than one of them felt pretty light, but until now I was thinking it was just leftovers saved for touch-ups."

Five minutes later they walked back into the living room area carrying four gallon paint cans, each stuffed with rolls of bills fastened with rubber bands.

Leigh Ann lowered the cans she was carrying onto the carpet beside the sofa. "I'm going to call Dale. He'll know what needs to be done next. I imagine the lab will want to check the cans for prints. At least I still had gloves on and we knew to stop touching the sides and tops after we found the first stash."

"Call, then afterwards we'll celebrate with a

nice dinner. Then I can show you the sculpture," Melvin said cheerfully, putting down the two containers he was carrying before edging his way over to the sofa and sitting down.

"Sounds wonderful," she whispered, listening as the phone rang at the other end.

Dale didn't pick up the call, so Leigh Ann left a voice mail. "Dale, we found some stolen money. I'll stick around at home for another half hour in case you want to come pick it up. If I don't hear from you before then, I'll drop it off by the sheriff's office on my way to Melvin Littlewater's house. I don't want to be responsible for it any longer than I have to. Call me as soon as you can, okay?" She put down the phone.

"Leigh Ann, you don't know when he'll check his messages. Unless you also notify Detective McGraw, he's going to be pissed thinking you're deliberately shutting him out of this. You'd be better off letting him share the credit. You really don't need an enemy in the sheriff's department right now."

"Maybe you're right. Let me get his business card out of my tote."

Suddenly Melvin stood up, holding his finger to his mouth in a gesture of silence.

"Someone's outside," he whispered, pointing across the room toward the patio, which was adjacent to the kitchen and dining area.

Leigh Ann looked over just as a glass panel

shattered on one of the French doors. Seeing a hand reach through, groping for the doorknob, she screamed. The .38 was in her tote bag on the dining room table, which was sitting less than six feet from where the intruder was trying to gain entry.

"You bitch! You're going to pay for ruining my life," Pierre Boone spat out. Struggling to turn the lock, he cut his hand on a jagged piece of glass and cursed as blood flowed, marring the white doorframe.

"Out the front," Leigh Ann told Melvin, flinching as more glass broke and splintered.

Grabbing Melvin's hand, she'd only taken a step when a gun went off and a bullet struck the wall just ahead of her. She turned to see Pierre aiming his pistol at them through the broken pane. She jumped back just before another bullet struck even closer to them, lodging in the wall.

"Upstairs," she whispered, leading Melvin as she dialed 911 with one hand. Pierre fired again, shattering the mirror above the sofa.

As they reached the second story, her call connected and she spoke quickly to the dispatcher even as she pulled Melvin down the hall to her bedroom. The second they were both inside, Leigh Ann closed the door behind them and turned the key in the lock.

There was a loud crash downstairs. Pierre had probably given up on the lock and kicked open the door. It was dark in the bedroom, but Leigh Ann knew the layout by heart. Moving quickly, she led Melvin to the dresser.

"Help me push this against the door," she said, putting his hand on the top. They both leaned into the effort and inched the chest into place.

Hearing uneven footsteps coming slowly up the stairs, like Pierre was limping, she unplugged a brass table lamp and stood on one side of the door, ready to use the lamp as a club if Pierre managed to get in. She'd lost track of Melvin, but before she could locate him her attention was diverted by the sound of the bedroom door-knob rattling. A second later, wood splintered, but the door only gave a few inches.

Leigh Ann heard Pierre grunting, trying to overcome the weight of the dresser. She was afraid it was only a matter of seconds before he got in.

"Pierre, take the money, all of it," Leigh Ann yelled through the door. "Kurt hid it in those paint cans downstairs. Take it and run while there's still time. I called the sheriff, and the deputies are on their way."

"I'll leave, but not before you're dead. You took everything from me. Now you'll pay," Pierre yelled, slamming against the door again and opening it farther.

He'd moved so silently she hadn't realized that Melvin was beside her until he reached across and pushed the bedroom door shut. Crouching down, his foot blocking the door, he quickly pushed the dresser away, then stepped back.

Leigh Ann instantly figured out what he was hoping to do and moved away, watching the door, ready to jump Pierre and try to grab the gun once he broke through.

She could hear him breathing out in the hall. Then he grunted and rushed the door, slamming into it with full force. The door flew open and Pierre stumbled in, off balance from the sudden lack of resistance.

Melvin lunged forward, tackling Pierre at the knees. "Got you now, bastard!"

Leigh Ann swung the brass lamp at Pierre's head and caught him on the back of the neck. Pierre yelled in pain and fell facedown onto the carpet, the pistol flying out of his hand. Melvin was now on top of Pierre, hanging on to him with both arms.

As the men wrestled on the floor, Leigh Ann spotted the pistol by the edge of the bed and grabbed it. She aimed the semiauto at the head of the man responsible for her husband's death. "Stop struggling and lie still, Pierre, or I'll blow the top of your head clean off!"

"You won't shoot me, you don't have the balls," Pierre said, trying to break free from Melvin's grip.

Melvin punched Pierre in the jaw. When the

man fell back, Melvin pinned him down with an iron grip on his foe's biceps and a knee to his thigh, which was stained with blood. Pierre groaned, blood seeping from what looked like a bullet wound.

Leigh Ann jammed the barrel of the gun into his neck. "I'll kill to protect the ones I love," she said, her voice vibrating with deadly intent.

Suddenly there was a loud crash downstairs—the sound of splintering wood as another door was kicked in. "Leigh Ann! Where are you?" It was Dale.

"Upstairs! We've got Pierre. Hurry!" she yelled.

Melvin looked in her direction and grinned. "Nice going, beautiful."

Her hand was shaking so badly she was afraid she'd pull the trigger by mistake, so she moved her index finger aside and took the gun away from Pierre's neck. "What makes you think I'm beautiful?" she teased halfheartedly.

" 'Cause I see with my heart."

There were quick footsteps in the hall and a second later Dale appeared, weapon in his hand. He flipped on the room lights and took in the scene.

"You guys have the worst dates ever," Dale said, putting away his pistol and bringing out his handcuffs. "Next time, why don't you just take in a movie?"

‚Ä¢ ‚Ä¢ ‚Ä¢

Dinner wound up being sandwiches from the vending machine at the police station while they gave their statements. Once they were done, Leigh Ann drove them directly to Melvin's home, parked, and followed him inside.

This was the moment she'd looked forward to and now dreaded at the same time. Today, she'd see the sculpture, and after that, it would be time for her to keep her word. Whatever the consequences, there'd be no more secrets between them.

Melvin walked to the table where he kept the whiskey bottle. "I don't need this half-empty reminder here anymore. I know who and what I am." He held it out. "Enjoy it. My gift to you."

She took it from his hands. "I'll keep it just as it is—half full—a souvenir of the adventure of a lifetime."

"Our adventure is only beginning—if you'll allow it," he said. "I've already had the sculpture fired, so I'm ready to show it to you. Are you ready to keep your end of our bargain—no more secrets?"

"I am," she answered, amazed at how steady her voice sounded considering her heart was lodged in her throat.

He felt his way into the study and reached up onto the shelf behind his work desk. Removing the dust cover, he presented the sculpture to her.

She took it from him with trembling hands and

sat down on the closest chair to study it. Twelve inches high, the figure was made up of two tones of porcelain clay, one-third cream, the other two-thirds a dark gray that was almost black. One of the things that caught her eye was that the line distinguishing light from dark wasn't straight or easily delineated. It was a blend.

The sculpture represented a woman in a short, loosely fitting sleeveless dress. She was sitting on the ground, legs crossed, just to the right of a standing lynx. The woman was half turned to the right from waist up, her left hand resting on the animal's shoulder, behind the animal's head. The woman's head was glancing back along her right shoulder. A curtain of windswept hair hid most of her features, and her right hand was up, clenched into a fist, as if making a challenge.

"It's incredible," Leigh Ann said in an awed whisper.

He sat next to her on the arm of the chair. "Lynx is the keeper of secrets. She knows many things, but seldom shares her knowledge. She also stands for purpose and action," he said. "The figure's left hand resting on the animal shows gentleness, the right, intent and willingness to fight."

"She's looking behind her, just like I've been," she said in a near whisper.

"Yes, and although the darkness that follows her casts a long shadow, the light within her is too powerful to extinguish."

"It's who I am inside," she said, her voice trembling with emotion.

"Do you like it?"

"It's amazing, and the best piece you've ever done."

"Good," he said, and smiled, pleased. "I knew you'd never accept this as a gift, so, once I was satisfied with the original, I decided to make a smaller copy, a maquette that I actually finished," he added, bringing the miniature sculpture out of a cabinet and handing it to her, taking back the larger work.

She looked at the piece now in her hands. It was as perfect as the other. "You've been working on two of them all along! I don't know what to say. What an incredible gift."

"The sculpture has my heart and your soul. We're a part of each other now," he said, pulling her into his arms. "No more secrets."

Her throat tightened so much it ached. It was time. "All right, you deserve to know everything," she said, and stepped out of his arms. Fear wound through her, almost choking the air out of her lungs, but after a minute to gather her courage, she took a deep, steadying breath, and began.

"Five years ago I was waitressing at the Bullfrog Tavern, and one night in particular the place was really packed. We were a waitress short, and to make it worse, a drunk at one of my tables was giving me a hard time." Her voice trailed off as she saw Melvin's body tense.

Leigh Ann began to tremble, but gathering her courage, forced herself to continue. "We'd been instructed to stop serving any patron who'd had too much to drink, ask for their car or pickup keys, and call a cab for them. When I tried to get his keys, the man insisted I get him just one more drink. After that, he promised he'd hand them over. I couldn't serve him any more alcohol, so I decided to give him a cup of coffee instead."

She paused for a moment, trying not to cry, but Melvin didn't break the silence, just sat rock still, waiting, nodding his head slowly. He'd already guessed.

"What I should have done was get my manager, but I was still new at the job and worried the boss would think I couldn't handle difficult customers."

Melvin still hadn't made a sound.

Biting back tears, she continued. "When I got back to the table with the coffee, he was gone. I ran out to the parking lot to try and find him but he'd already left. I forgot all about it until two days ago."

Melvin nodded. "When we visited his parents?"

"Yes, his photo was on the wall in the Jonas entryway. The man I let get away that night was Ronald Jonas. Until that moment I'd never made the connection or seen his photo. He was the drunk I should have stopped the night of your accident."

She looked at Melvin, expecting to see disgust on his face, but he simply stood.

Figuring he'd want her to leave, she went to get her purse. "I'll go now."

"Why?" he said.

There was no anger at all in his tone, only curiosity. Melvin wasn't slow, but maybe it just hadn't hit him yet. "Why? If I'd taken his keys, or gone to get my manager, you wouldn't have been in that accident and lost your sight. I'm responsible for what happened to you and I'm so very sorry," she said, her voice breaking on the last syllable.

Each second that ticked by felt like an eternity to her. She wanted to run out the door, but she owed him the chance to react.

"You're not responsible for what happened, Ronnie Jonas was. You'd tried to do the right thing, going for coffee. You had no way of knowing he'd leave."

"I should have done *something*. . . ."

"Life's filled with 'what ifs,' Leigh Ann. What if I'd driven down that highway five minutes earlier, or later, or just pulled off the highway?" He expelled his breath in a long, slow hiss. "I've learned a lot about myself—and life—these past five years. Had I heard this, say four years ago, I might have blamed you. Back then, I was drinking *my* life away, angry at the world. I'm past that now. I got hit by a drunk driver.

That's the beginning and the end of that story."

He held out his hand, and when she took it, he kissed the center of her palm. "I've accepted what happened to me. As much as I wish it were different, my sight's gone for good. I've been given a new gift instead, a vision that goes deeper inside than ever before. I can see anything now through my senses and my imagination."

"You've adapted, but—"

He shook his head. "There are no negatives. Before I met you I was empty inside. Your voice, your touch, your courage, they brought me back to life. Can't you see it, Leigh Ann? *Your* light pushed back my darkness."

She felt the tears running down her face. "You're a beautiful man, Melvin, inside and out. When I saw that photograph, I thought you might be angry, maybe even hate me. . . ."

"No, Leigh Ann, I love you. Let go of the past and take what's before you today. Can you do that?"

She stepped into his arms. "This is where I choose to be. I love you. I have for a long time."

He cupped her face and took her mouth in a slow burning kiss. As Leigh Ann melted against him, he lifted her into his arms. "I want you in my bed, taking from me, and giving me everything. No more holdbacks."

Melvin carried her gently toward the doorway. "Stop!" she whispered.

"What? Now you change your mind?"

She laughed. "No, silly. You're about to slam my legs into the doorjamb."

He laughed, then they laughed together. "Okay, now that I've been properly embarrassed, you guide me to the bed. After that, I'll be the one guiding you."

The thought was intriguing and formed all kinds of images in her head, all of them X-rated. "Turn to your left, just a little. That's it, now straight ahead."

He carried her through the doorway and took three angled steps toward the bed. "How close am I?" he whispered.

"One more step, then turn me just a little to your right."

"Together, we can make this work, sweetheart." He took a step, brushed up against the bed, and lowered her to the soft mattress.

He bent down and undressed her, kissing her in ways that made her moan softly with pleasure. "I want you to burn for me, to need me as much as I do you. It's our time," he murmured.

"I like the darkness in here," she whispered, reaching out to him.

"Yes, and there's balance in that, too. *Feel,* use your heart and your hands to explore, to learn . . . to live."

Welcoming the darkness, Leigh Ann surrendered to the night.

Twenty-One

Leigh Ann and Melvin arrived at The Outpost a half hour early, and as they reached the back door it swung open. Leigh Ann jumped back, startled.

"What are you—" Leigh Ann began.

Ambrose, looking half asleep, held a finger to his mouth, signaling them to be quiet. "Hi, guys," he whispered, stepping aside to let them in. "Keep it down. Jo's still asleep."

Leigh Ann led Melvin down the hall to the break room. "You mean Jo's been here all night?" she whispered back. "What's going on?"

"Any news of Ben?" Melvin asked.

"About ten last night, just as I was about to convince her to go to the house and get some sleep, she got a visit from that army officer," Ambrose said.

Leigh Ann sucked in her breath. "And?"

"He told her that the rescue operation had been successfully completed and that everyone involved had been evacuated by helicopter. He assured her that he would stay on duty until he learned what Ben's exact status was and would call her, day or night, as soon as he knew."

Leigh Ann nodded. "Jo stuck close to the

computer all night, hoping to hear from Ben himself."

"Yeah, and I stayed with her, talking, trying to keep her sane. She finally dozed off at her desk about two hours ago. You can start getting ready to open up, if you want, but I'll stick with her. She'll need to see a friendly face when she wakes up."

"I just did," Jo said, walking across the storeroom to meet them. Going up to Ambrose, she threw her arms around him and gave him a hug. "Thanks for having my back last night, brother."

"No prob," Ambrose said.

"Morning, boss," Leigh Ann said, noting that Jo looked exhausted. "Let's see what we can scrounge up for breakfast before we have to open the doors. Melvin and I also have some good news to share."

"Other than you took down Pierre Boone's ass last night?" Ambrose said.

"How'd you find out so soon?" Melvin asked. "Oh, never mind. You were at the computer all night."

"Following every news report we could find," Jo replied, nodding. "But give us the details, the local sources never get it right."

After running back to the Stuart house to shower, Jo returned to her office. More alert now, she stayed close to her computer and kept her cell phone in her pocket. Though waiting for word was taking a huge toll on her, she made a point of leaving her office every half hour and talking to the customers who came to admire Melvin's exhibit or watch Ambrose's silversmith demonstrations.

When lunchtime arrived, Leigh Ann brought her a sandwich and sat across the desk from her. "Staring at the screen isn't going to make time go by any faster," she said gently.

Jo expelled her breath in a whoosh, stood, and made a face at the monitor. "You bucket of chips and wires, give me what I want!"

A familiar tone sounded on the computer and the Skype screen popped into view. Jo jumped, simultaneously grabbing her headset. Leigh Ann hurried around the desk, praying this would be good news, but ready to help Jo if things didn't turn out so well.

Moving the mouse to click on the green video button, Jo looked at Leigh Ann. "It's Ben!"

A grainy image appeared and quickly became sharper. Ben was staring back at them. From the background, he appeared to be back in his own quarters. He looked exhausted, sunburned and scratched, and there were crutches propped up against the back of his chair.

"Ben! You're alive!" Jo said, half laughing

and half crying. "But the crutches. You're hurt!"

"I'll be fine, just a cracked tibia and sprained ankle. Took a hard landing," he answered, his voice still sounding a little underwater because of the connection.

"Well, don't you *ever* scare me like that again! I was so worried. I miss you so much," she added in a softer tone.

Leigh Ann smiled. Since she didn't have a headset she had no idea what Ben said next, but Jo's smile could have lit up a room. Moving away, she left the office, closed the door behind her and went to the others to give them the good news. "He looked a little banged up and is on crutches, but otherwise seems okay."

Ambrose pointed outside the window. "Here comes that lieutenant, and he has a smile on his face for a change. Let's see if we can get any more details."

Sergeant Stuart's a hero," the lieutenant told them as they gathered near the cash register in the main room. "Though his leg was injured in the crash, he protected the rest of the crew for three days. They're all expected to fully recover from their injuries."

Jo smiled. "That's the Ben I know," she said.

"This calls for a celebration," Ambrose said.

"Yes, a party! Complete with a barbecue and a

country-western band. We can have it right outside," Leigh Ann said.

"Guys, I *have* to get some sleep," Jo said, giving them a weary smile.

"You do that, hon. We'll handle everything," Leigh Ann said.

That evening Leigh Ann found herself sitting beside Jo on one of the three dozen folding chairs facing the band. Somewhere between twenty and thirty people were already there, helping themselves to the fixings laid out on the long buffet table.

"Everyone loves a party," Leigh Ann said, sipping a Coke and watching another pickup coming up the drive.

"How did you find a band so quickly?" Jo asked.

"Del. These boys play at high schools in the area, and he knows the skinny guy playing the bass guitar. They're doing it for free in honor of our community's latest hero."

"I'm so proud of Ben," Jo said, smiling.

"So are we all," Leigh Ann answered.

Ambrose came over to join them. "Ben's going to call you tomorrow, right?" He had to raise his voice to be heard over the band.

Jo nodded. "He promised we'd have a long talk. The best part comes from knowing he'll be grounded until he mends, and not long after that his unit will return stateside and I can go visit him. Leigh Ann and the rest of the staff can do without me for a few days."

"We've all missed him, you know," Ambrose said, leaning closer to her ear.

"Yeah, but I'm not sharing him when he comes home. He'll be all mine—and the army's," she said, then smiled.

As the band began a slow-moving country-western song, John led Melvin to Leigh Ann's side.

"Here you go, nephew."

"I saved you a seat right beside me," Leigh Ann said.

Melvin remained standing. "No, come on. The band's playing a great song—romantic and slow. Let's not waste it."

"I didn't know you liked dancing."

Melvin smiled. "I'll take any excuse to have you in my arms—but just to stay safe, you better lead."

Dear Reader,

Aimée Thurlo was a true professional, dedicated to her love for books and writing, and only her sudden, fatal illness prevented her from completing the final draft of *Looking Through Darkness*. We were working as a team, but the last read-through was always hers. Knowing that we were running out of time, we quickly went over the manuscript together. I took notes, planning on entering the changes—later. It was clear that there were more important issues at hand.

We spent those remaining two weeks at home, talking about everything imaginable from our past and present, experiencing every possible emotion, both of us struggling with the certain knowledge that the end was near. Fortunately, we also had the opportunity to hold hands and recall some of the pleasant memories from the forty-three years we'd been together, and, for a moment, dream of the plans we'd made for the future.

Aimée and I had wanted to retire, or at least slow down, but that had never included quitting doing what we loved. Writing was in our blood, and we'd still hoped to create more trading post stories. The Outpost was a lively place, with interesting people, and something always going on. And, after all, we had a great editor who was part of our team.

Melissa Singer had been with us from our very first hardcover novel, *Second Shadow* in 1993, to what was to become Aimée's very last manuscript—*Looking Through Darkness*. Writing with a partner was a blessing to us, and with Melissa's contributions and insights we had a wonderful ally. She'd helped guide us on the journey that encompassed twenty-three novels over the twenty years we've worked with Forge. At the end, Melissa also felt my loss. Thank you again, Melissa, for your friendship and support.

This is not the final chapter, however. Aimée's legacy will live on, and people around the world will be reading Thurlo books for many years. Those who got to know Aimée discovered that she was a kind, talented woman who made easy connections with strangers as well as friends. She will be greatly missed by those who loved her and her stories. Aimée Thurlo was a remarkable woman who left us far too soon.

David Thurlo

Books are produced
in the United States
using U.S.-based
materials

Books are printed
using a revolutionary
new process called
THINKtech™ that
lowers energy usage
by 70% and increases
overall quality

Books are durable
and flexible because
of smythe-sewing

Paper is sourced
using environmentally
responsible foresting
methods and the
paper is acid-free

Center Point Large Print
600 Brooks Road / PO Box 1
Thorndike, ME 04986-0001 USA

(207) 568-3717

US & Canada:
1 800 929-9108
www.centerpointlargeprint.com